Disney

FROZEN

Colouring

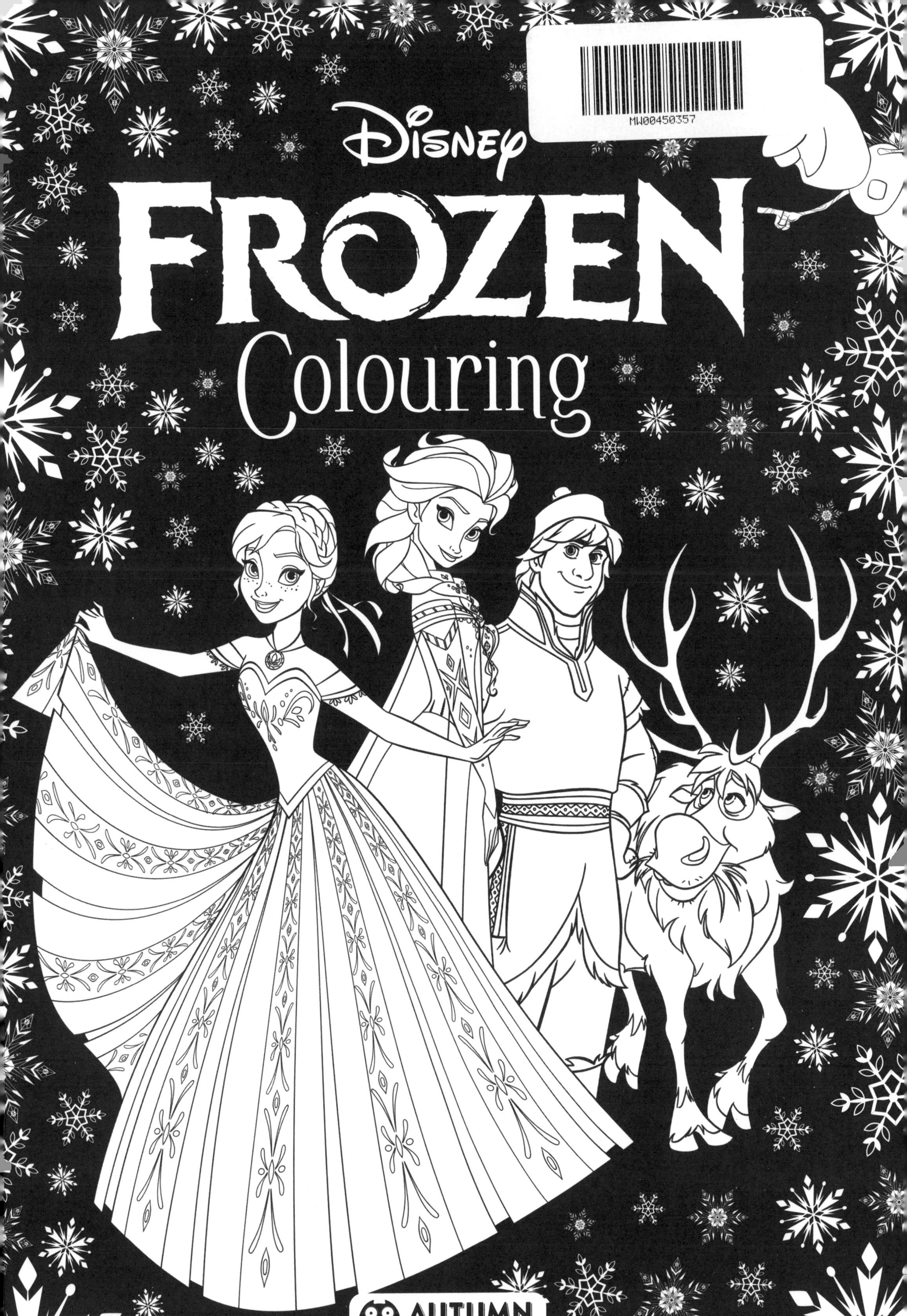

AUTUMN PUBLISHING

AUTUMN
PUBLISHING

Published in 2021
Published in the UK by Autumn Publishing
An imprint of Igloo Books Ltd
Cottage Farm, NN6 0BJ, UK
Owned by Bonnier Books
Sveavägen 56, Stockholm, Sweden
www.igloobooks.com

0921 001
2 4 6 8 10 11 9 7 5 3 1
ISBN 978-1-80022-276-2

Printed and manufactured in China

The snow glows white on the mountain tonight, Not a footprint to be seen...

In the beautiful kingdom of Arendelle, a princess is born with a secret power that becomes so strong she lives in solitude for most of her childhood. But one day, her magic is finally revealed, and the whole kingdom is frozen in an eternal winter.

Rediscover the wonderful world of *Frozen* and breathe life and colour into the characters, scenes and artwork of one of the most beautiful Disney films. A symphony of snowflakes, ice palaces, star mandalas and wintry patterns are combined with intricate line art of endearing and mischievous *Frozen* characters. Immerse yourself in a fairy-tale world bordered by rugged mountains, snow-capped hills and trees adorned with frozen crystals. Colour in rich Nordic decorations and patterns, Scandinavian clothing, embroidery and objects based on the real-life location of this hugely successful film franchise. Finally, use your colours to reimagine the poignant story of two sisters separated by fate, struggling to overcome fierce obstacles in a story full of love, friendship and courage.

With simple crayons or coloured markers, set off on an icy adventure and relive the enchantment of *Frozen*!

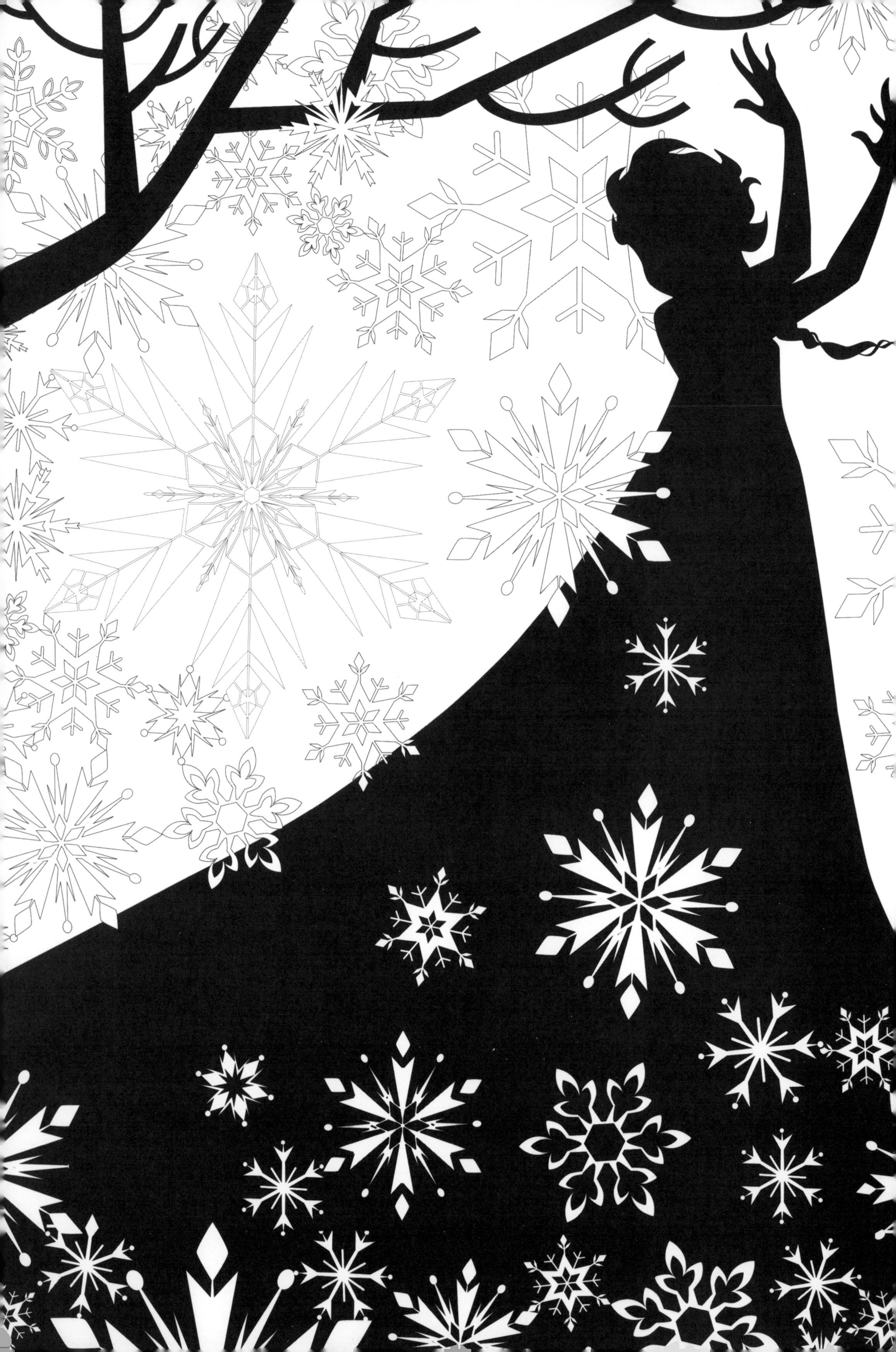

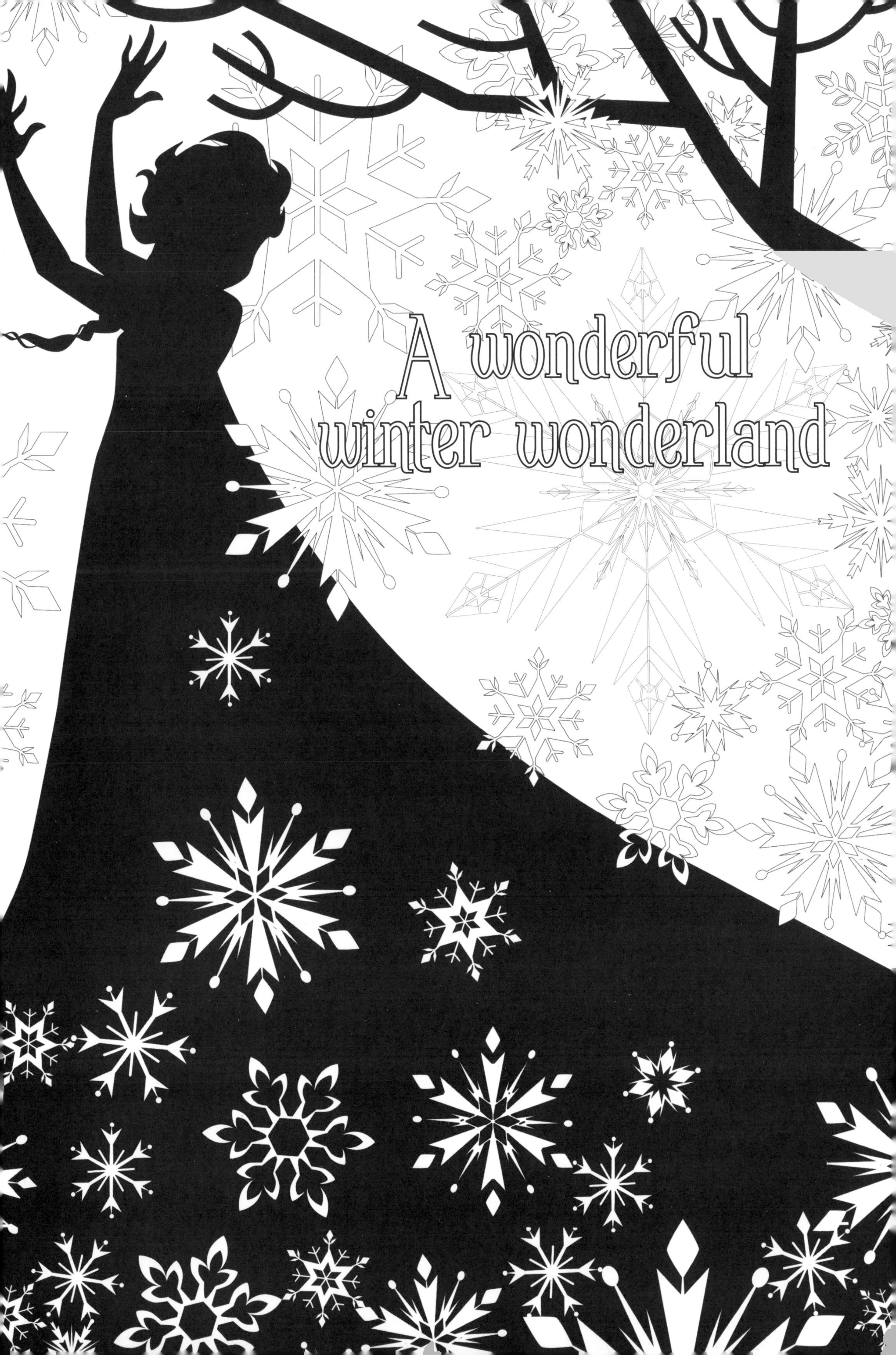
A wonderful
winter wonderland

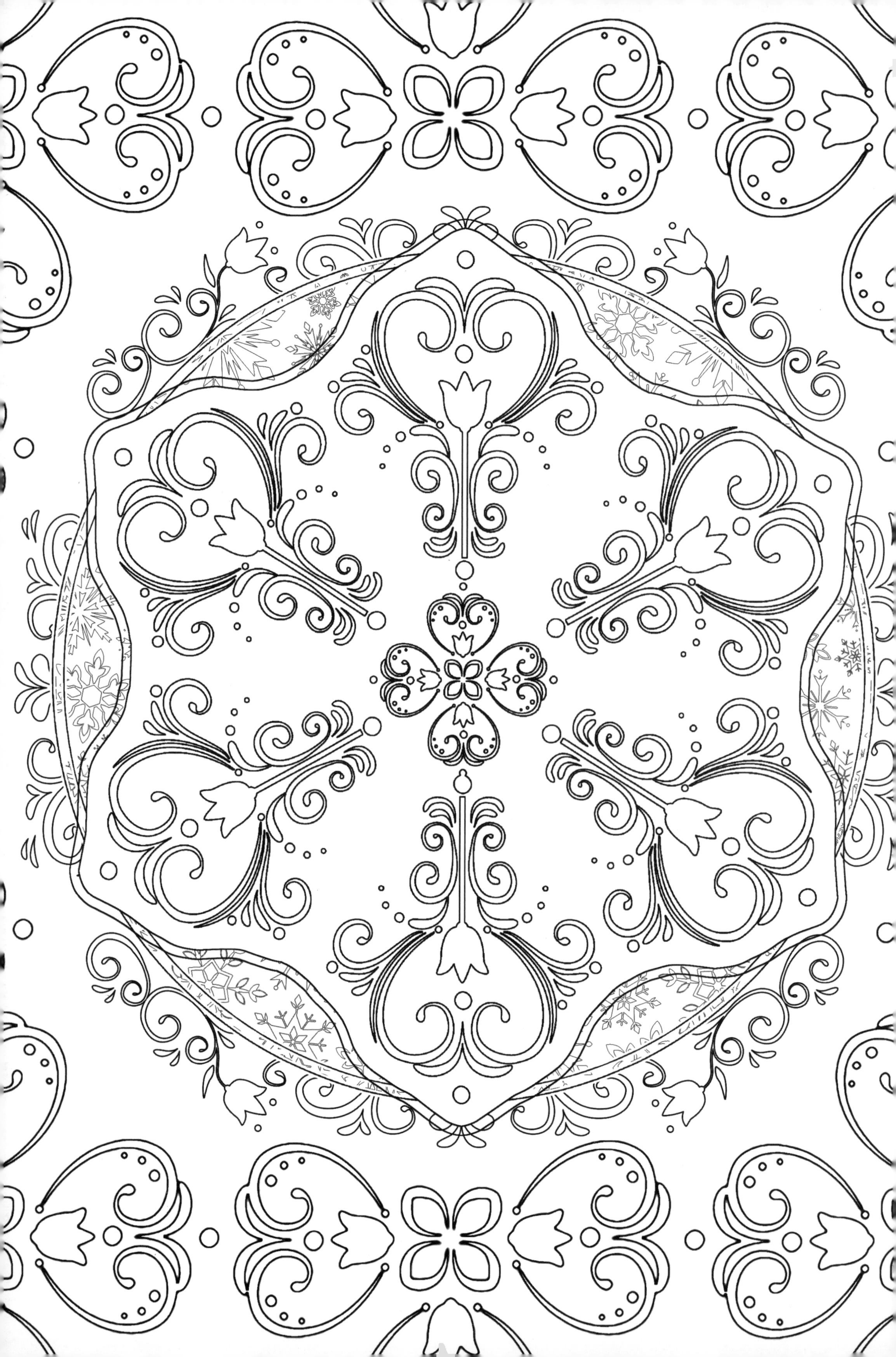

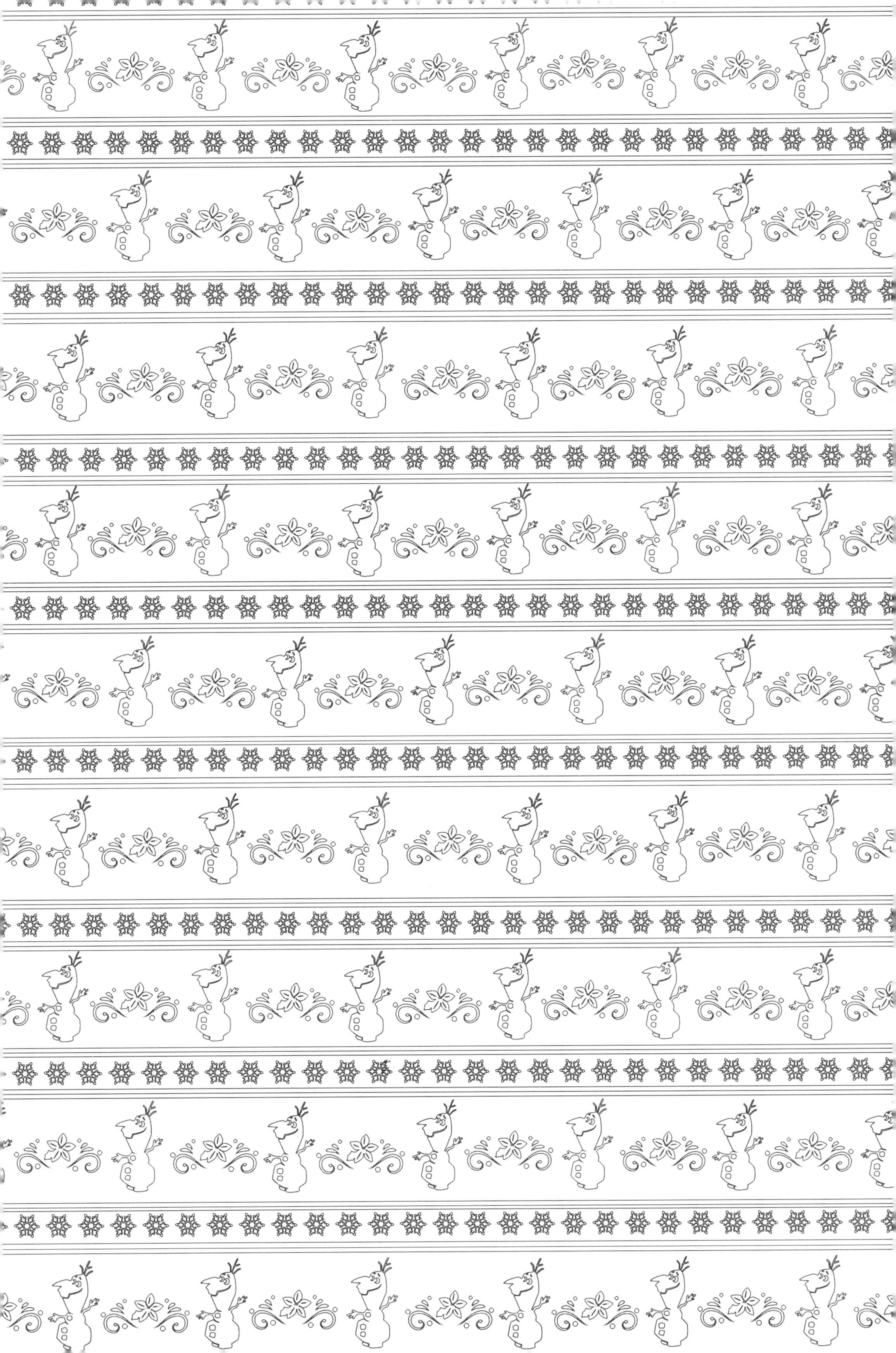

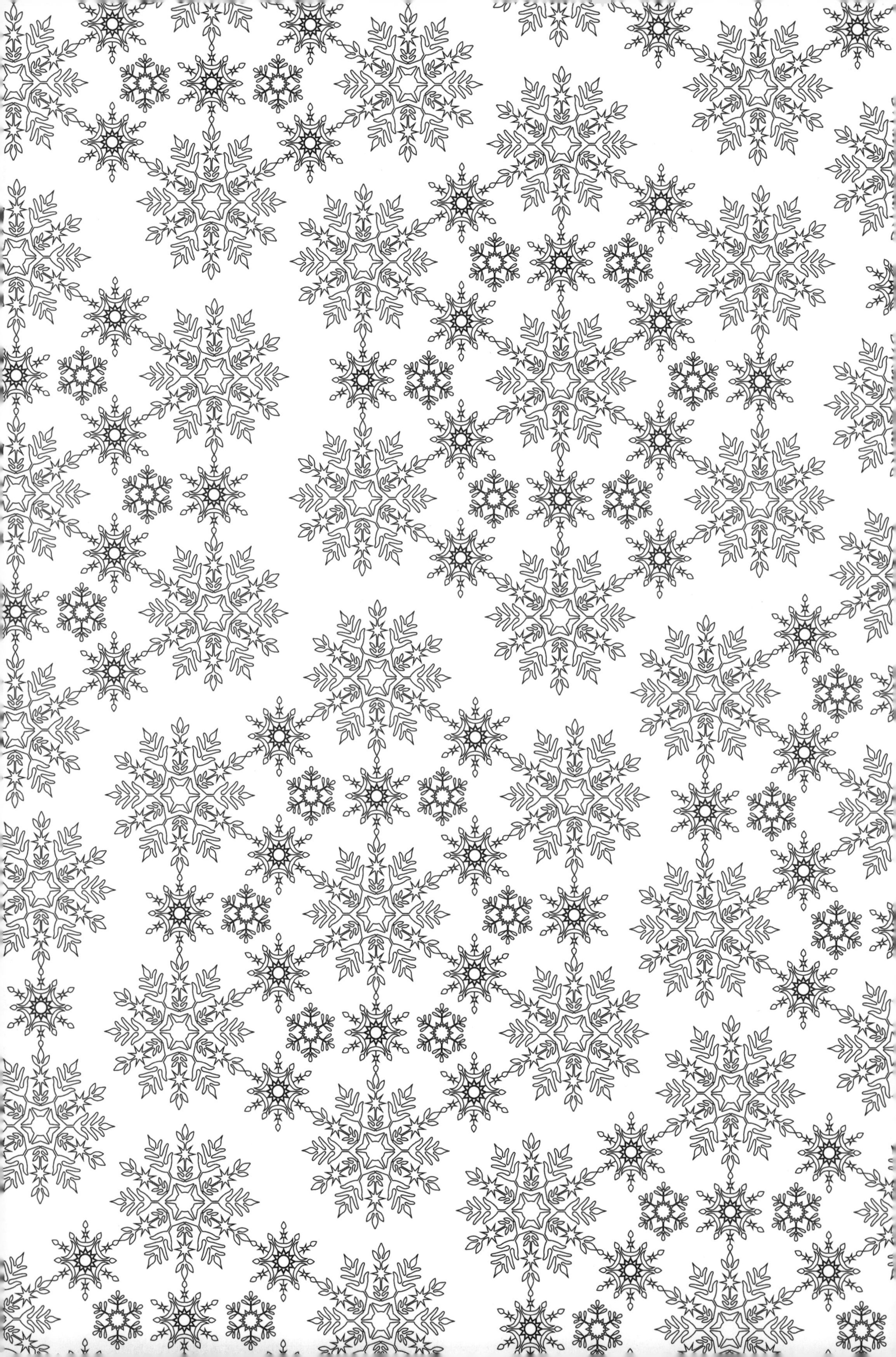

A BOND

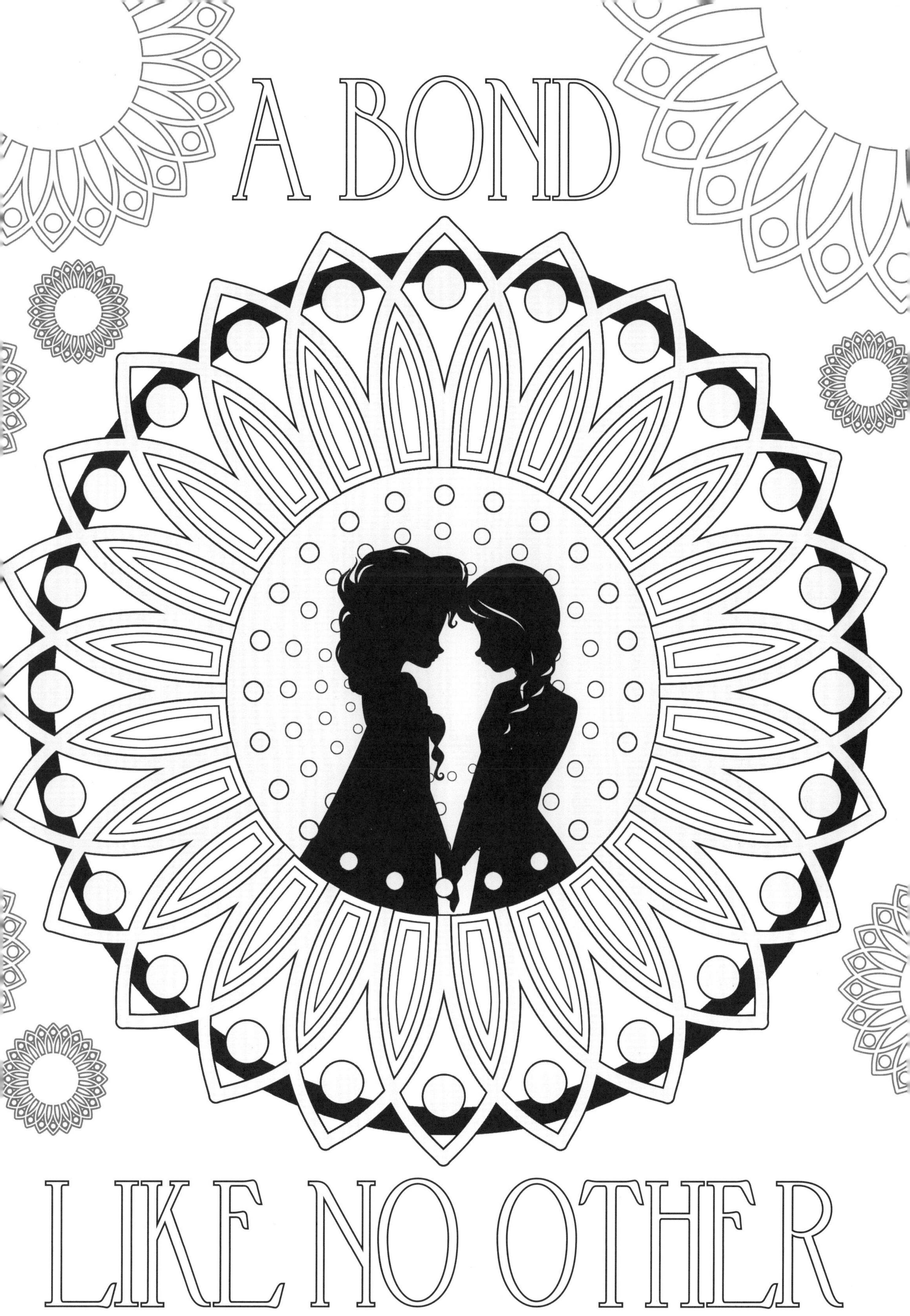

LIKE NO OTHER

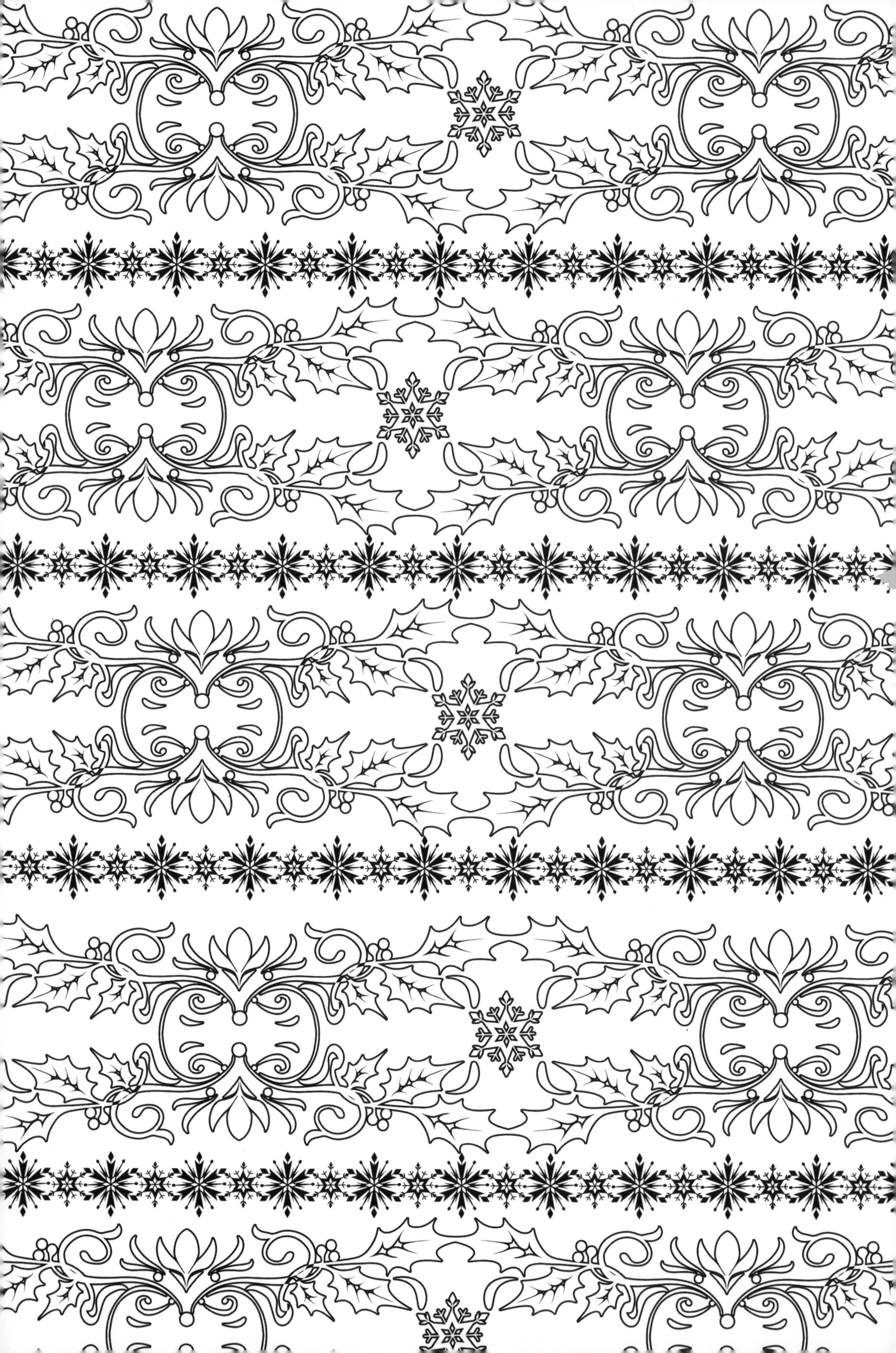

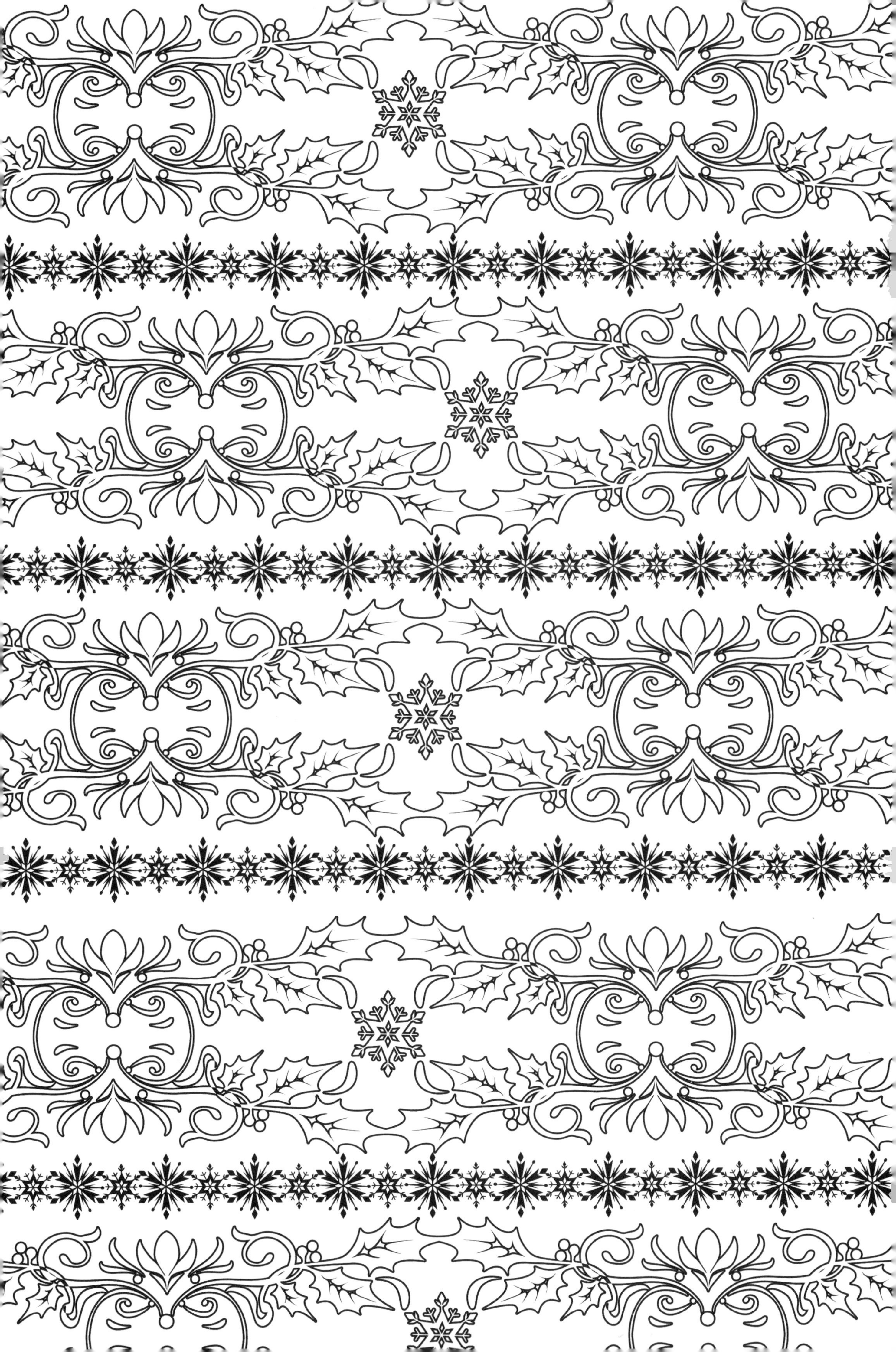

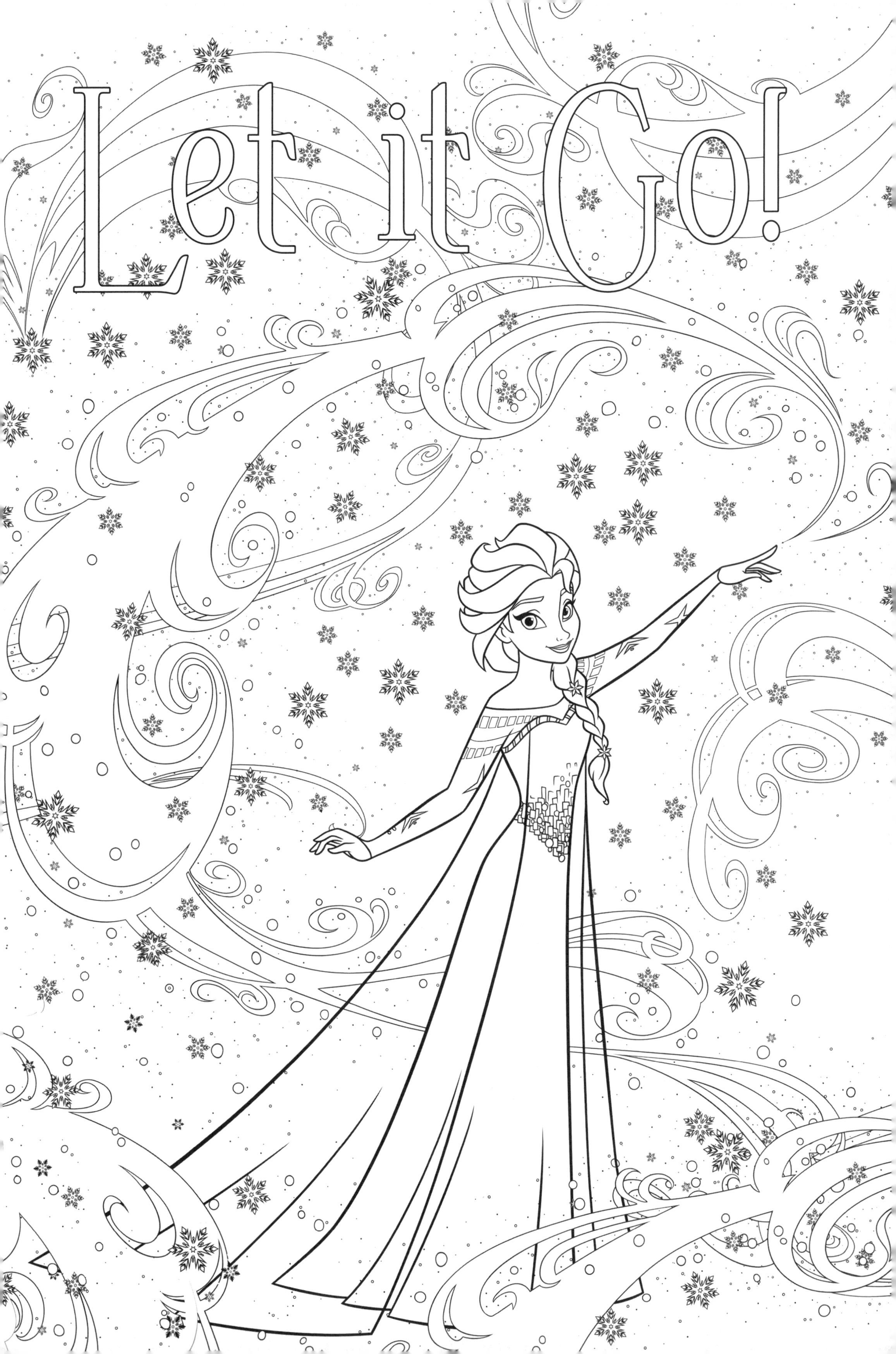
Let it Go!

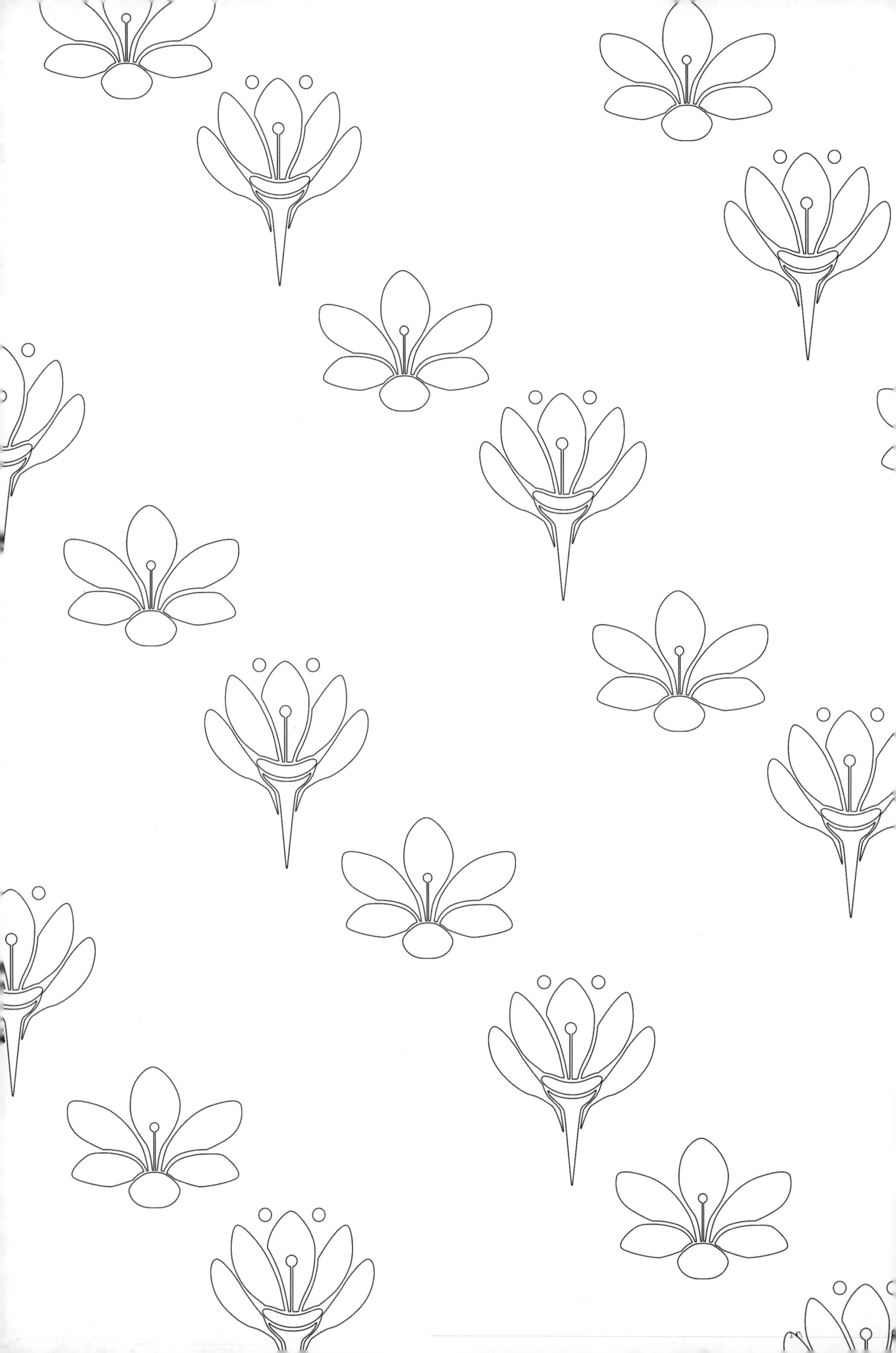

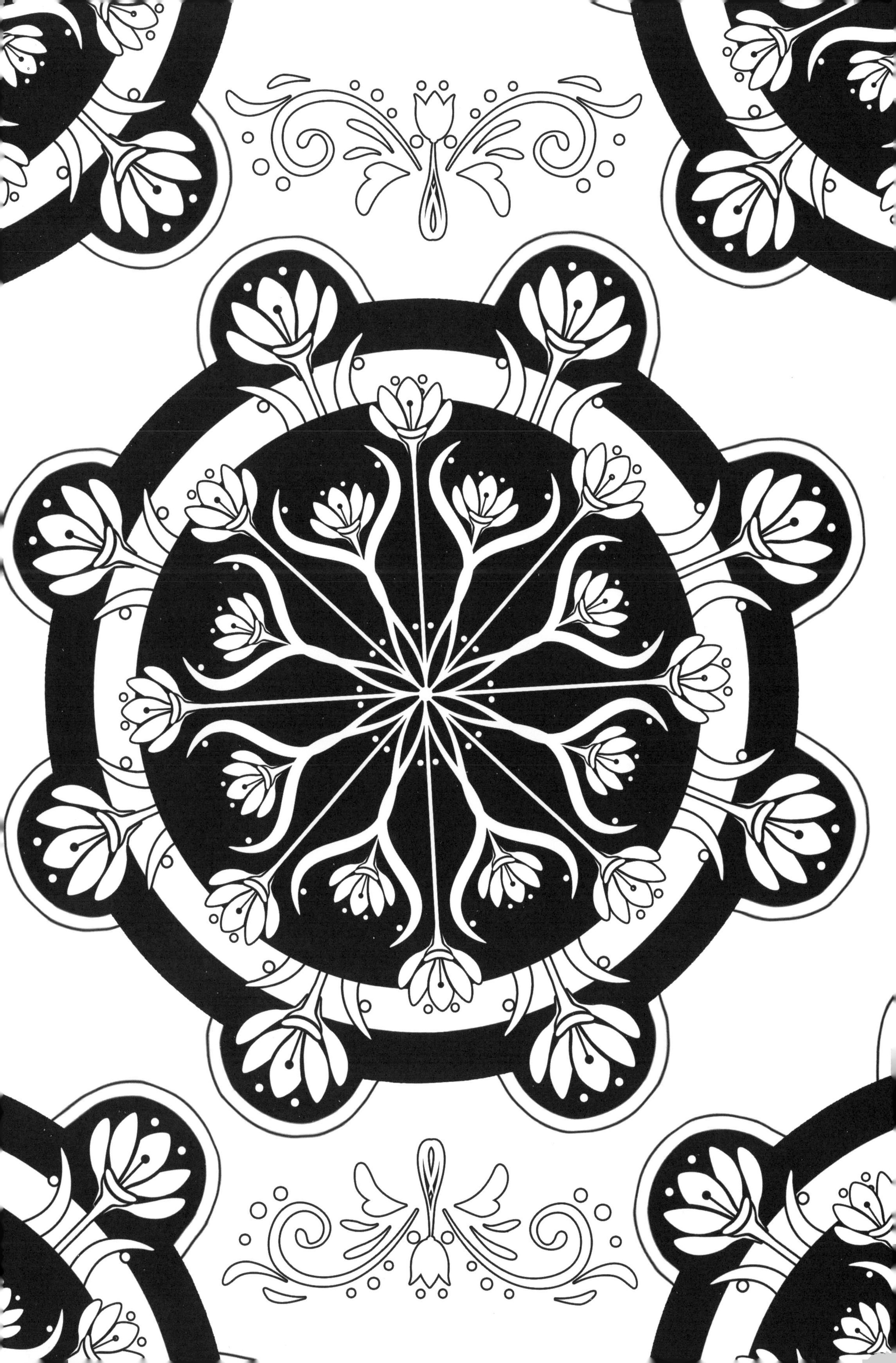

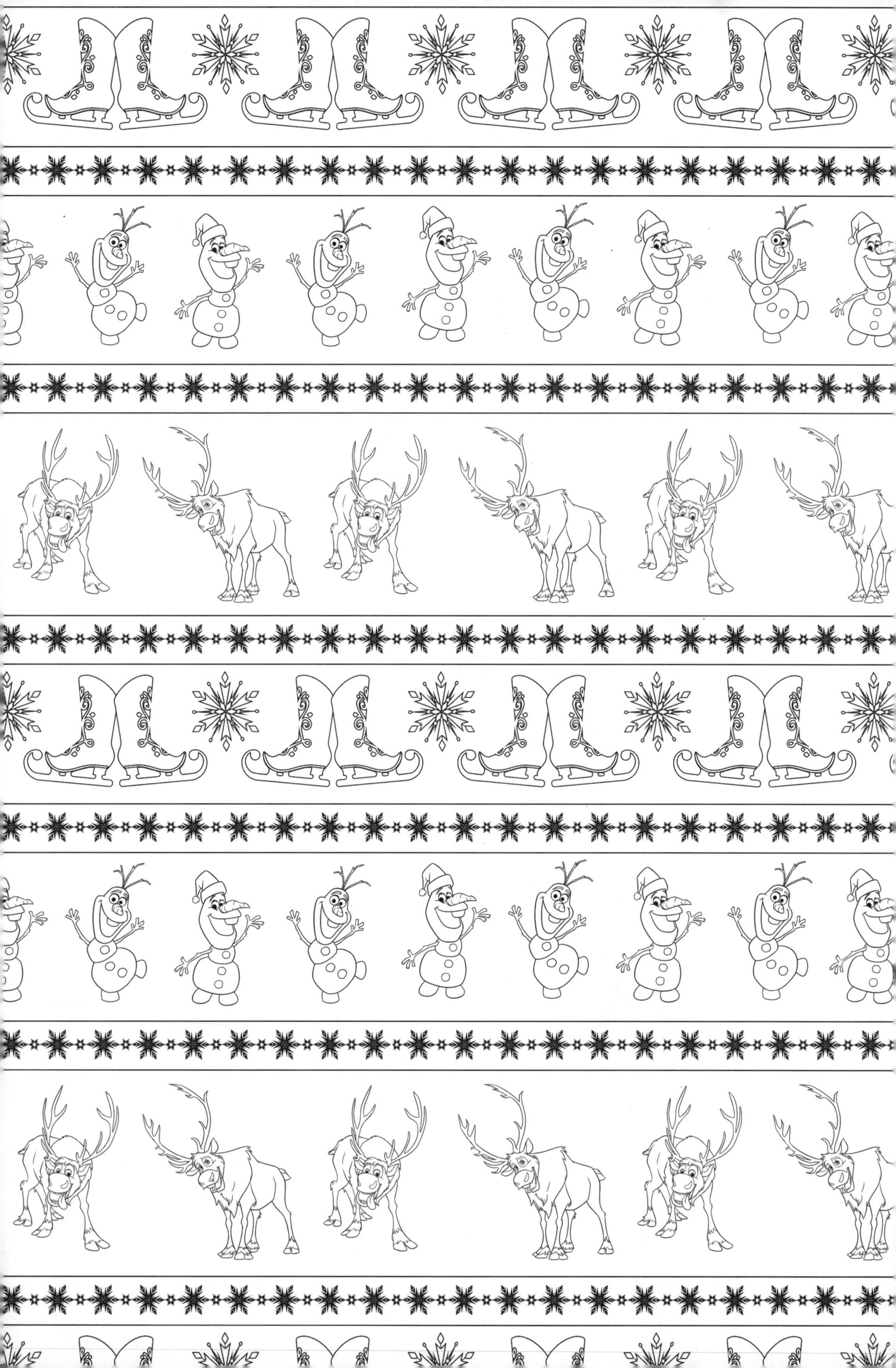

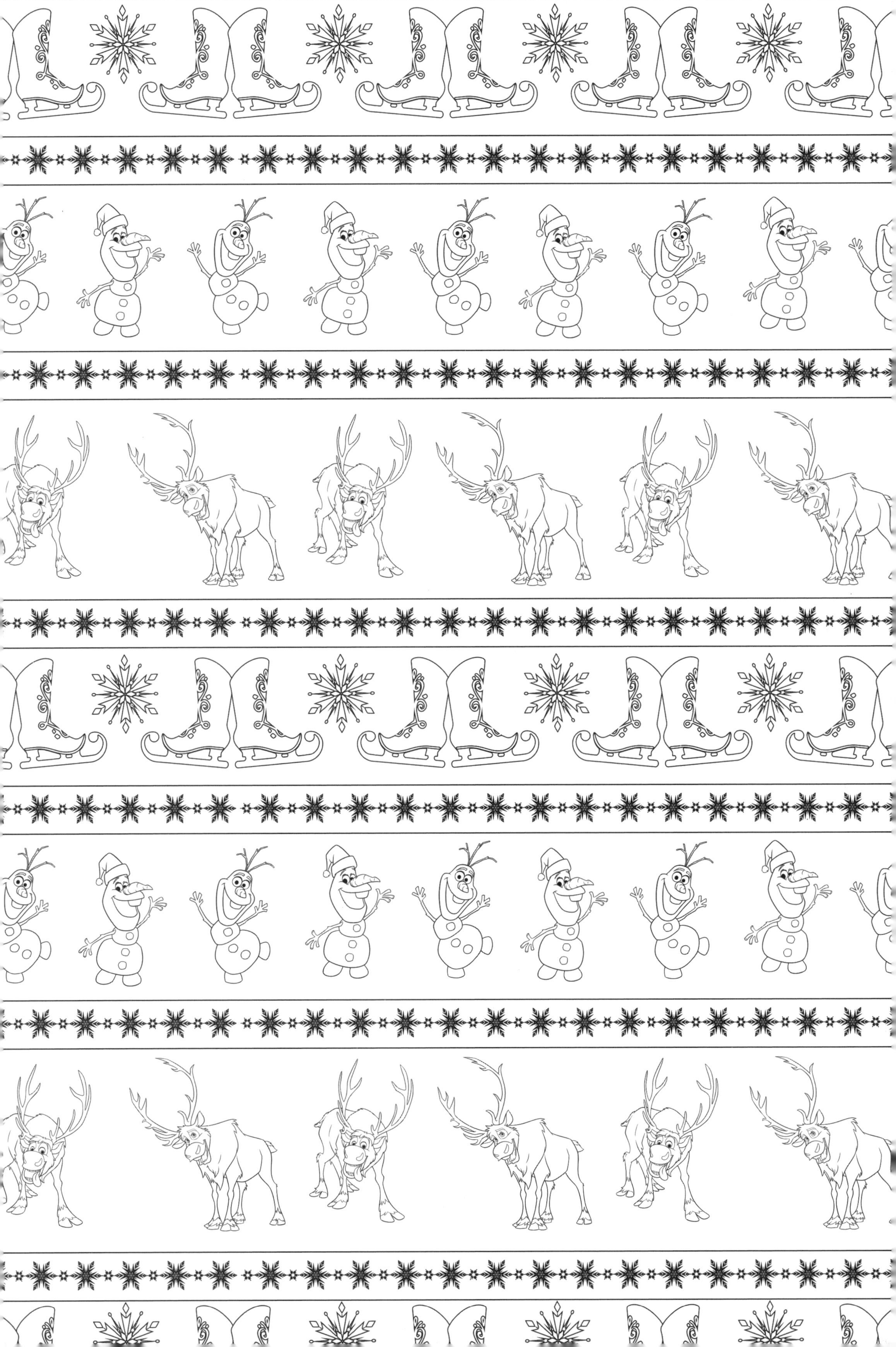

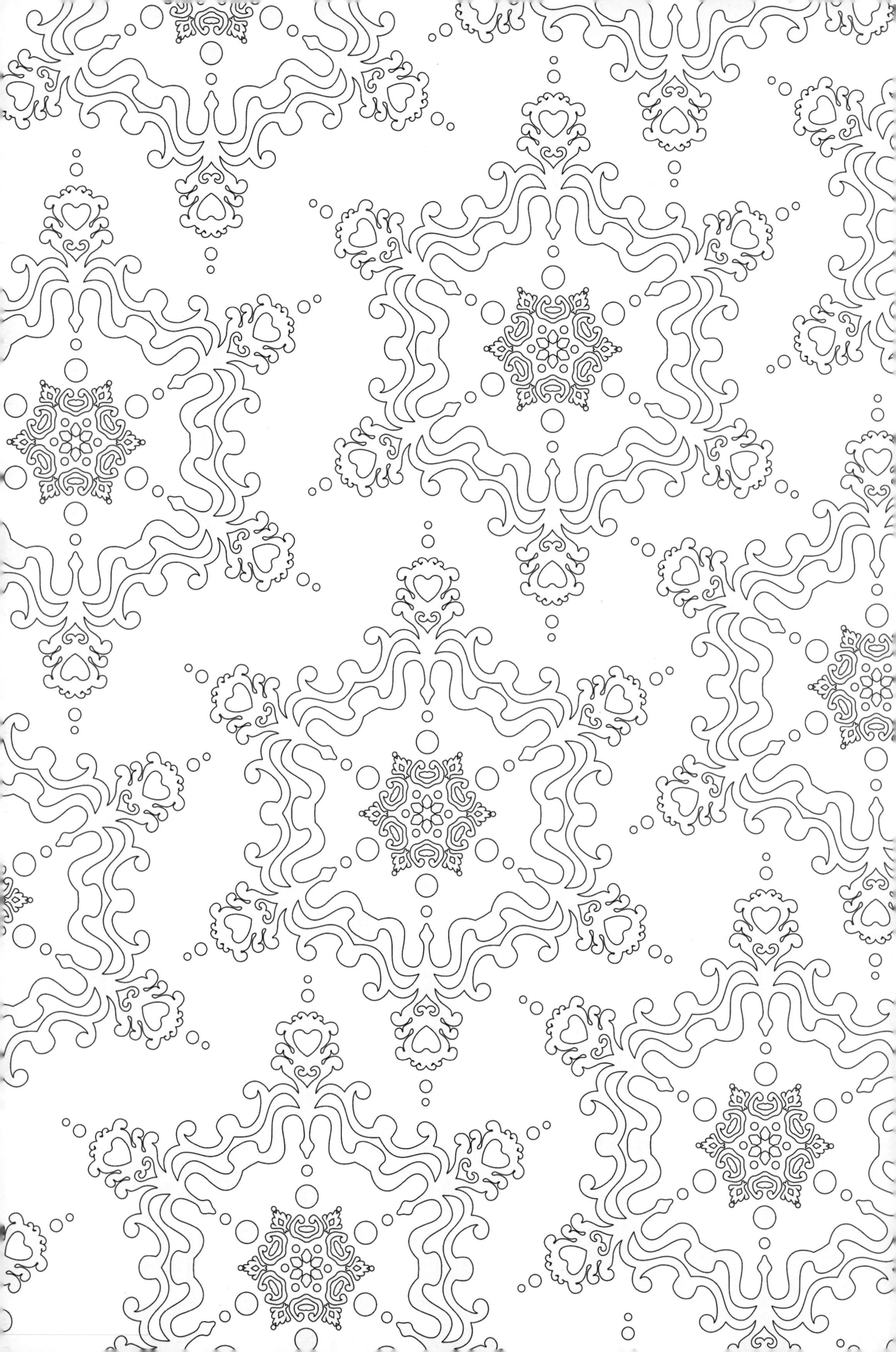

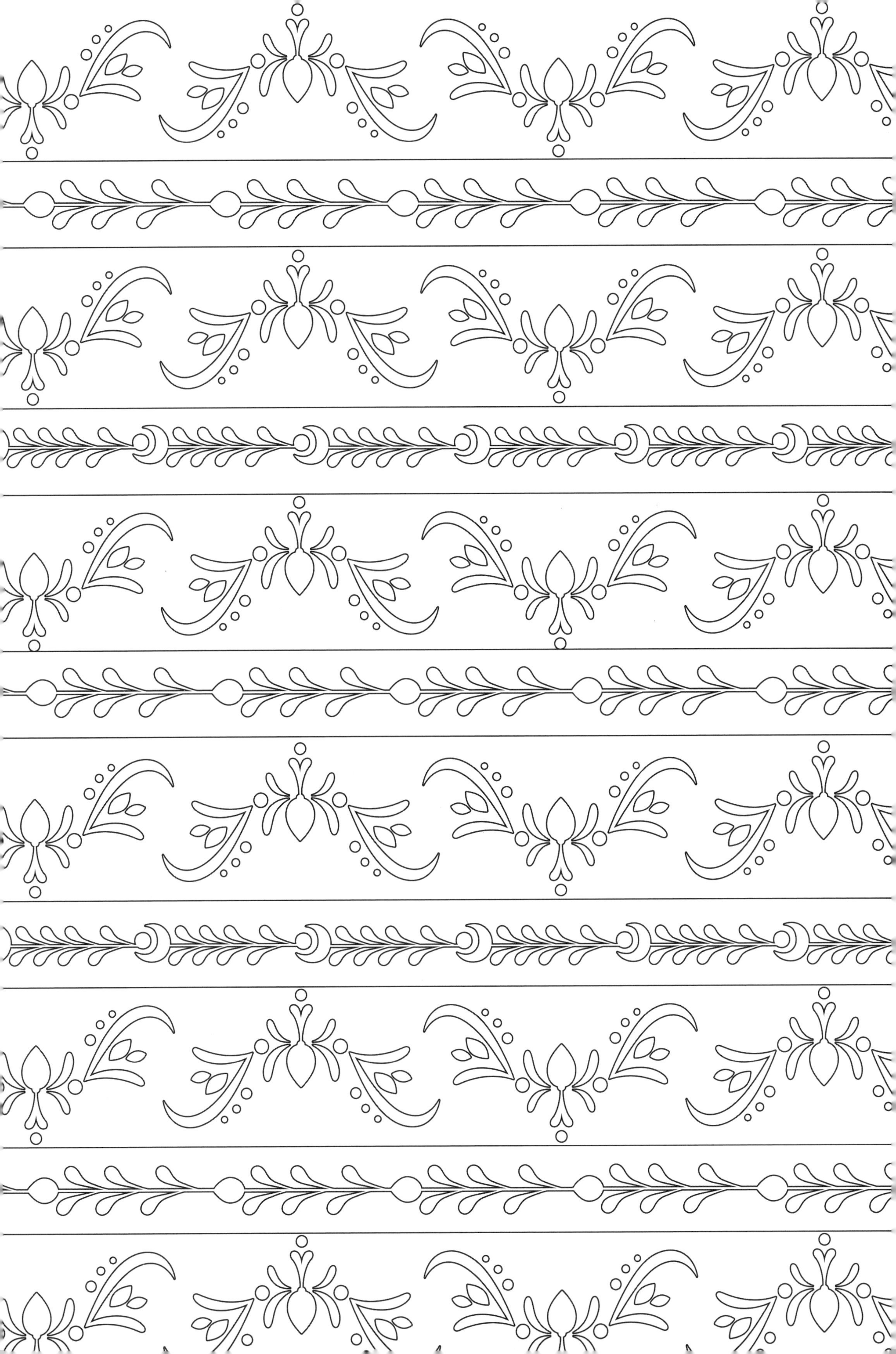

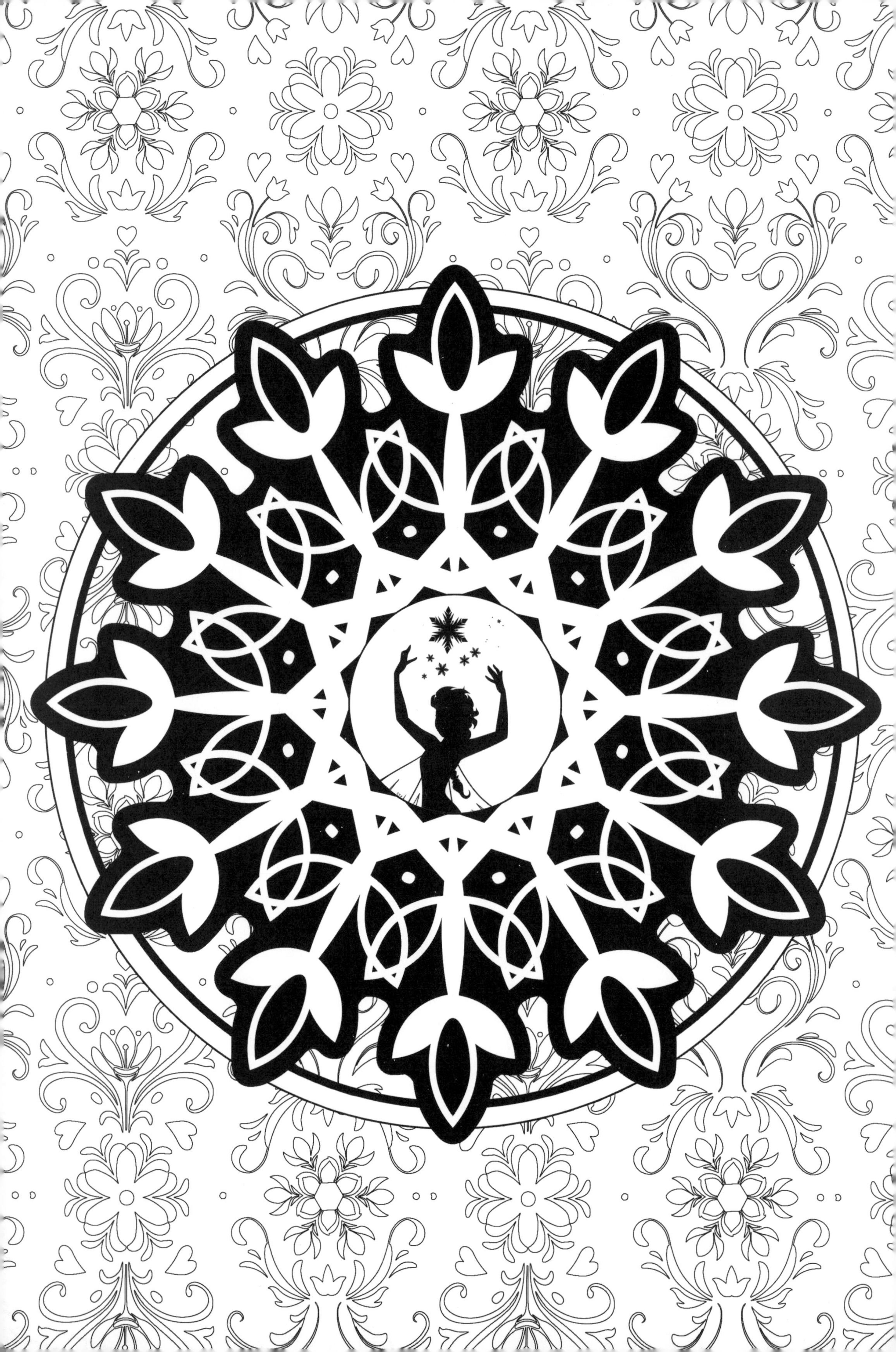

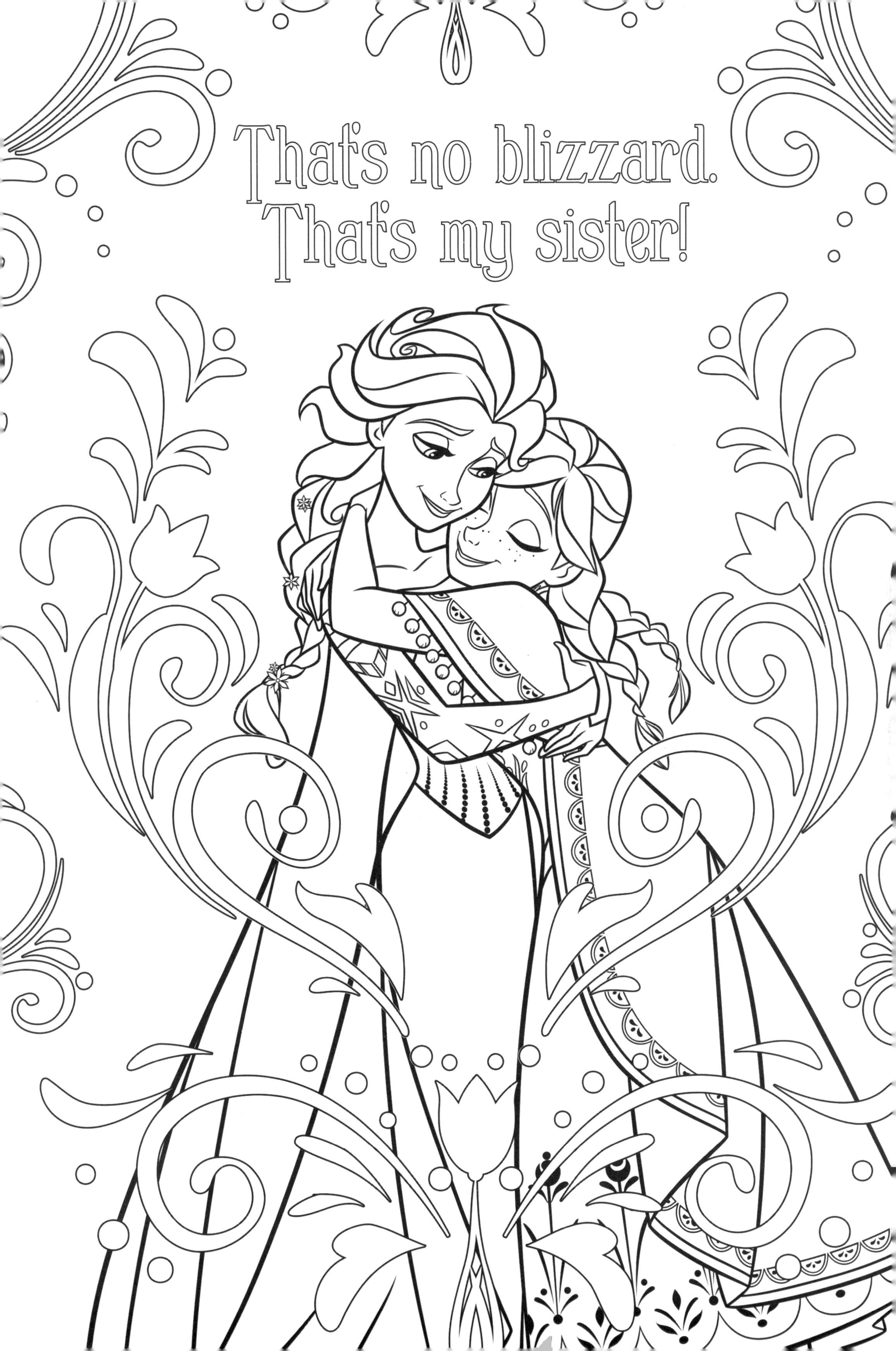
That's no blizzard.
That's my sister!

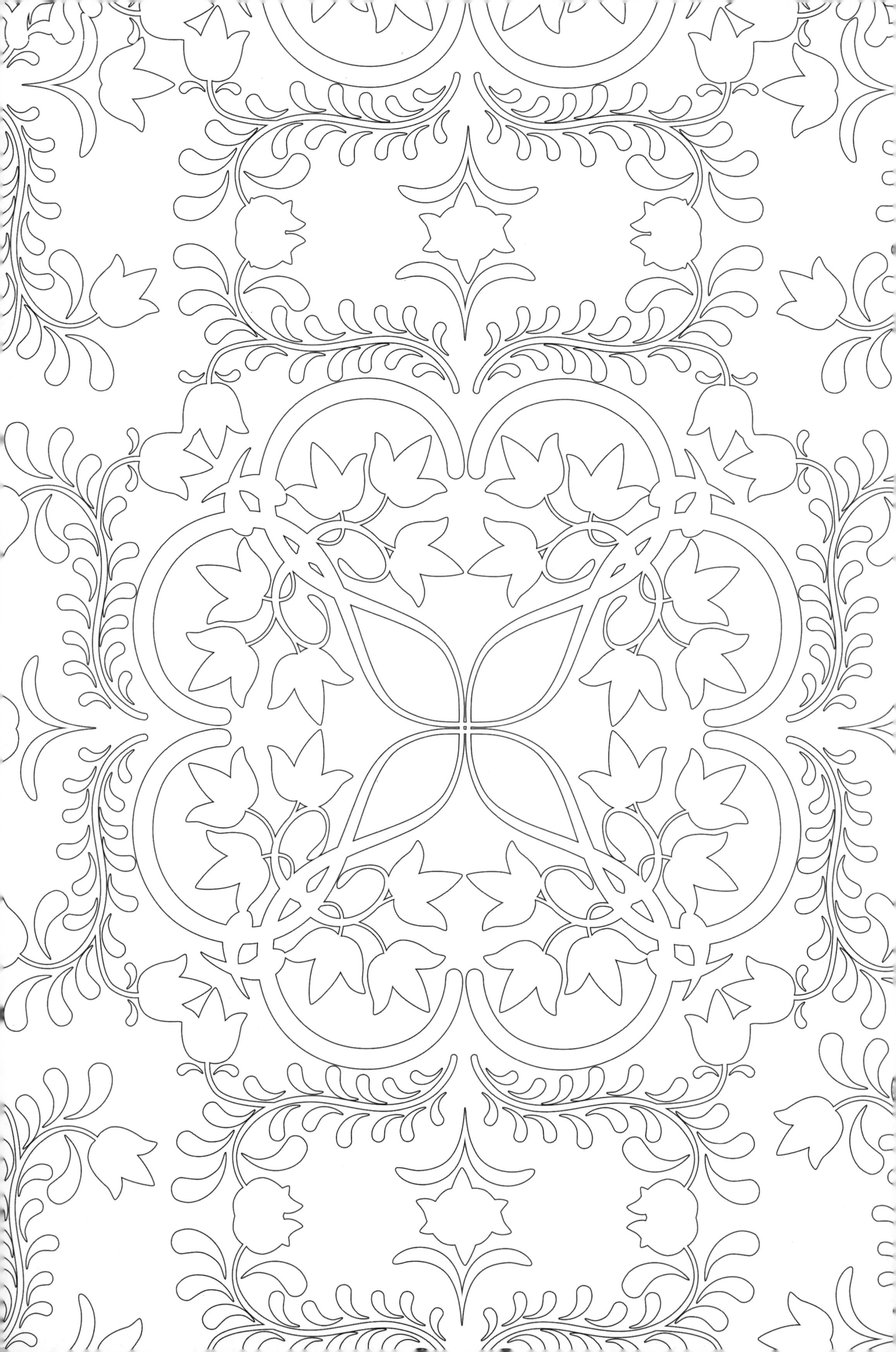

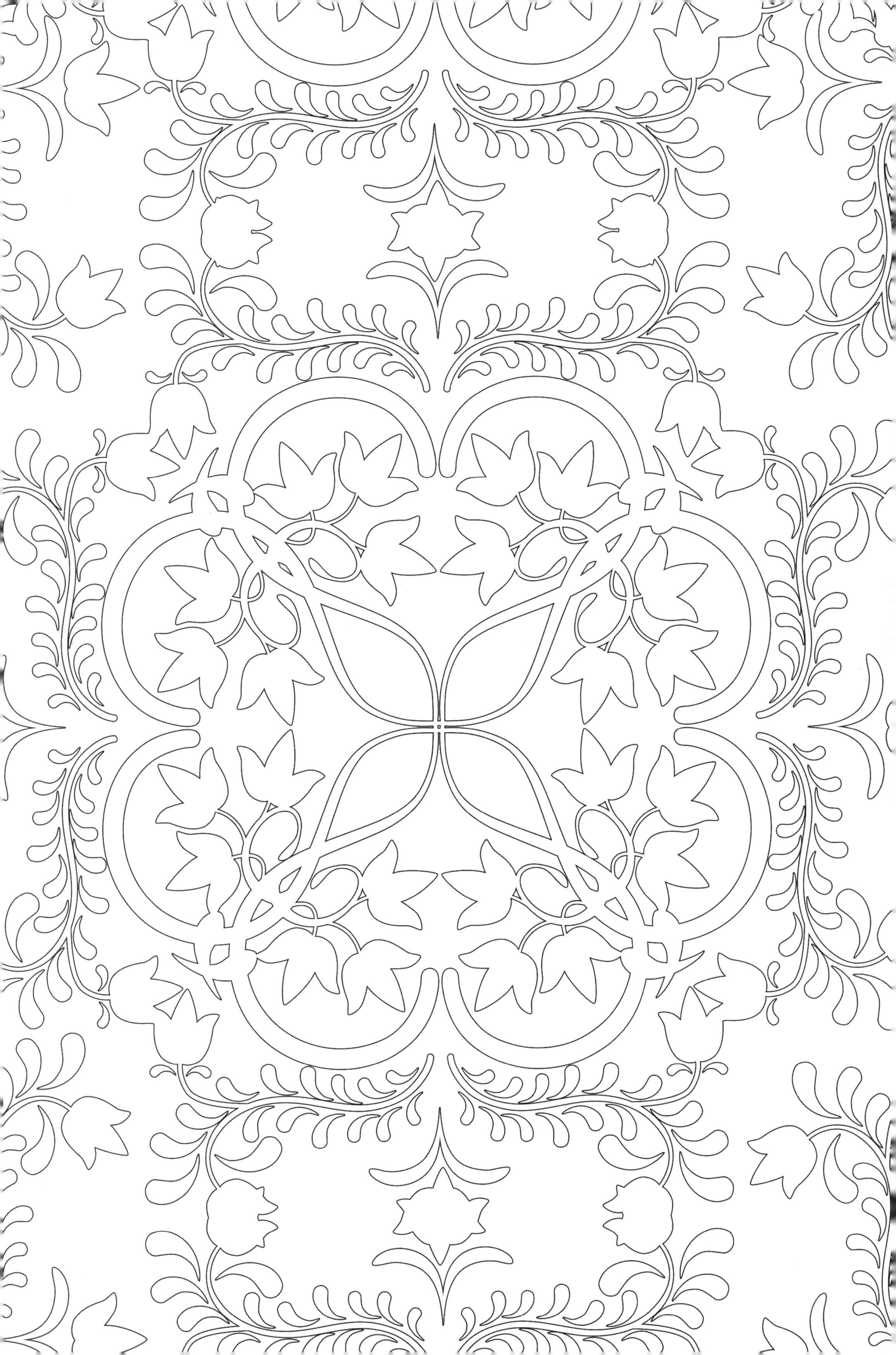

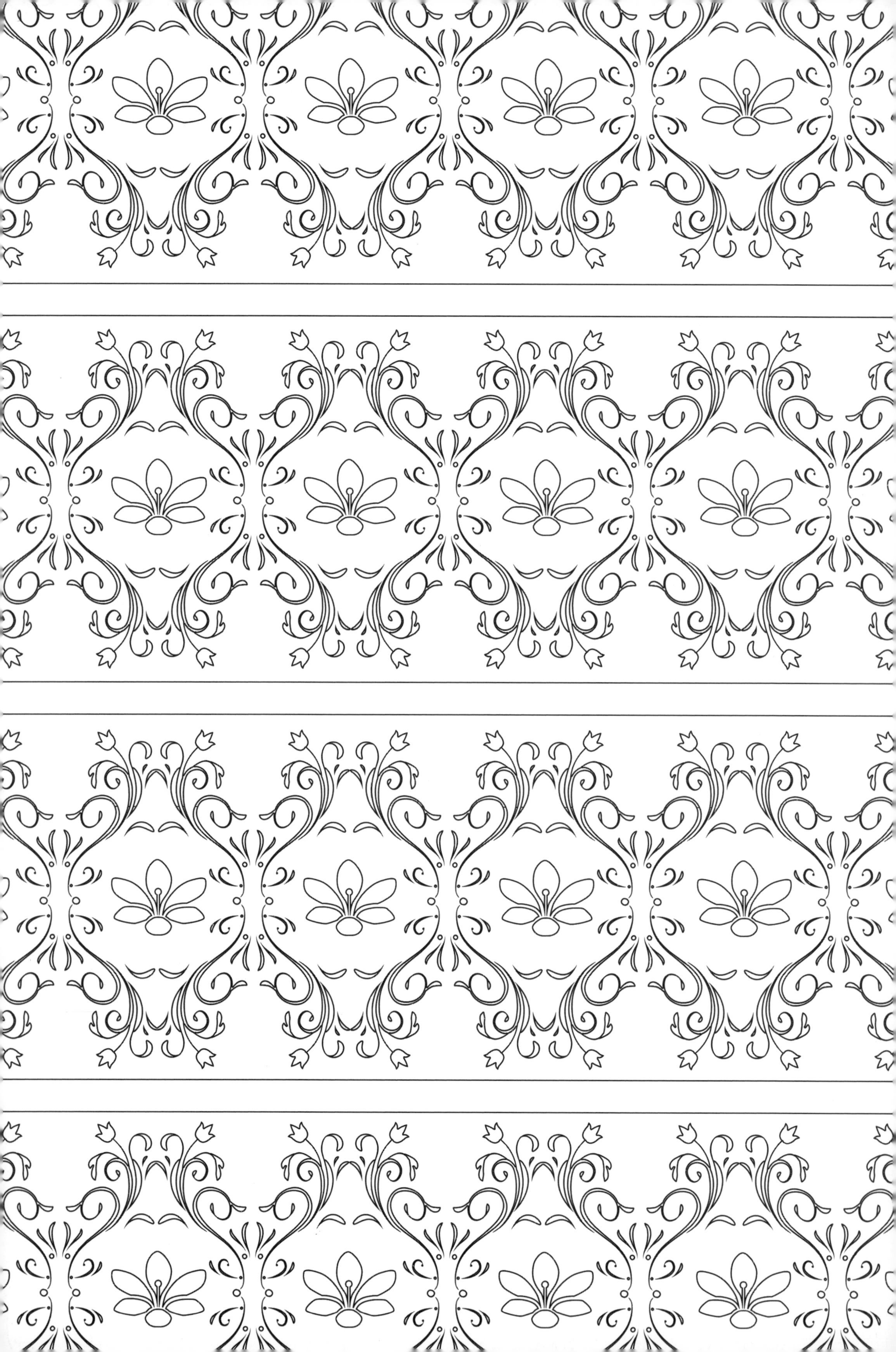

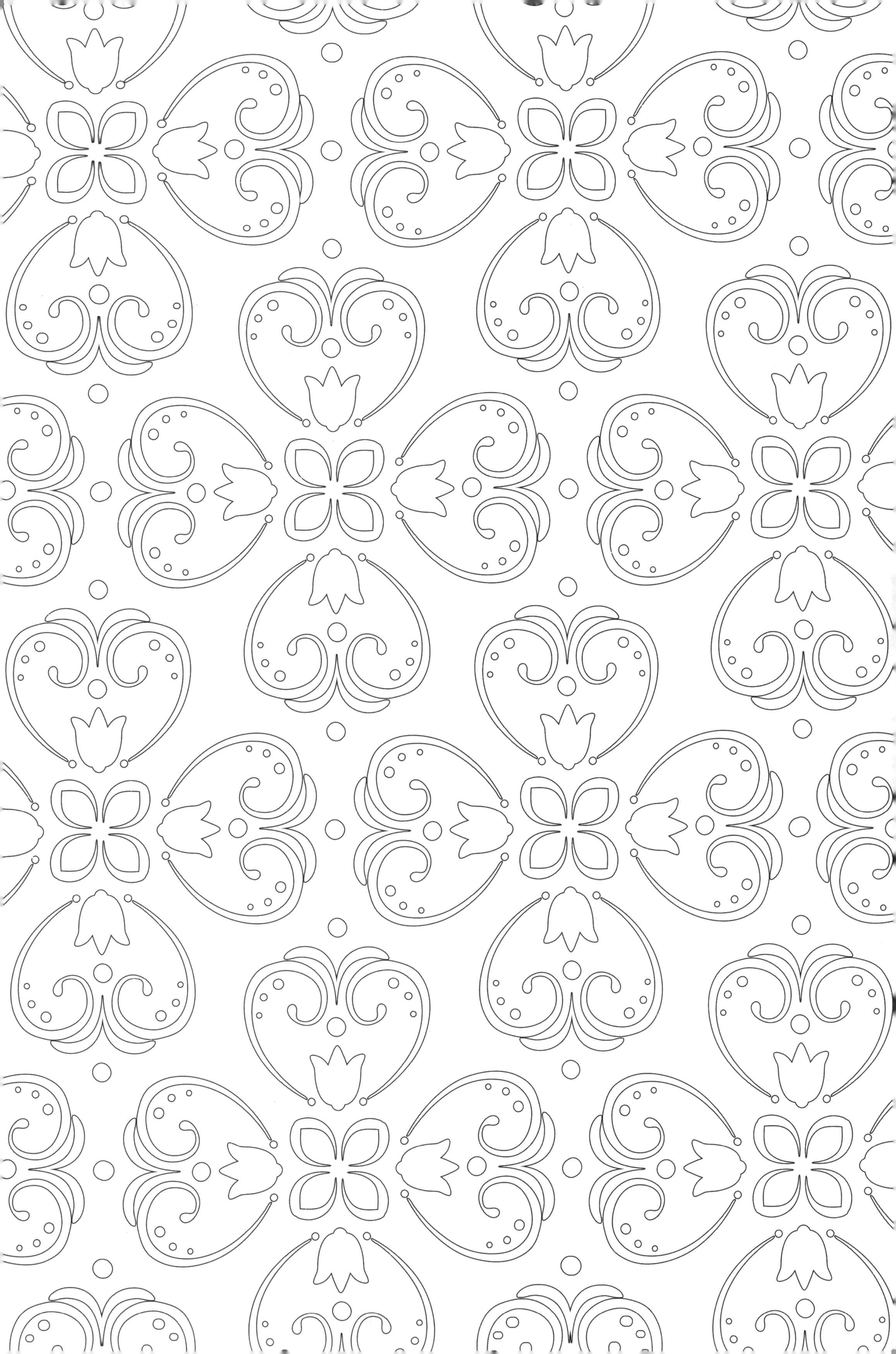

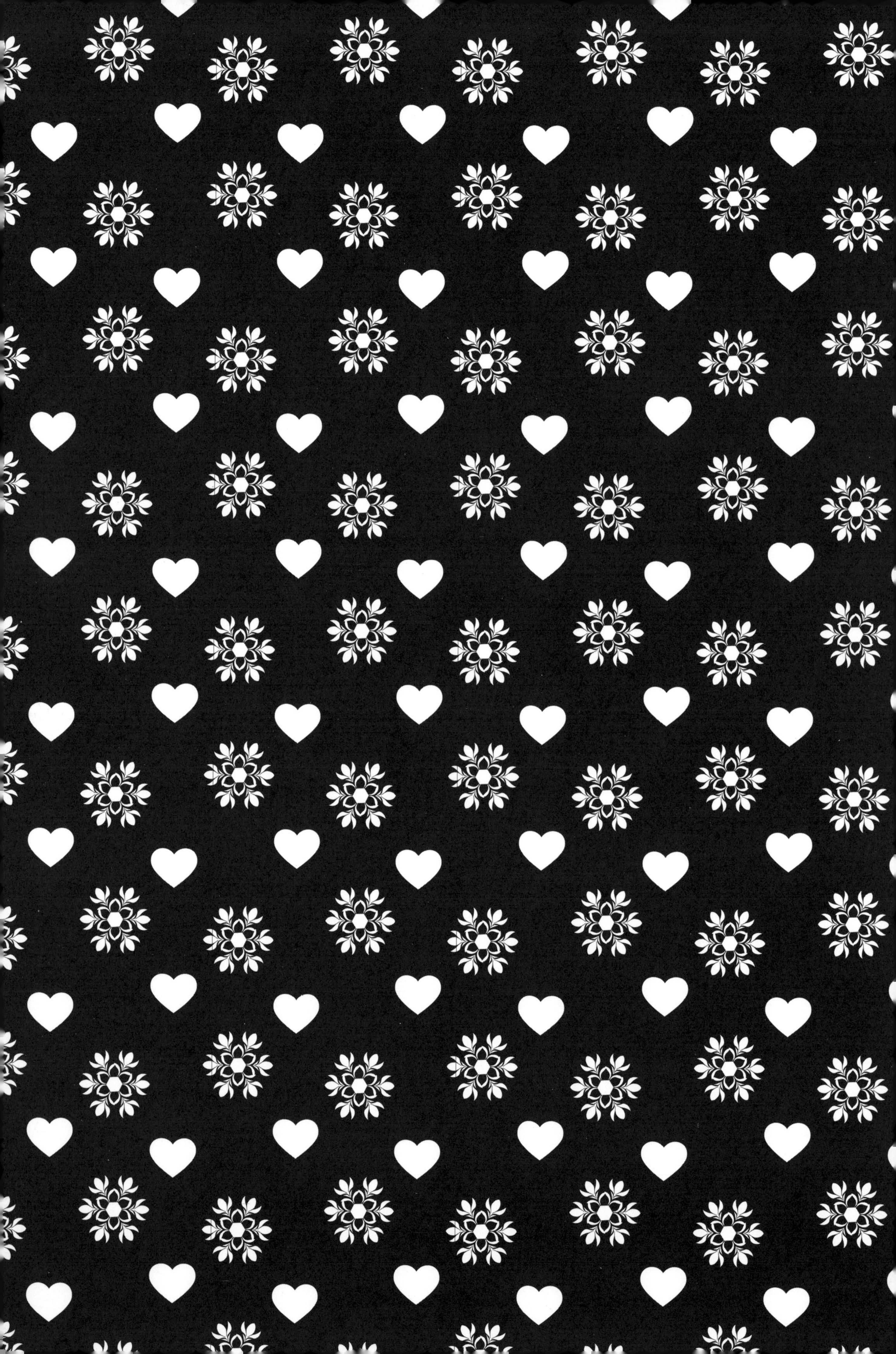

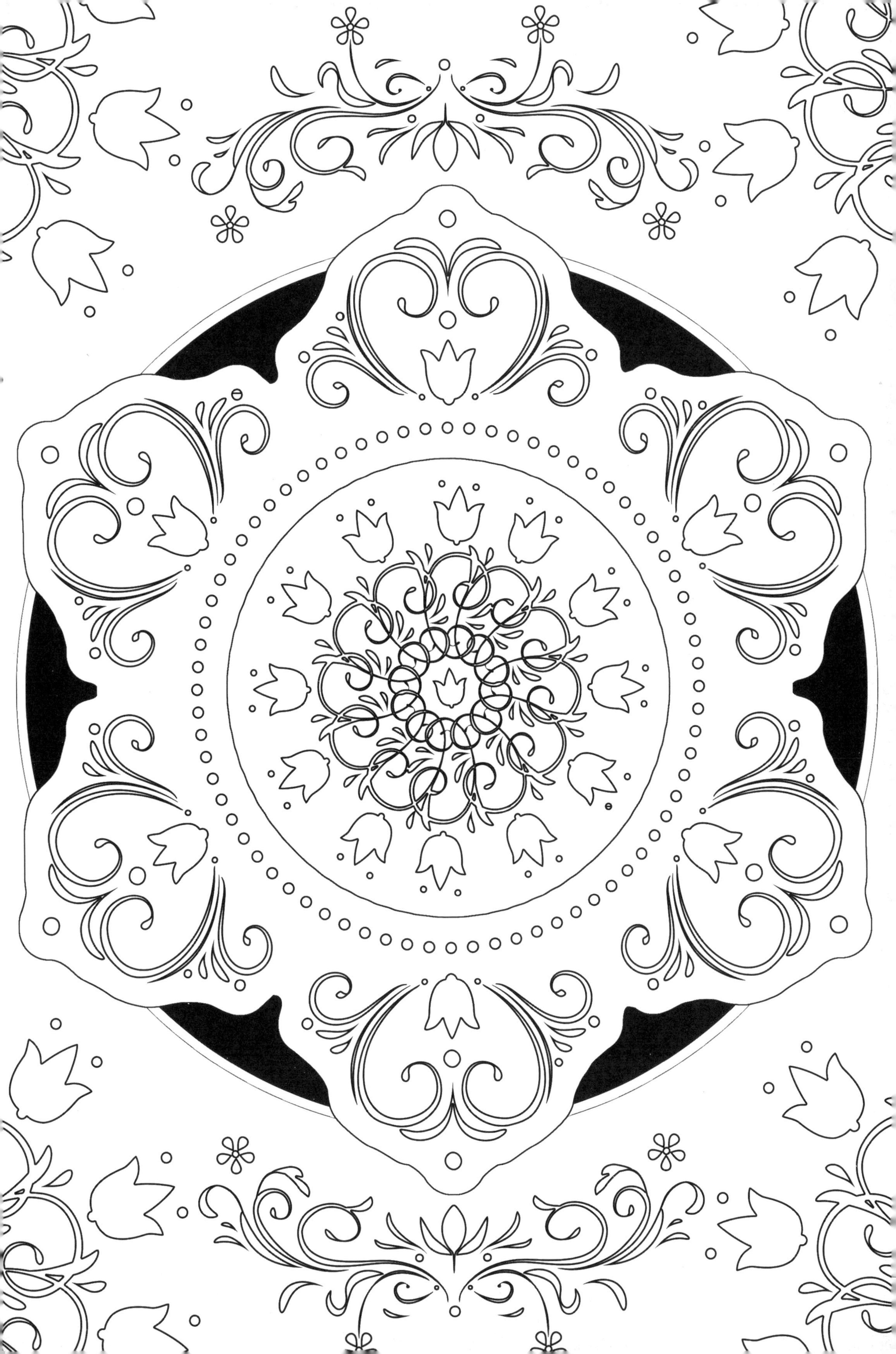

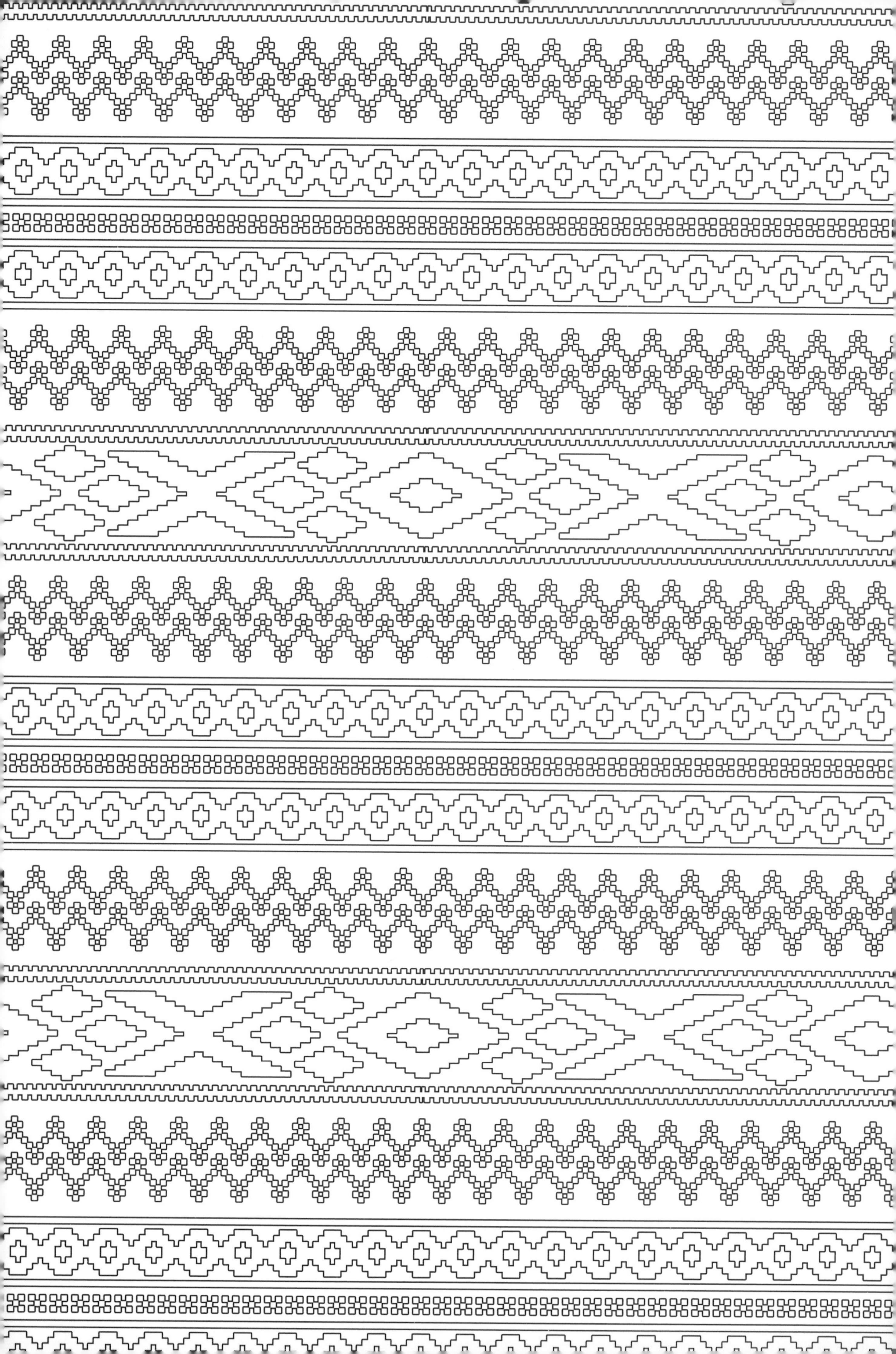

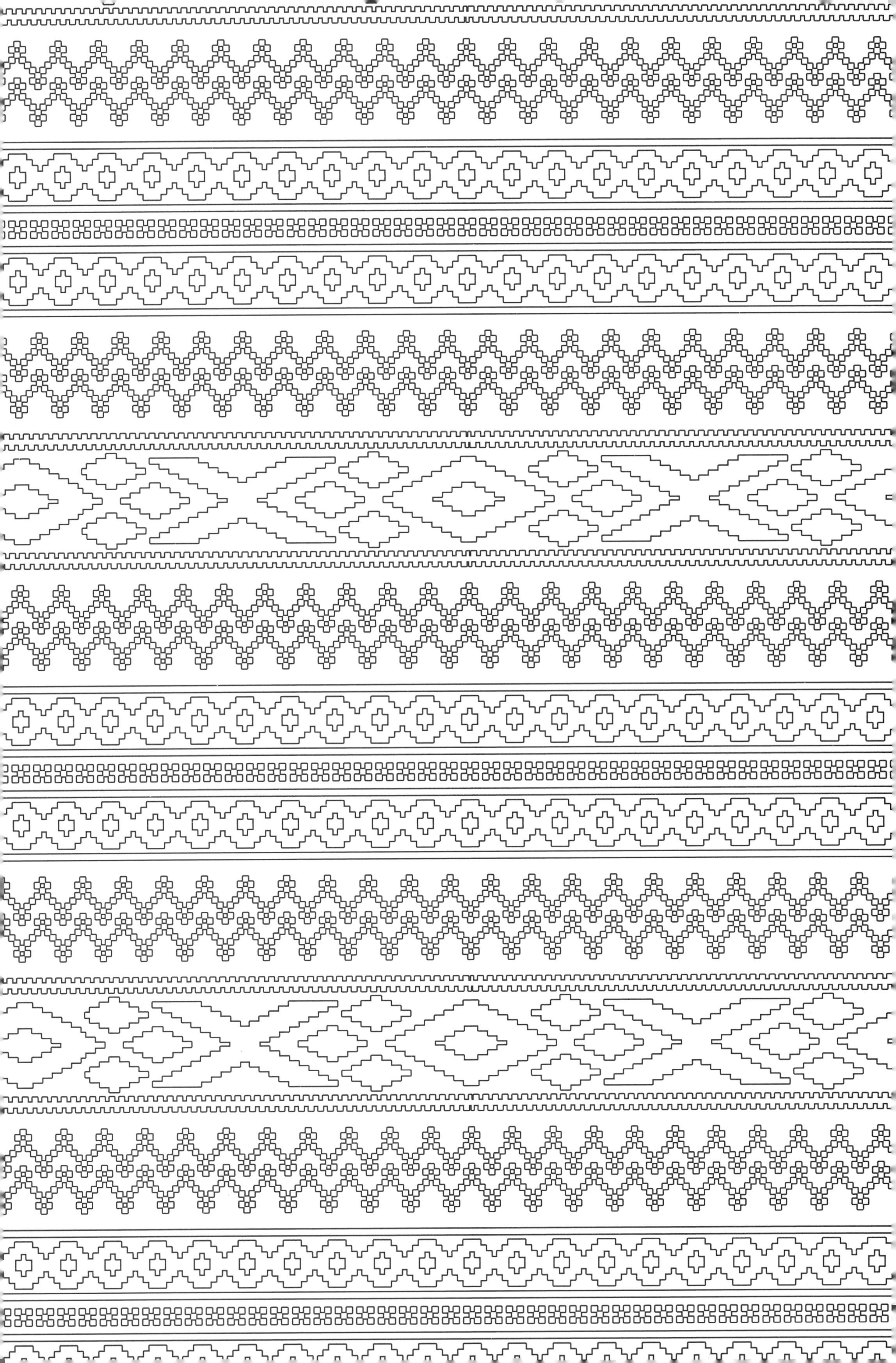

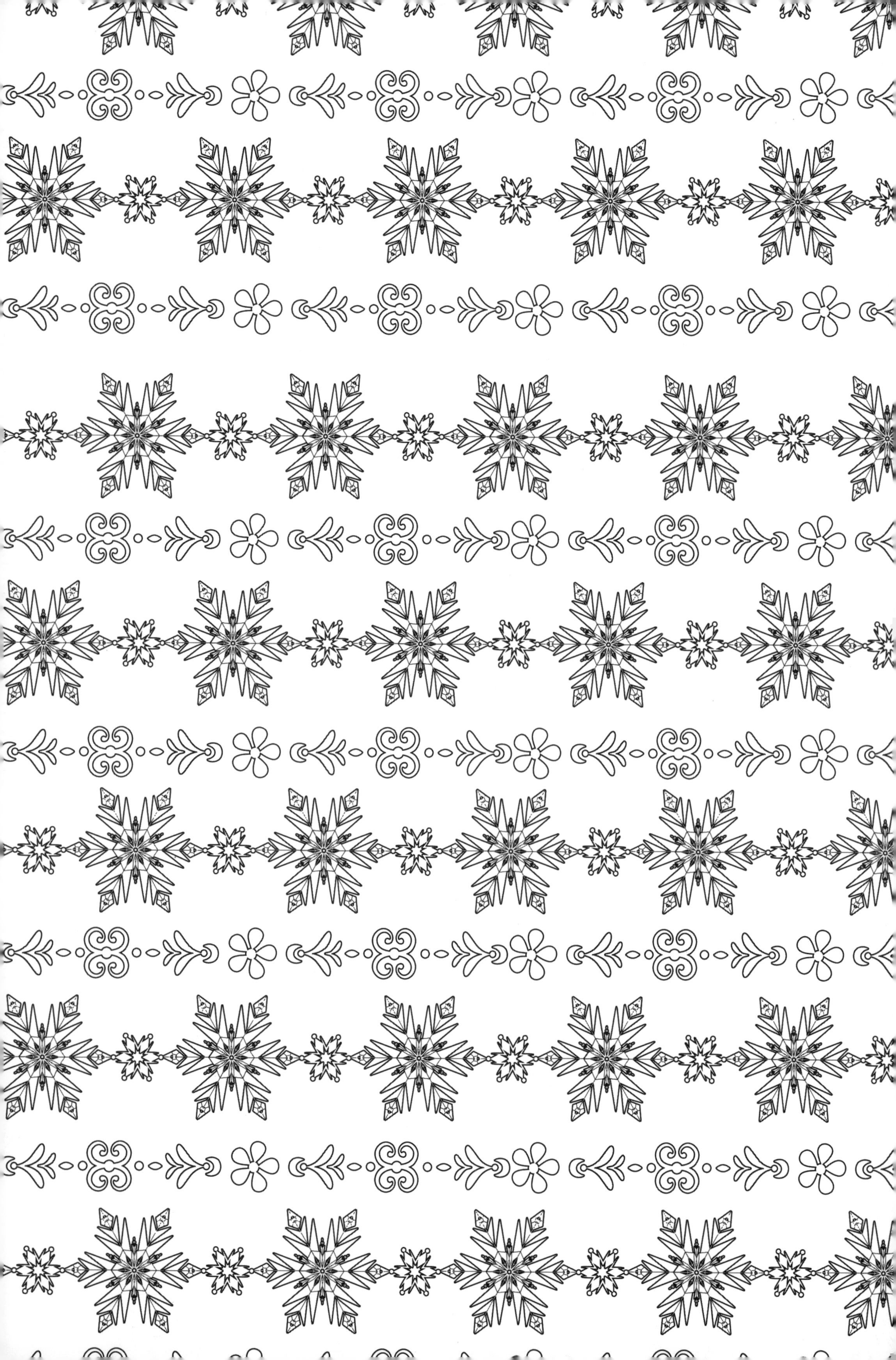

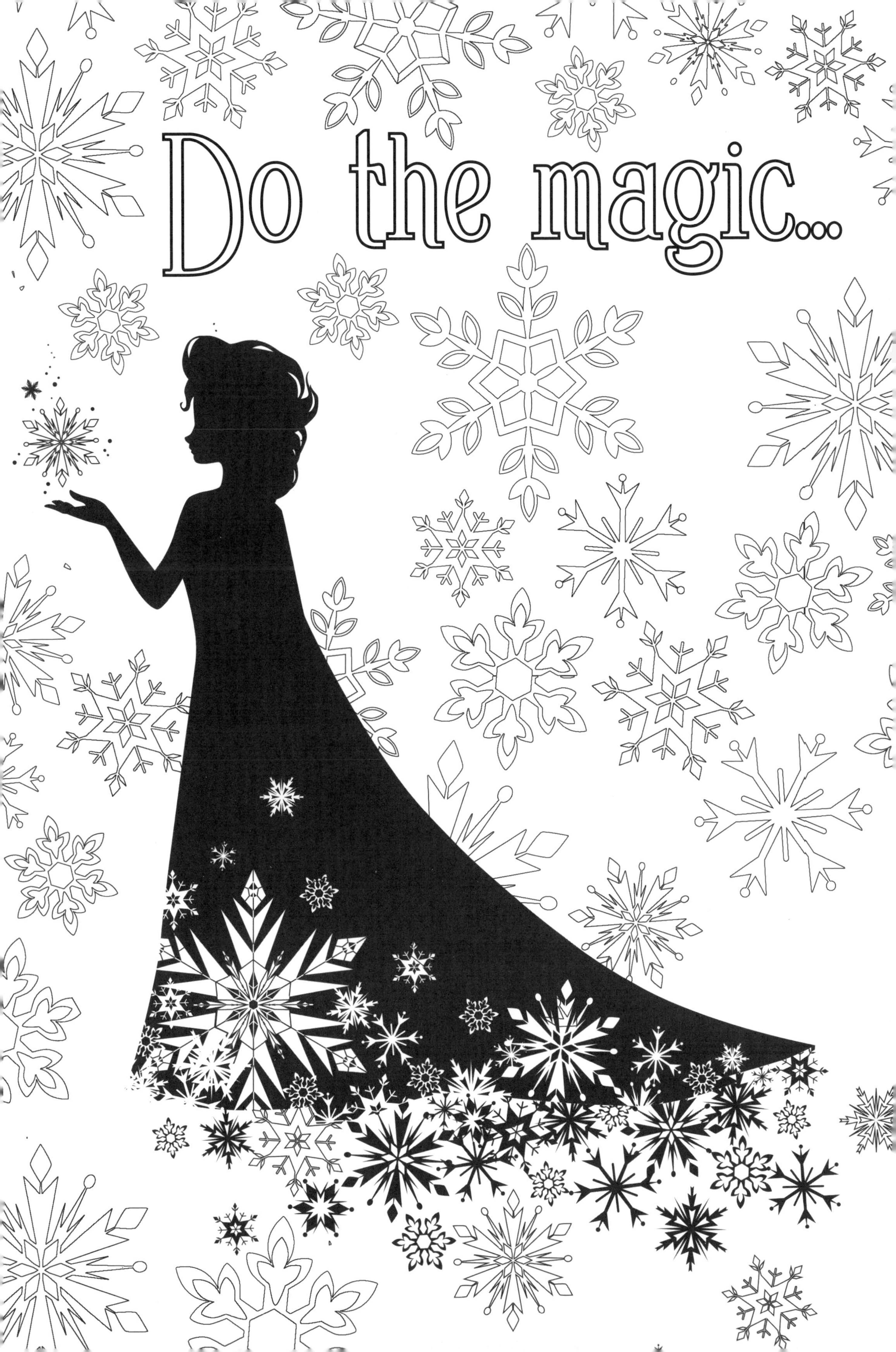
Do the magic...

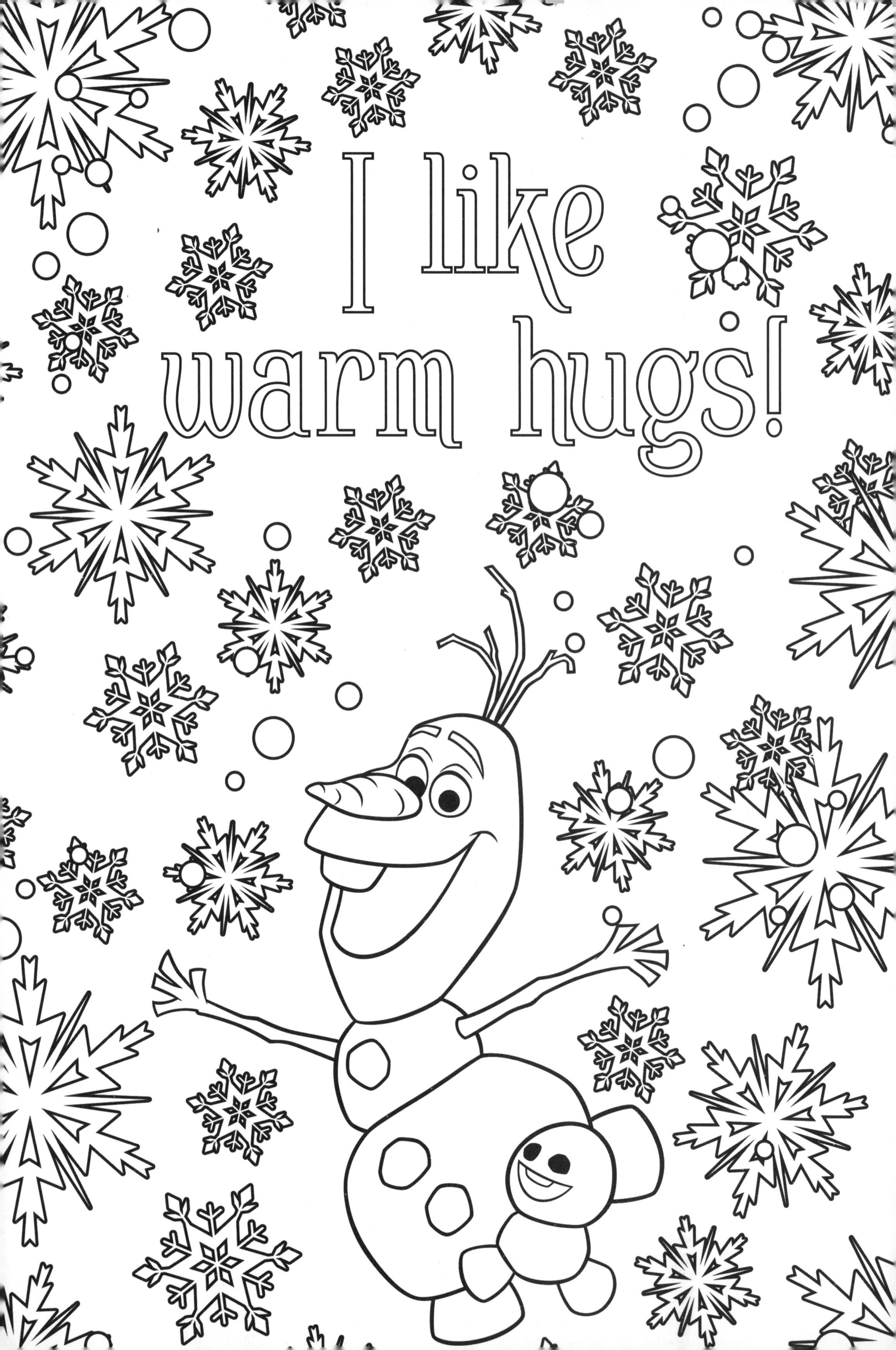
I like
warm hugs!

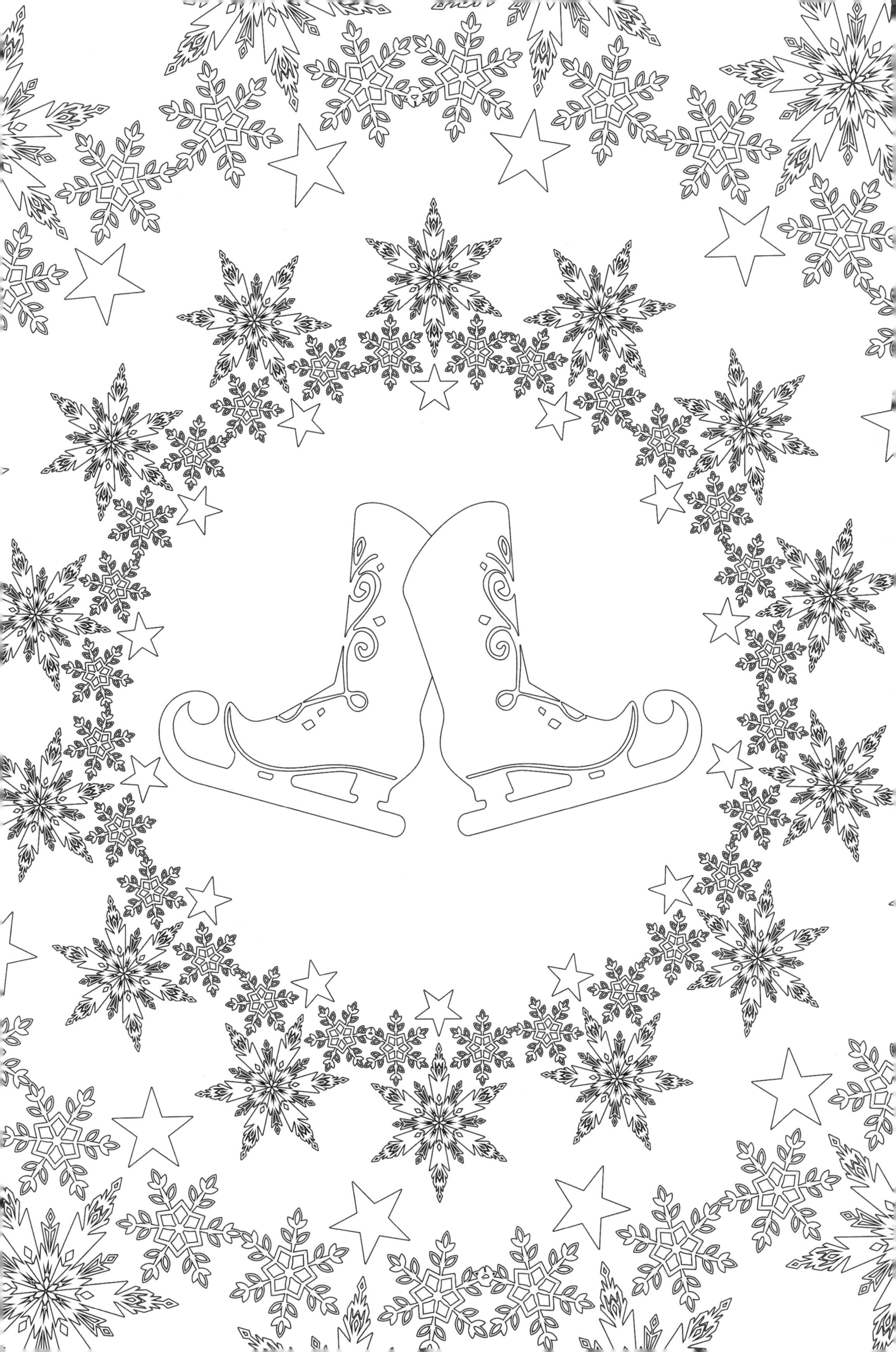

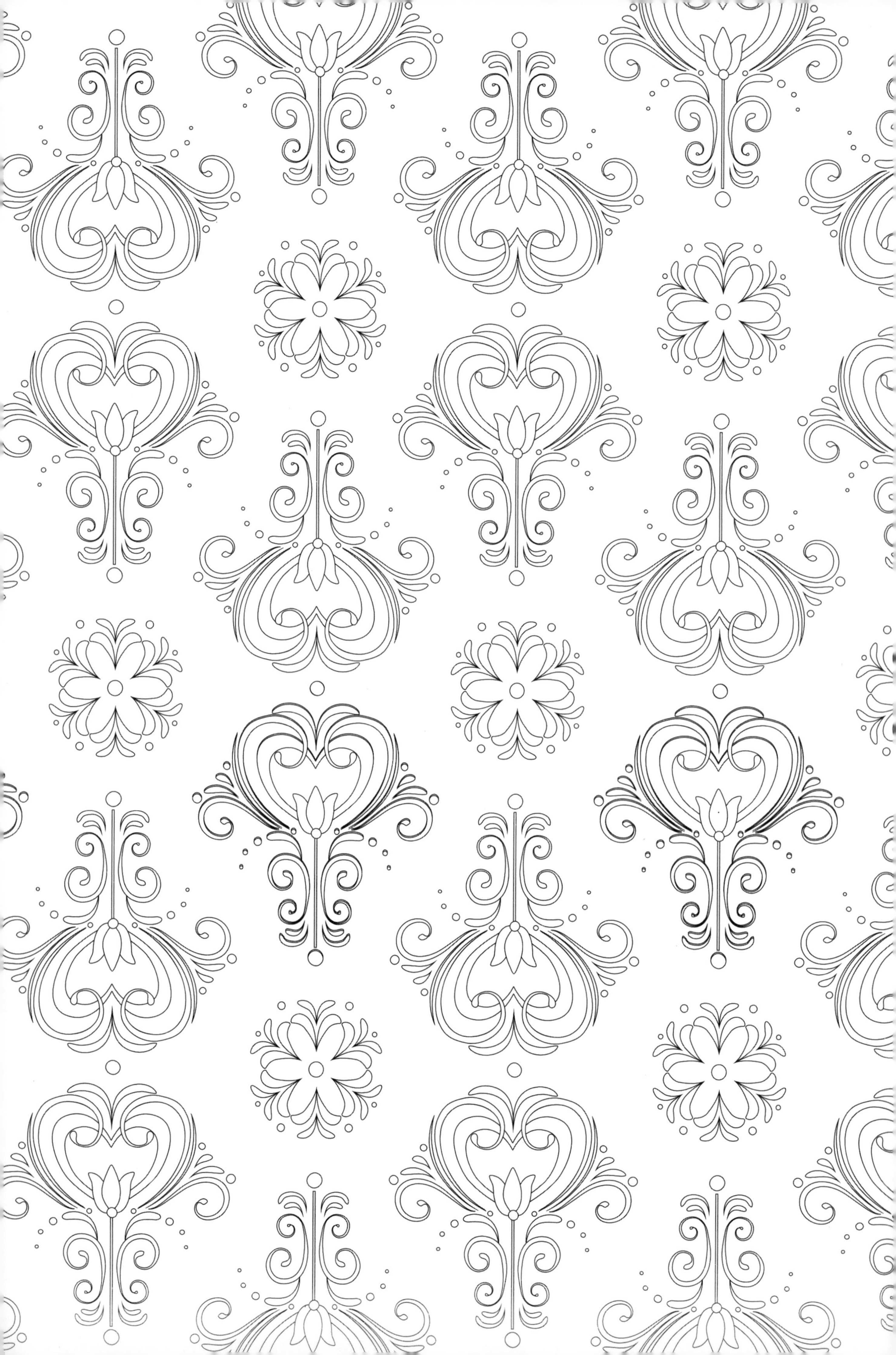

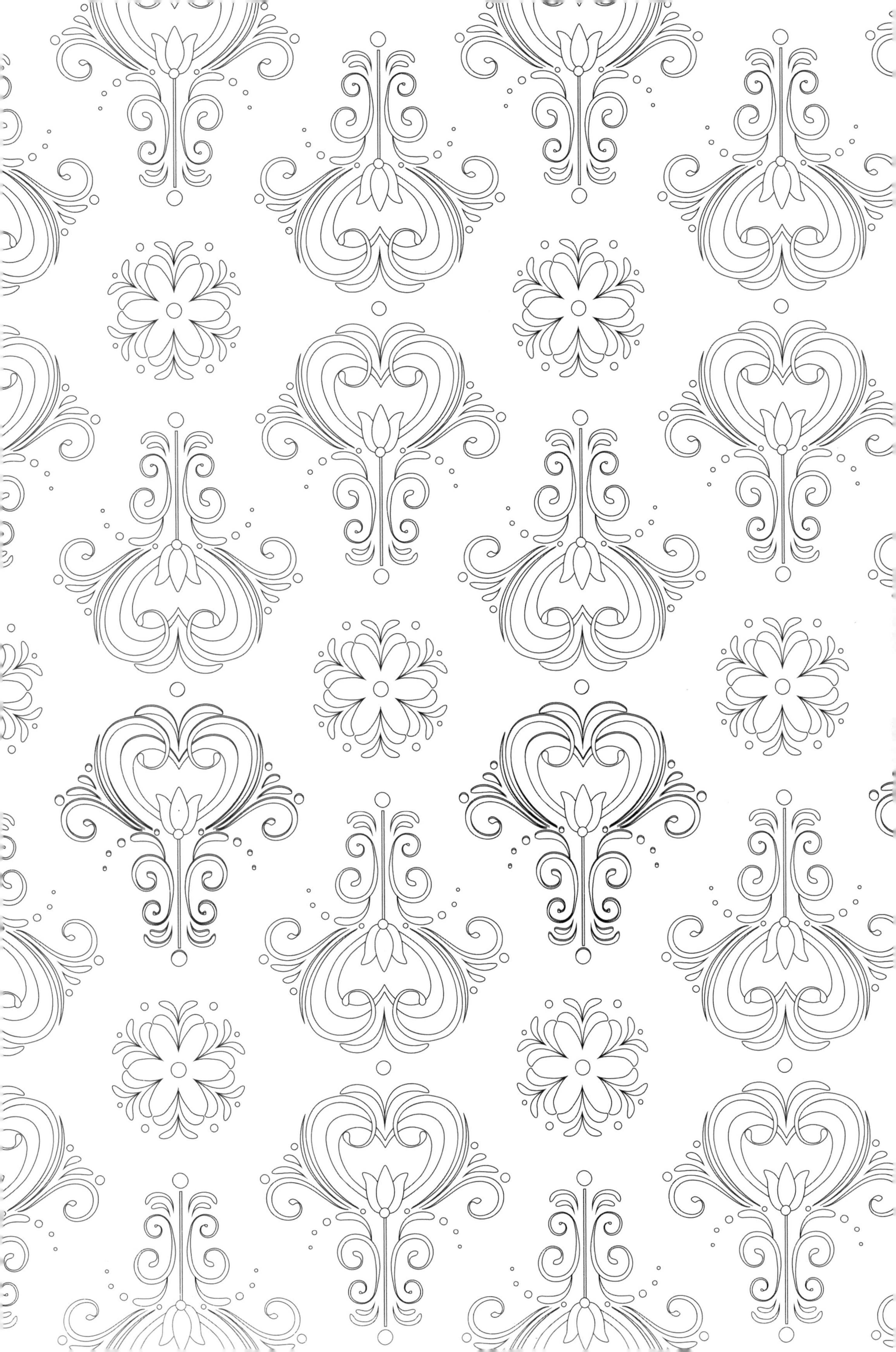

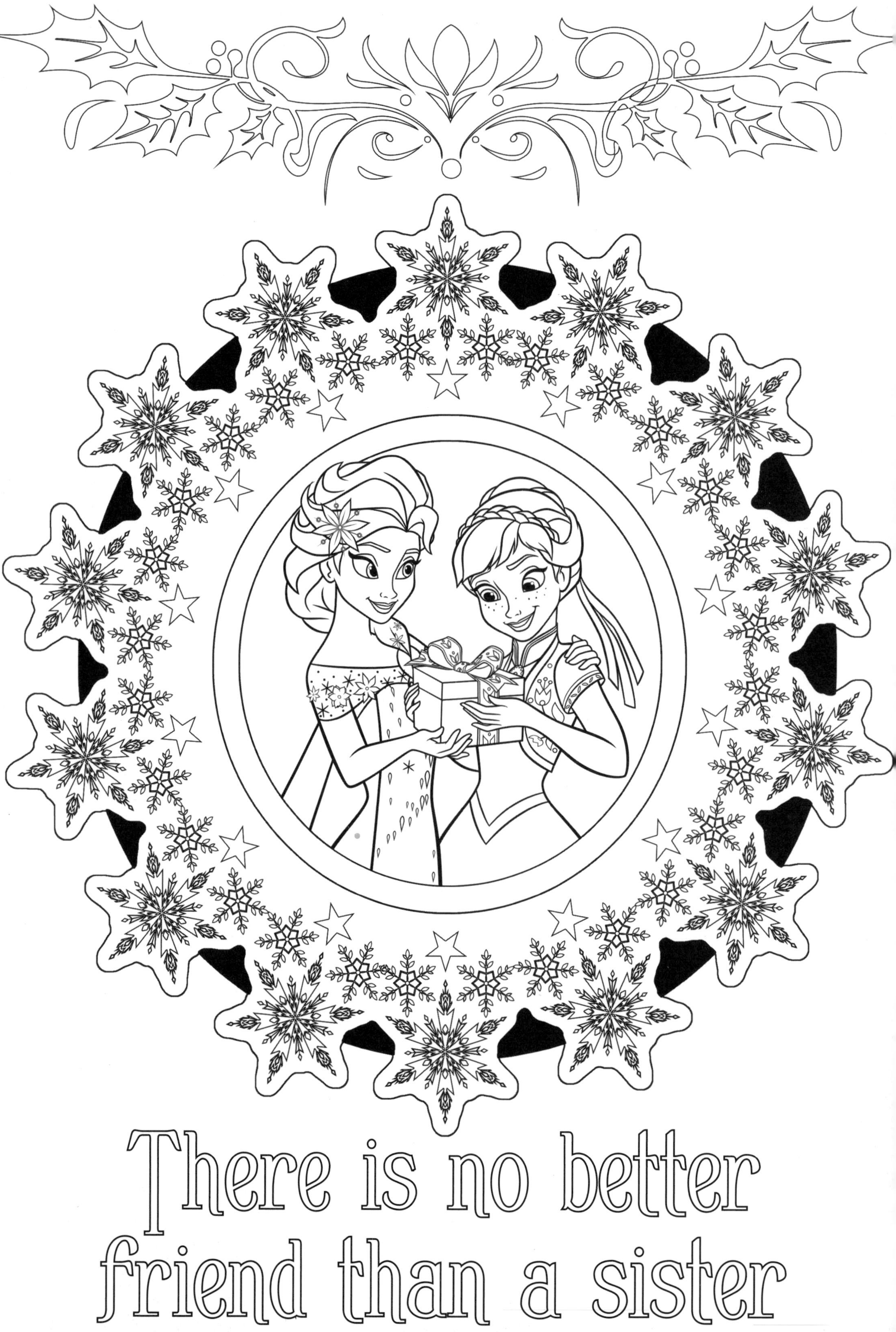

There is no better
friend than a sister

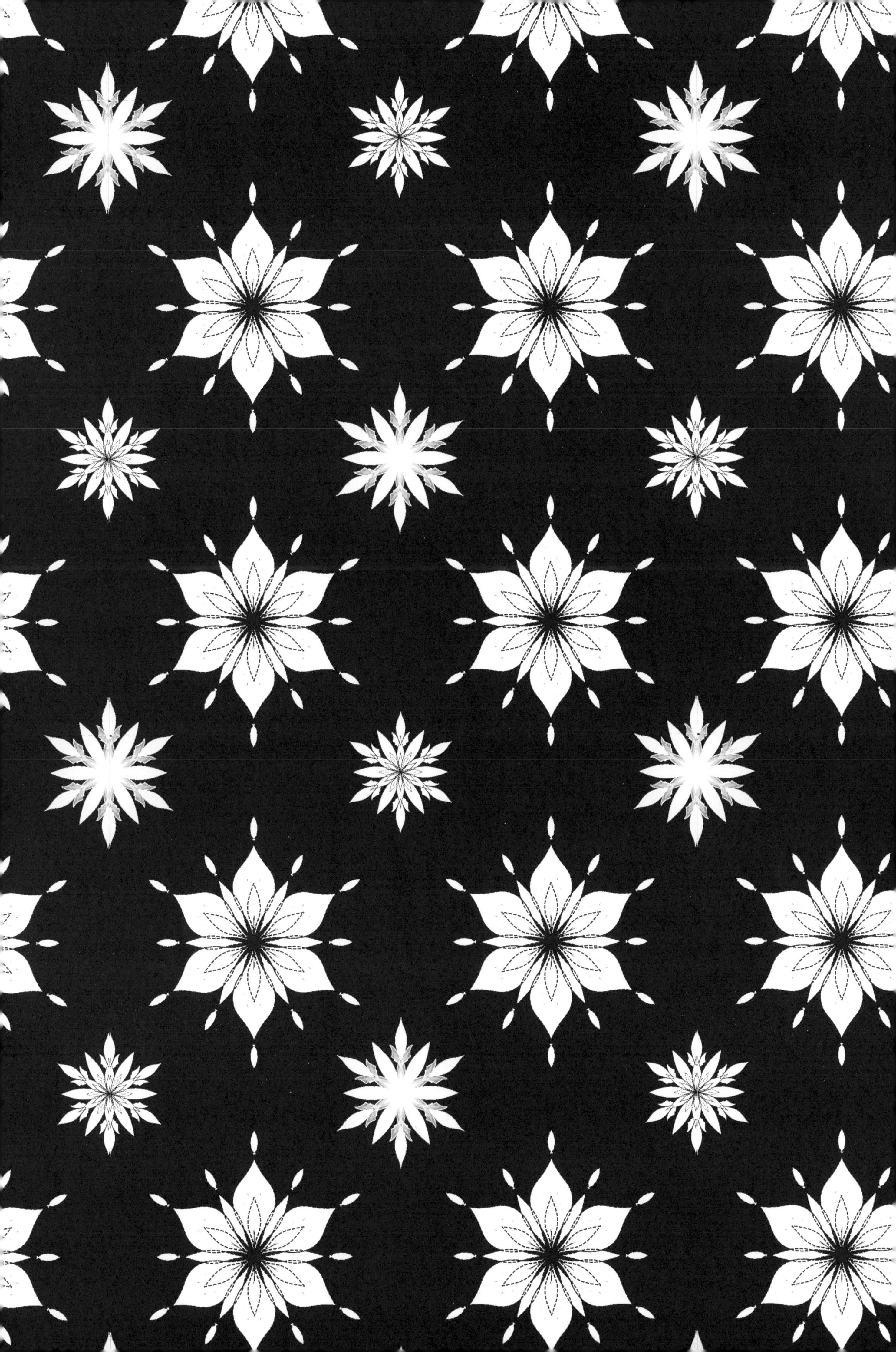

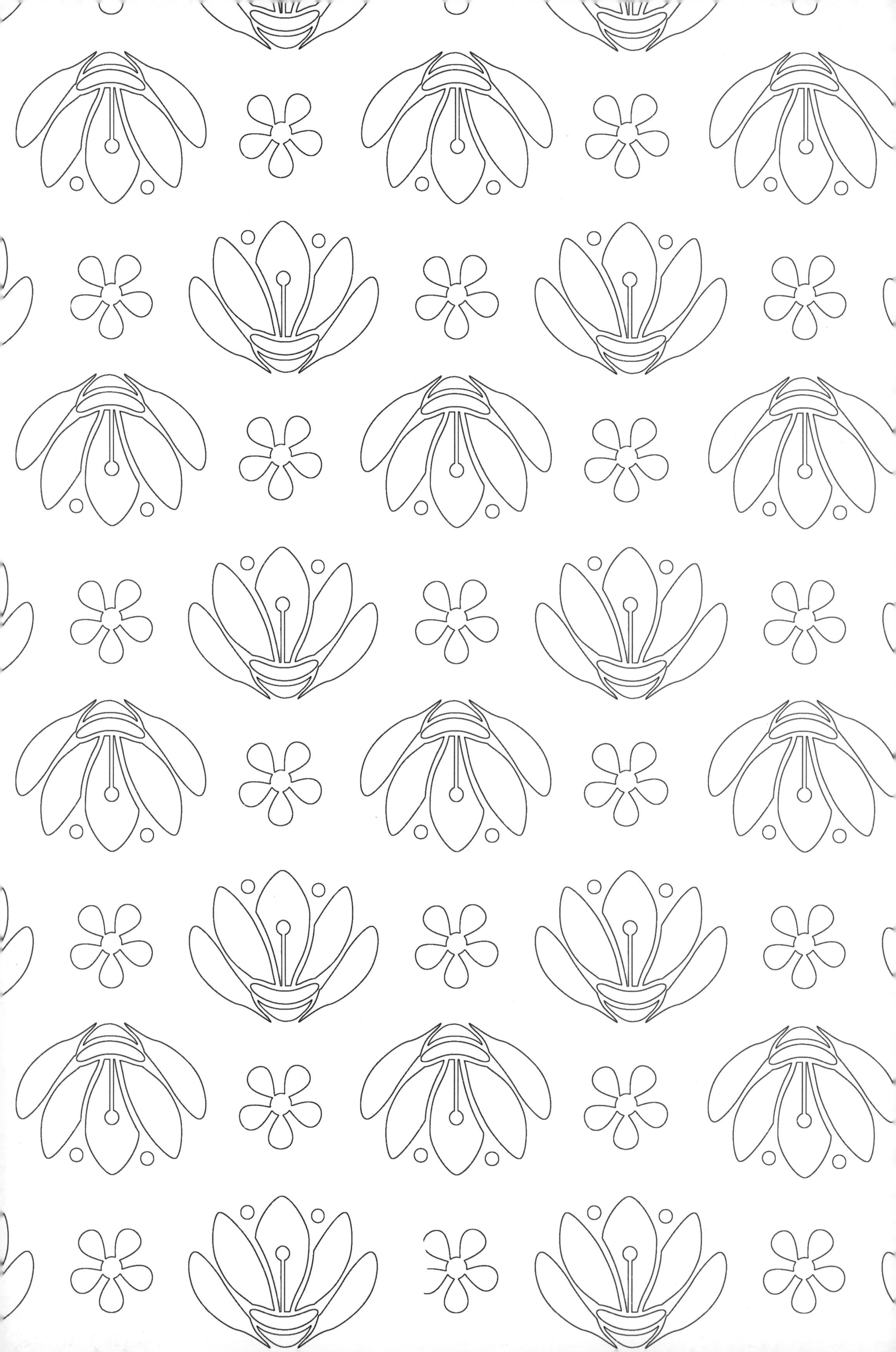

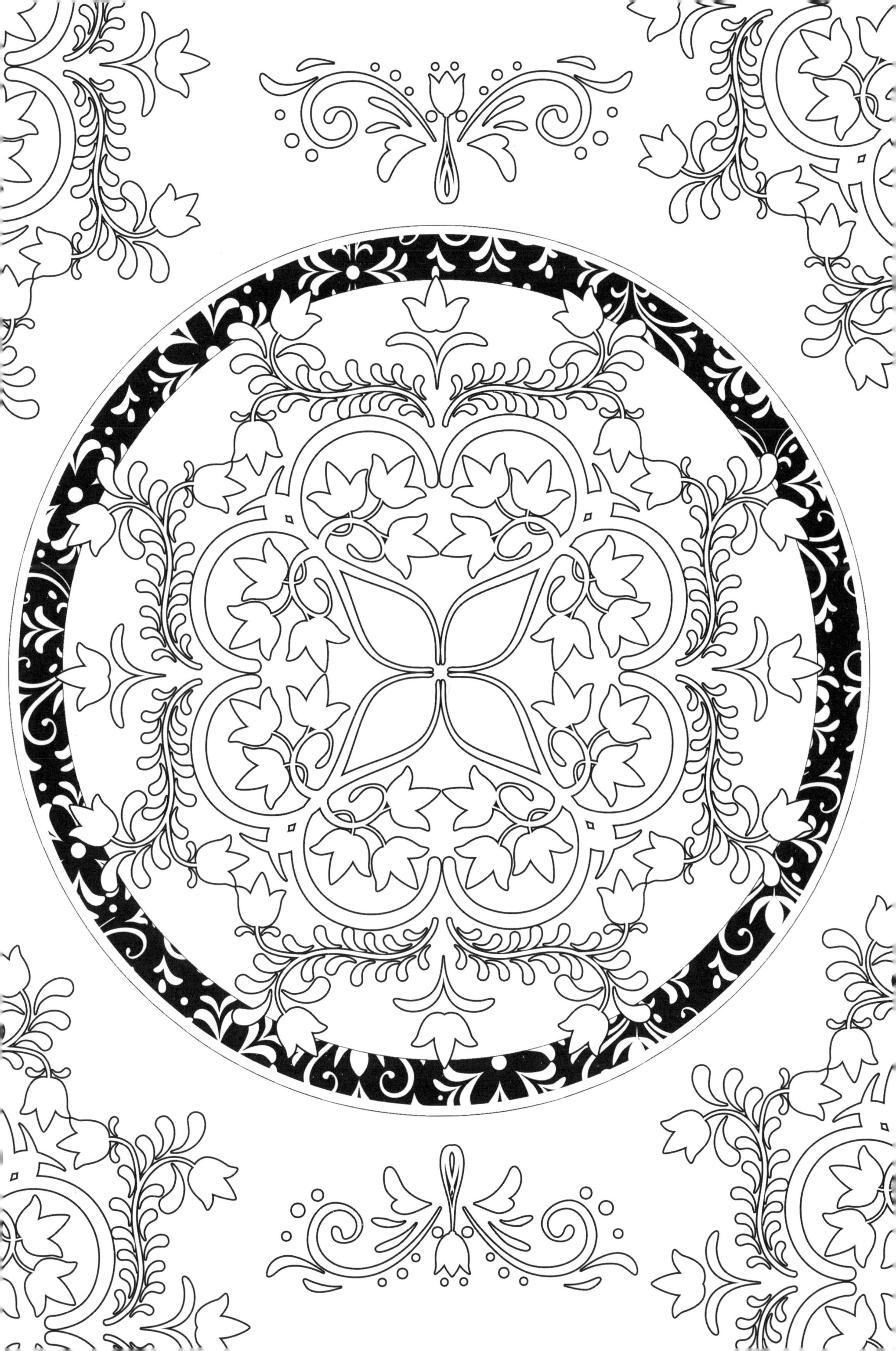

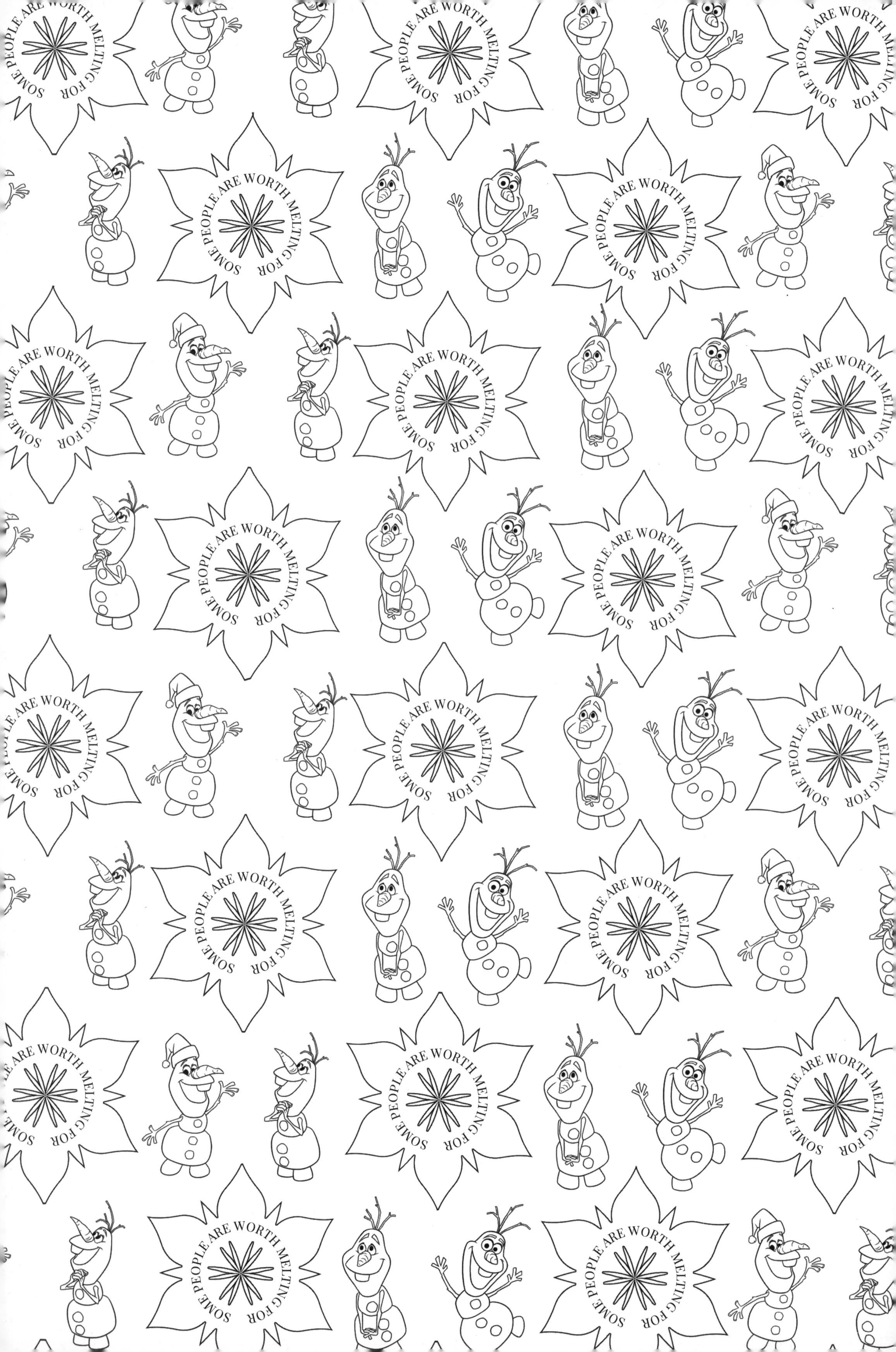
SOME PEOPLE ARE WORTH MELTING FOR

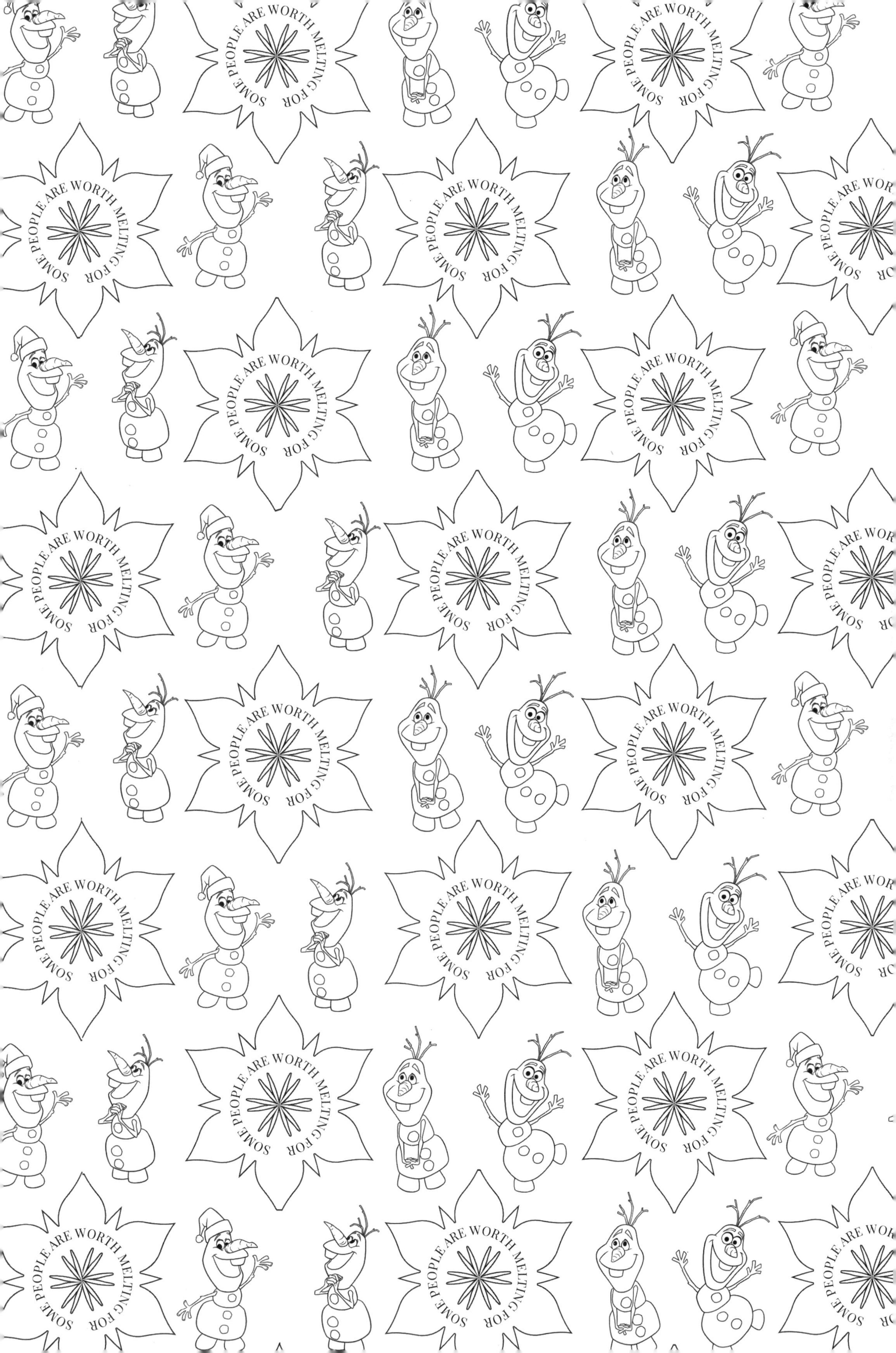
SOME PEOPLE ARE WORTH MELTING FOR

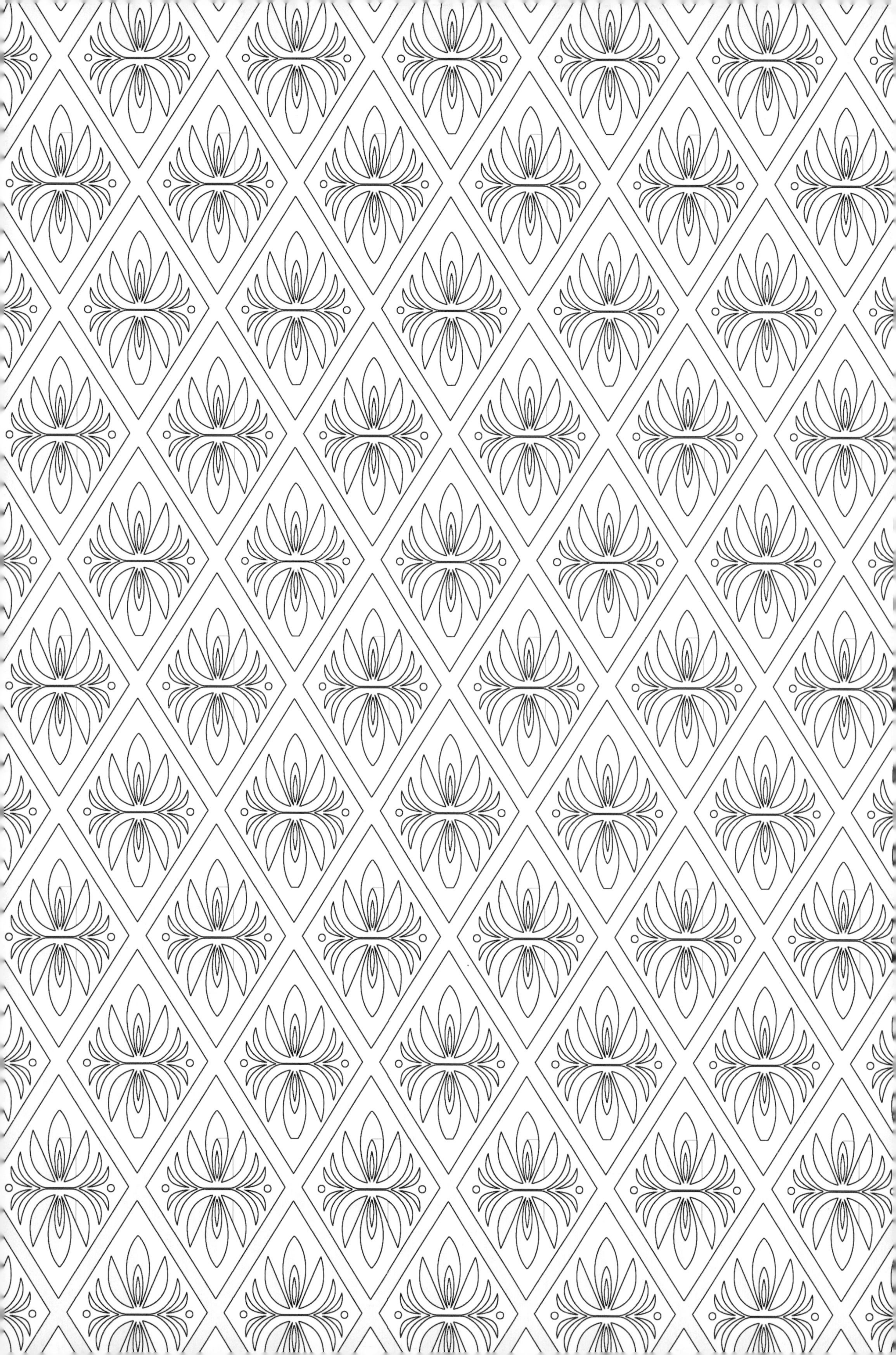

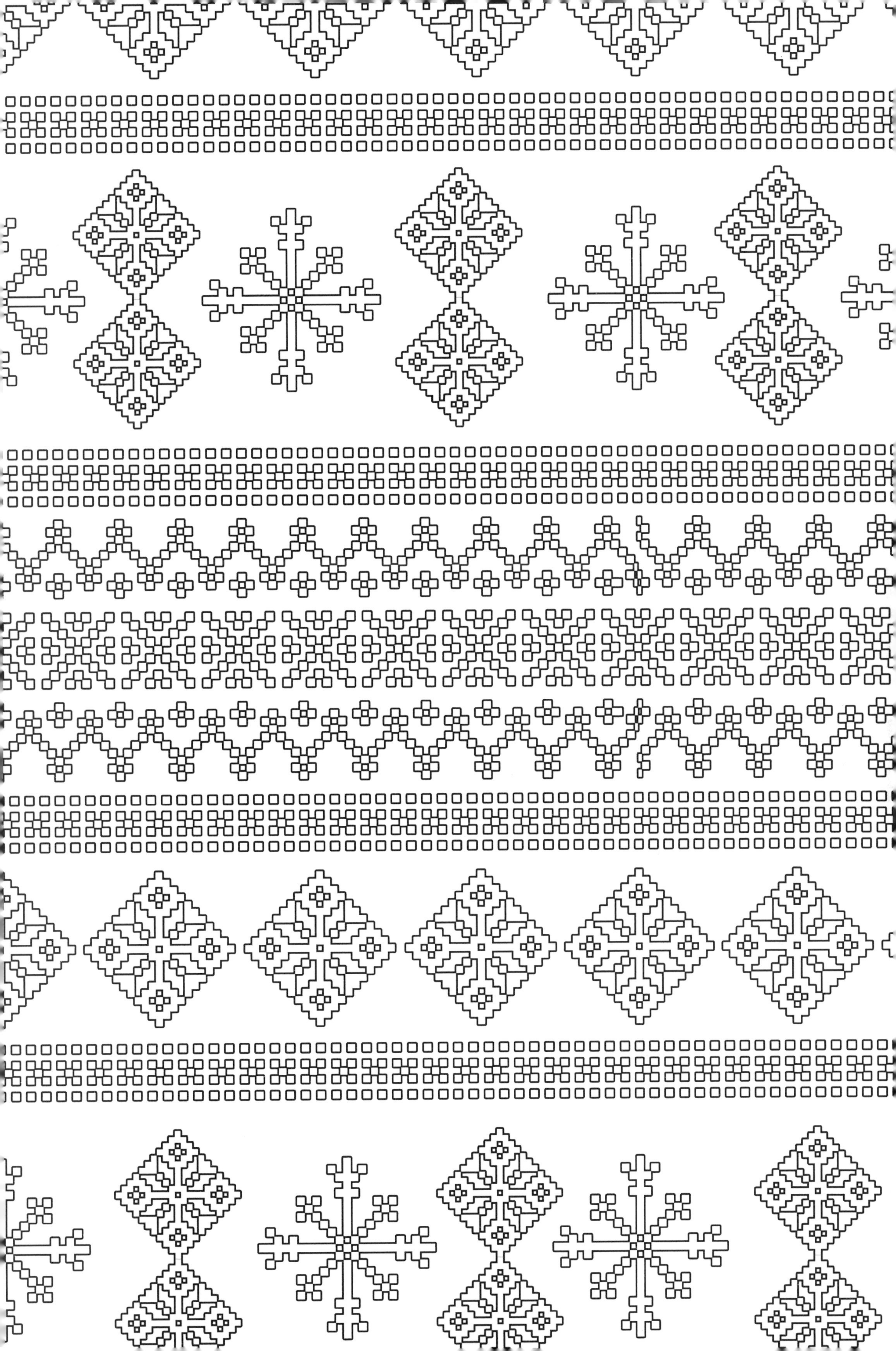

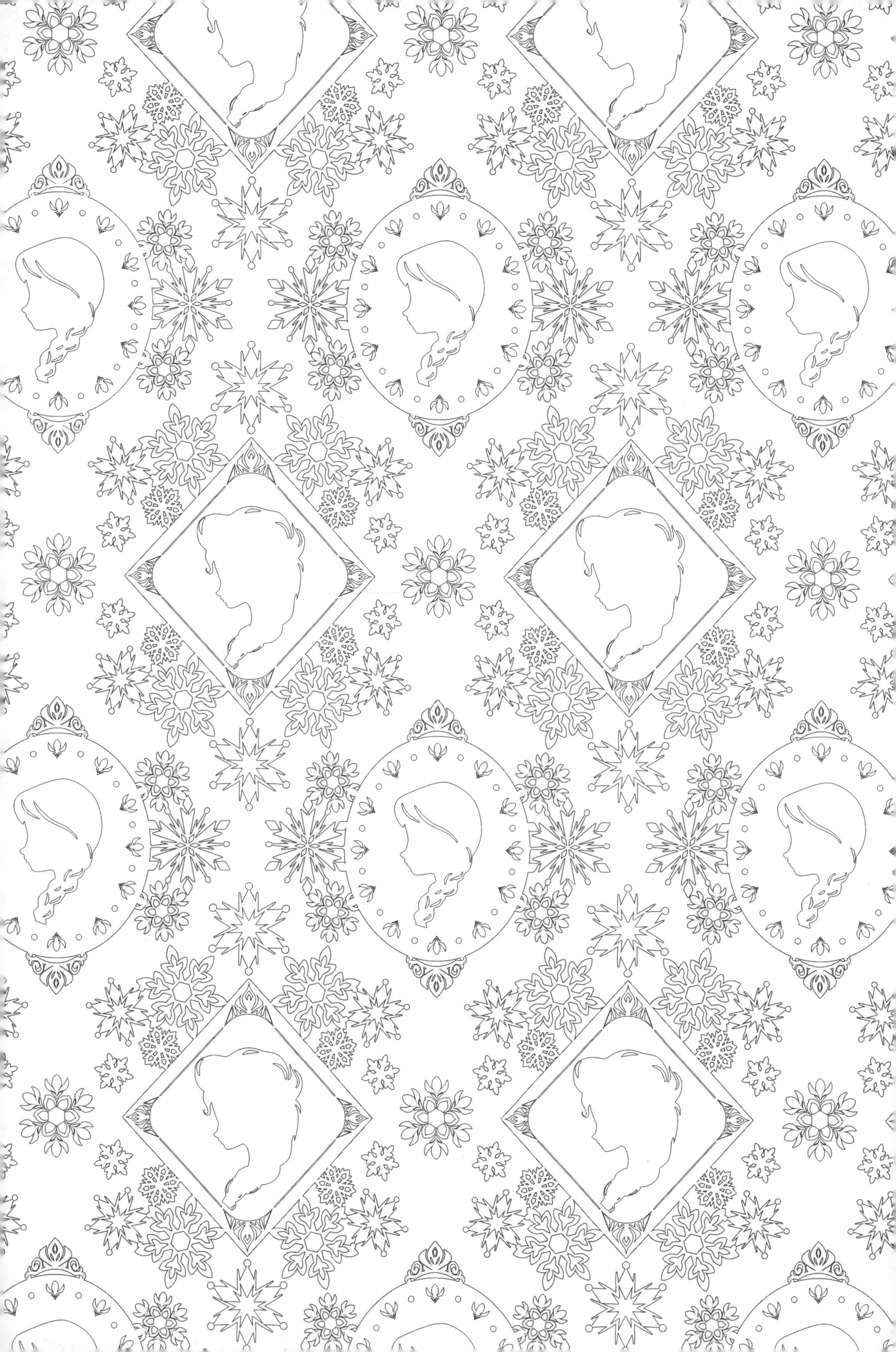

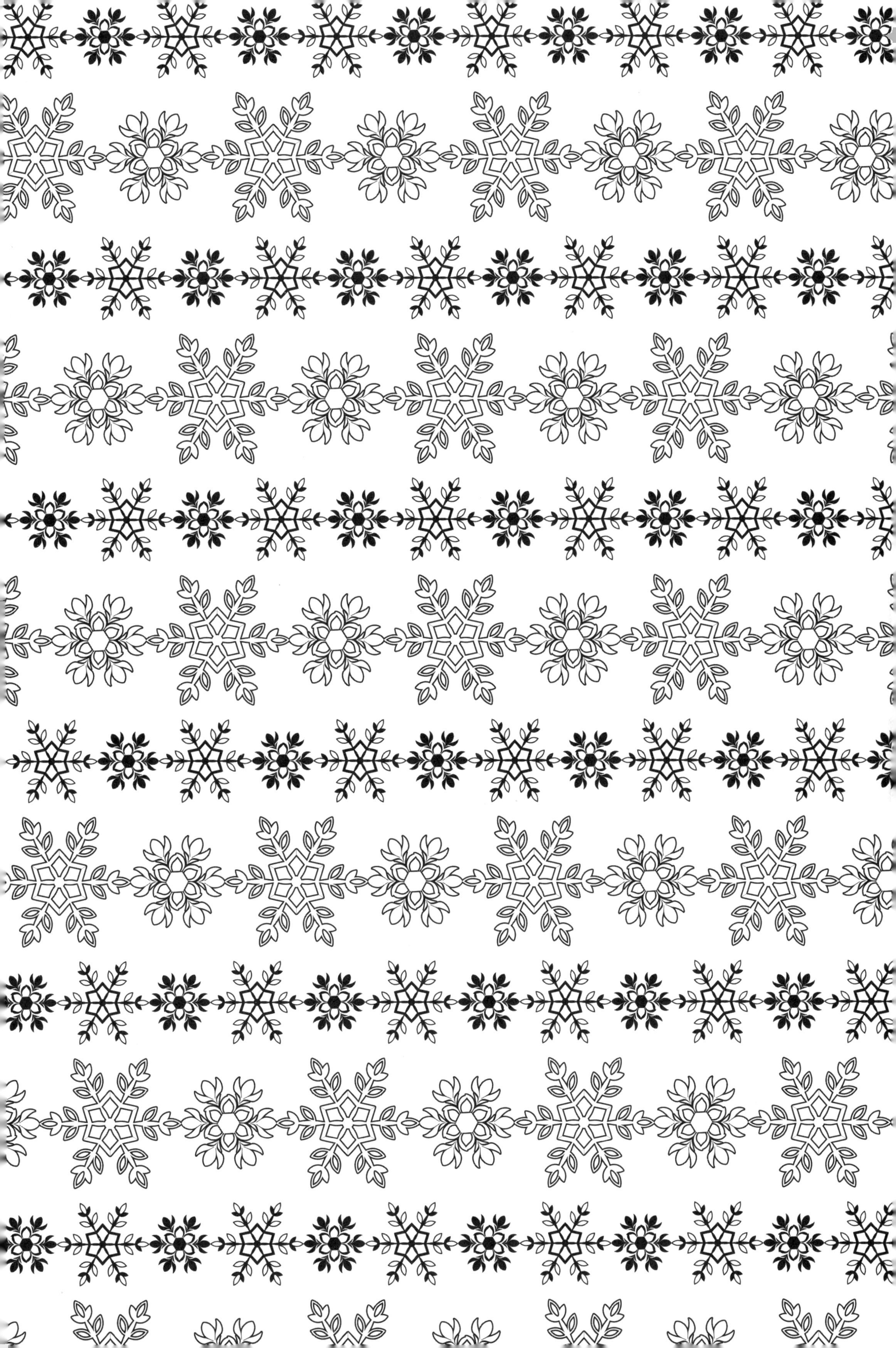

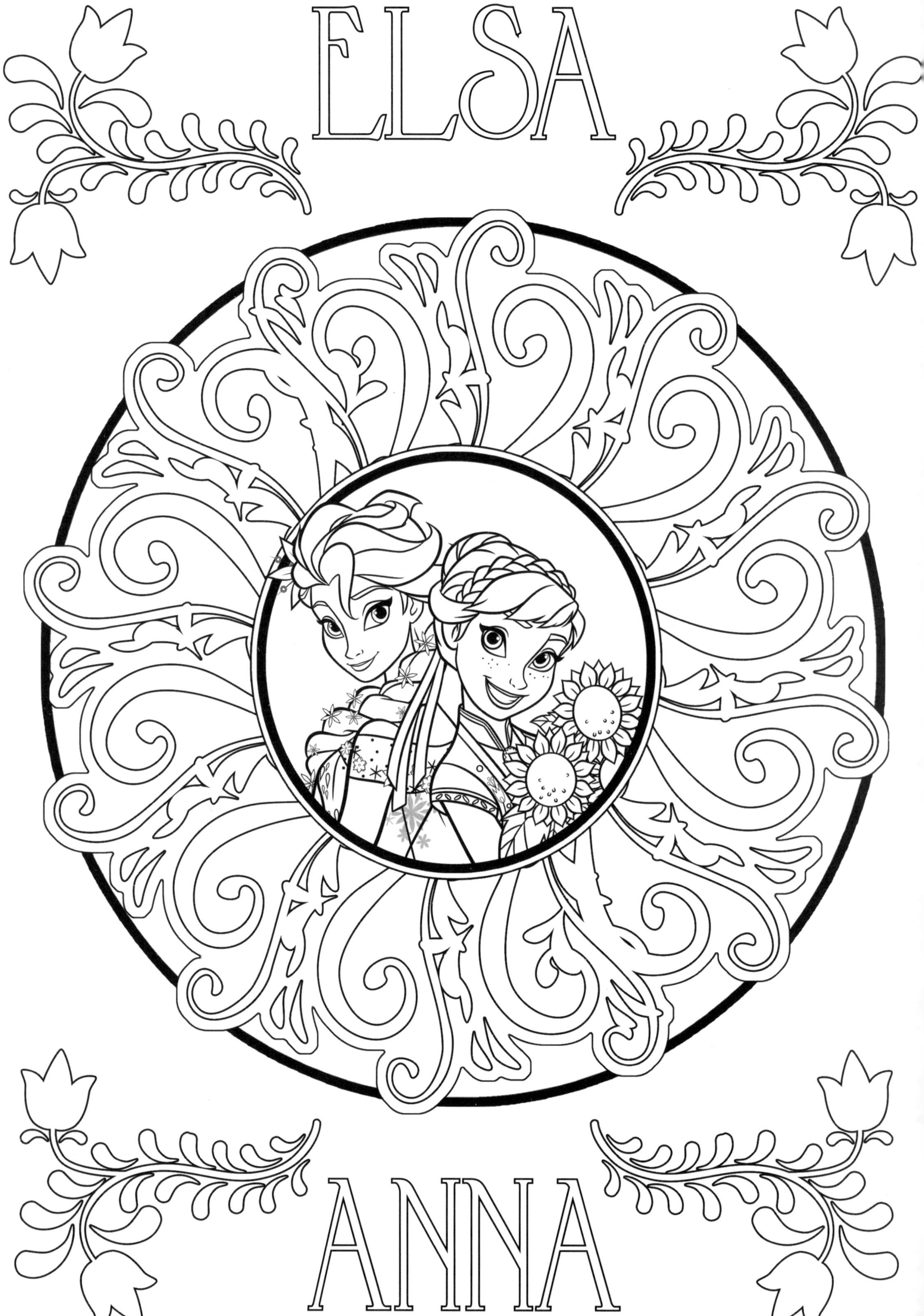
ELSA
ANNA

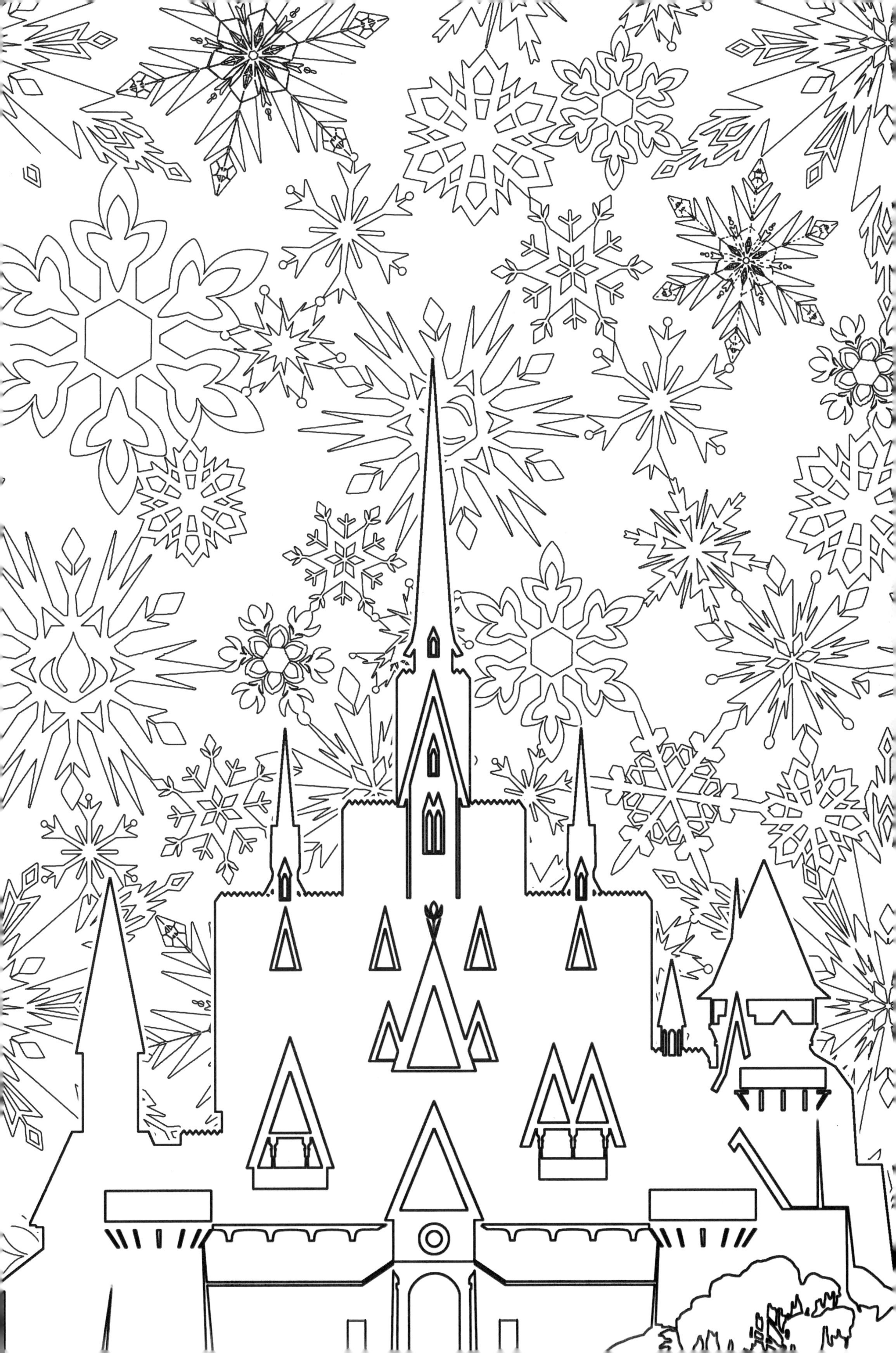

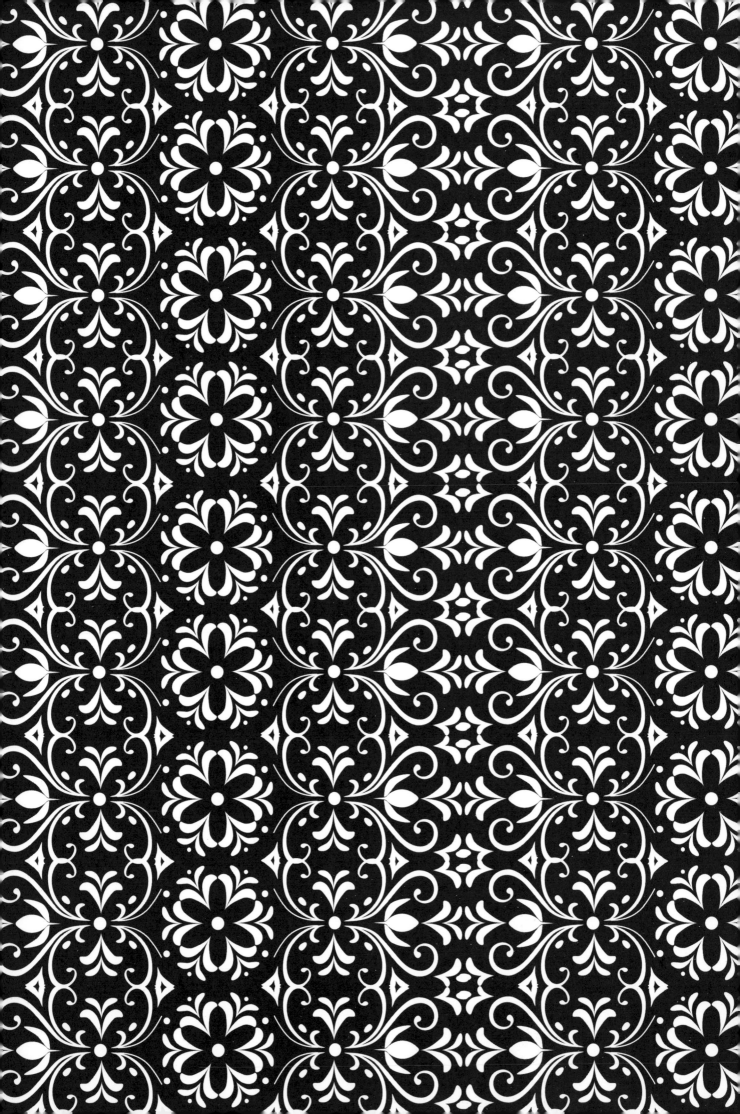

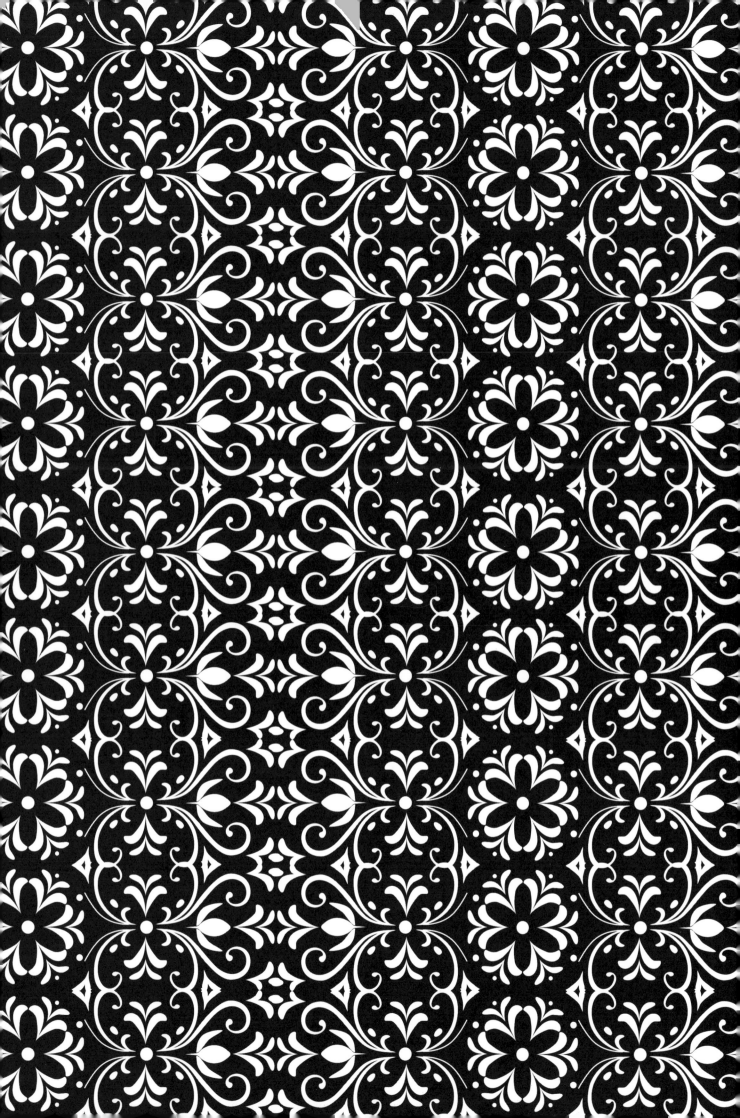

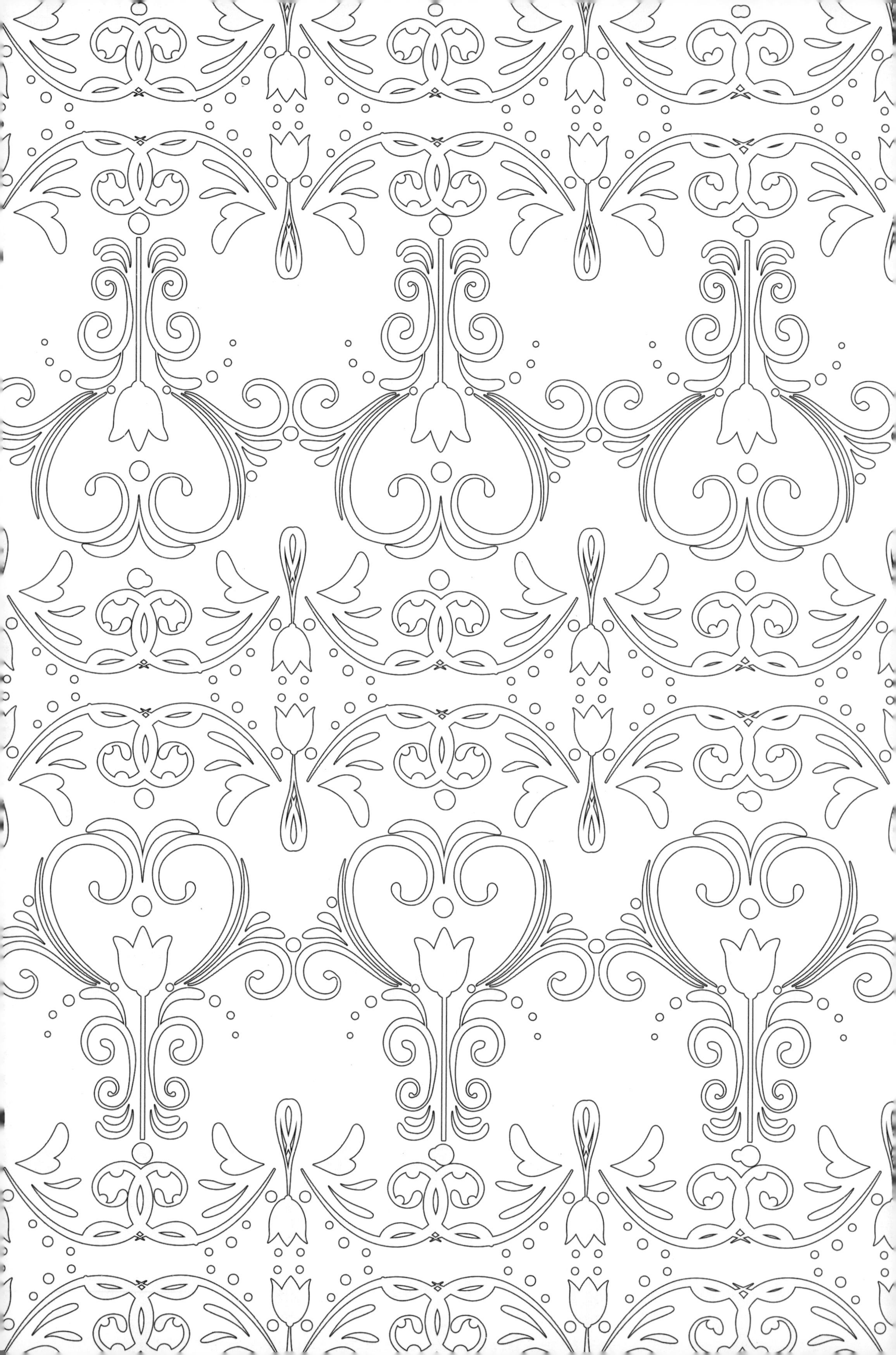

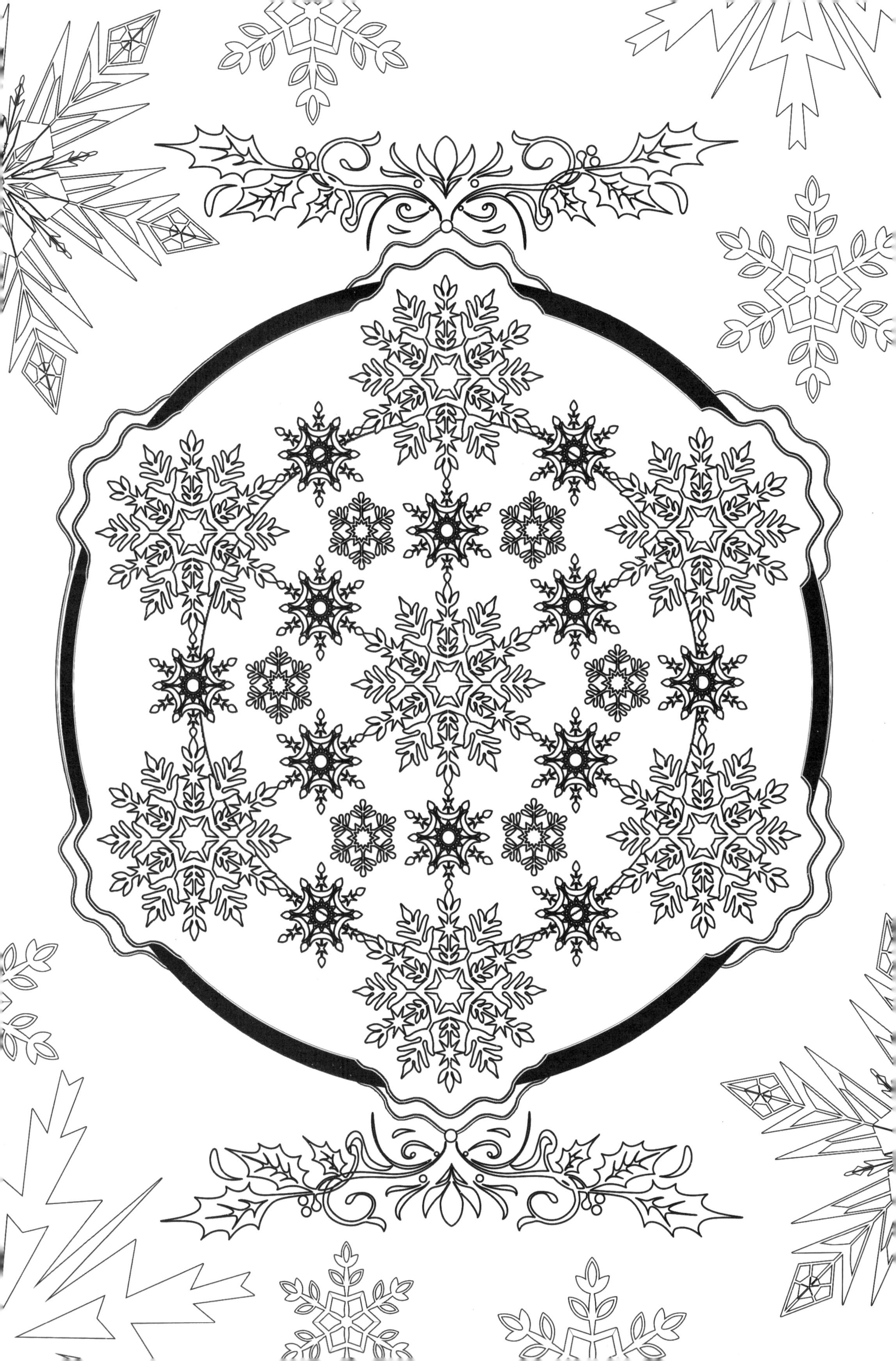

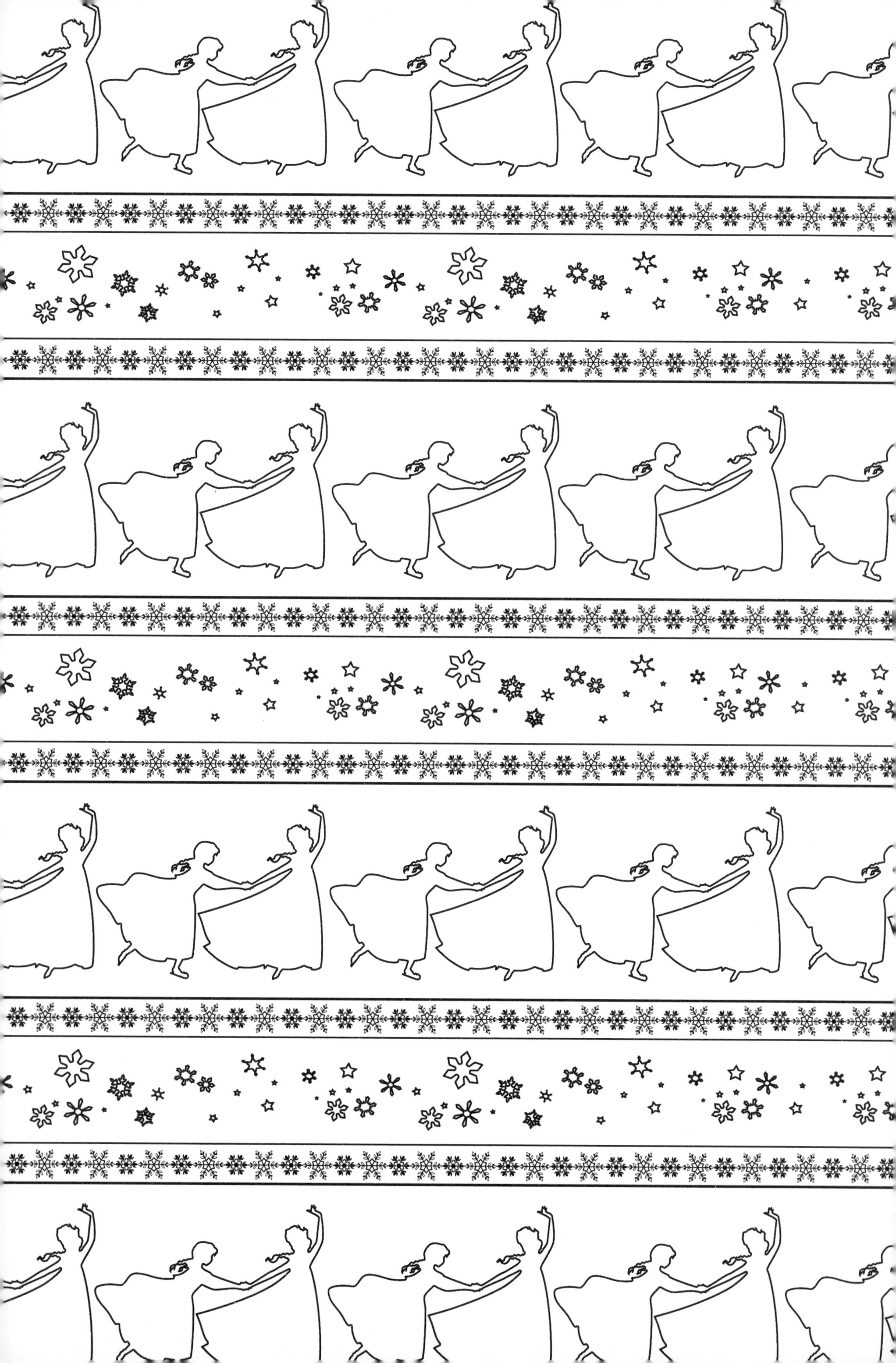

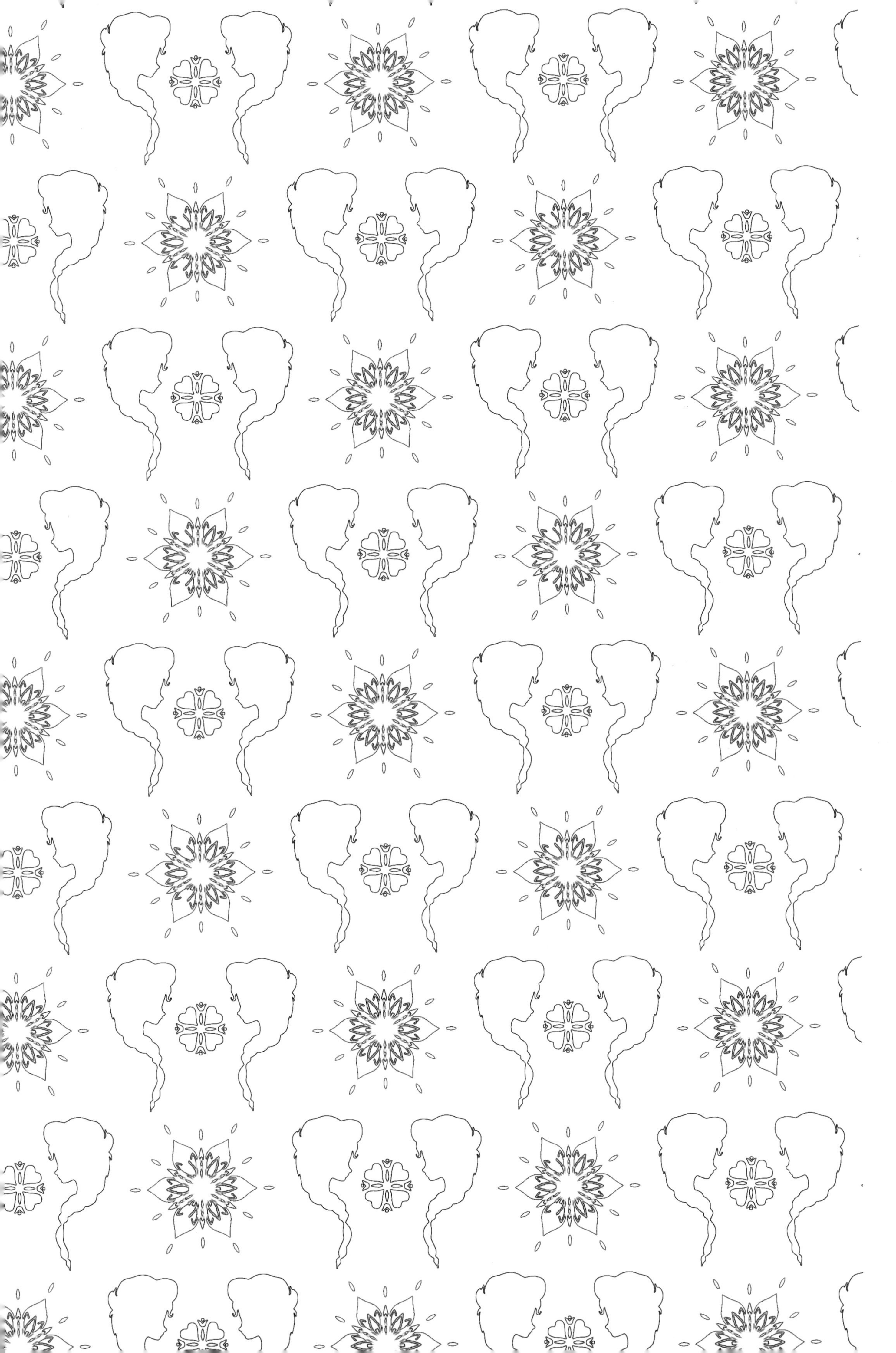

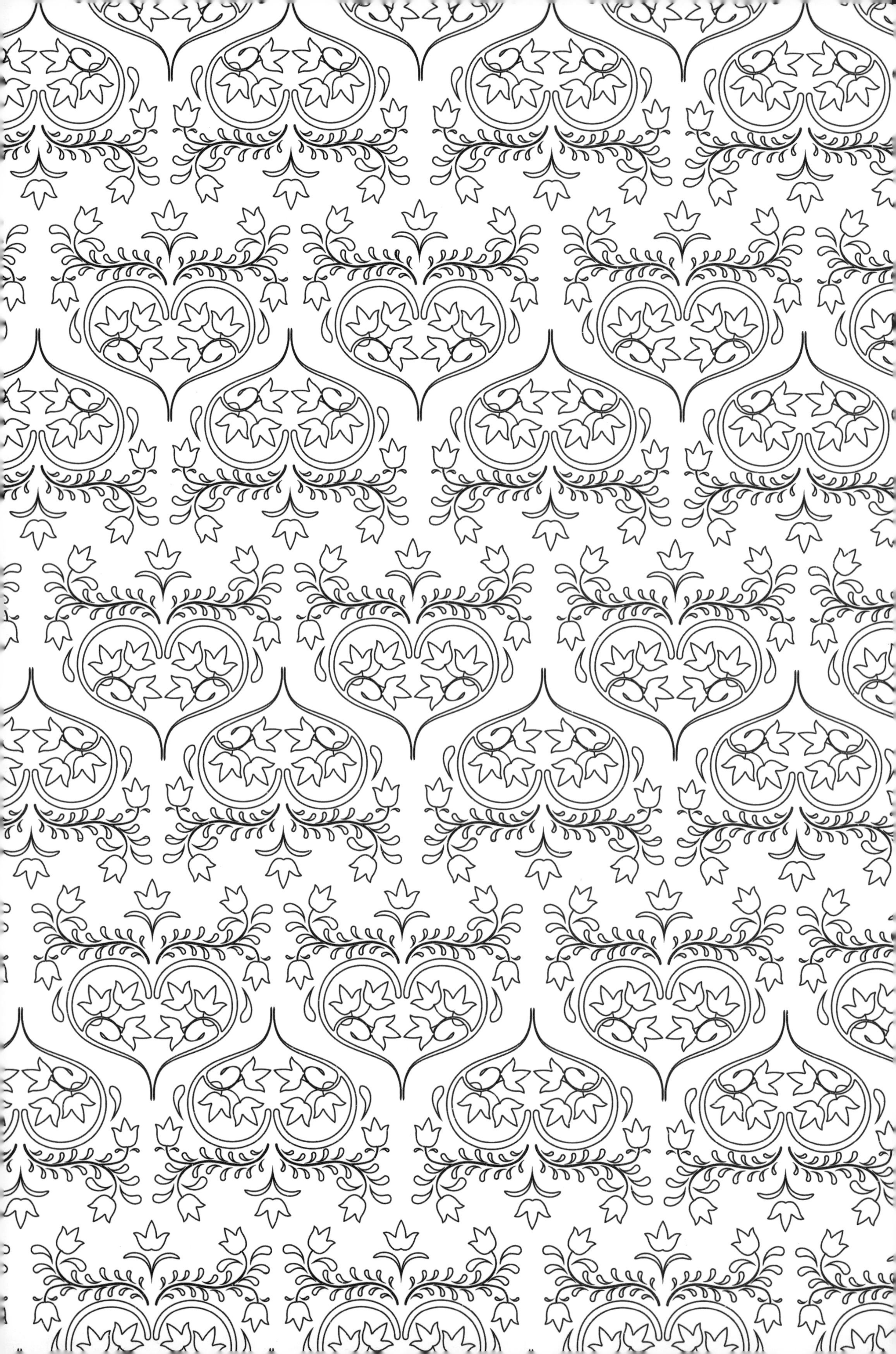

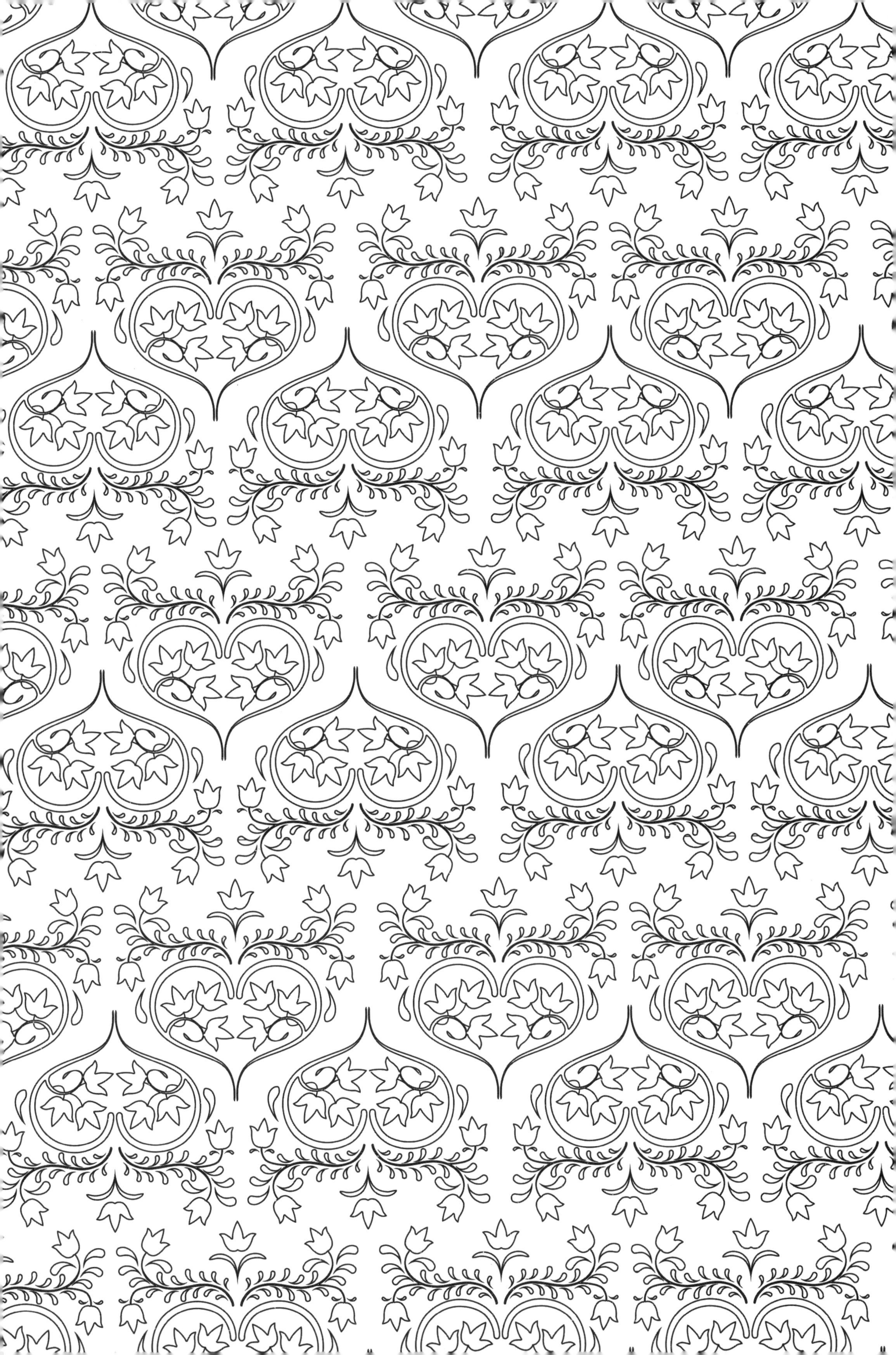

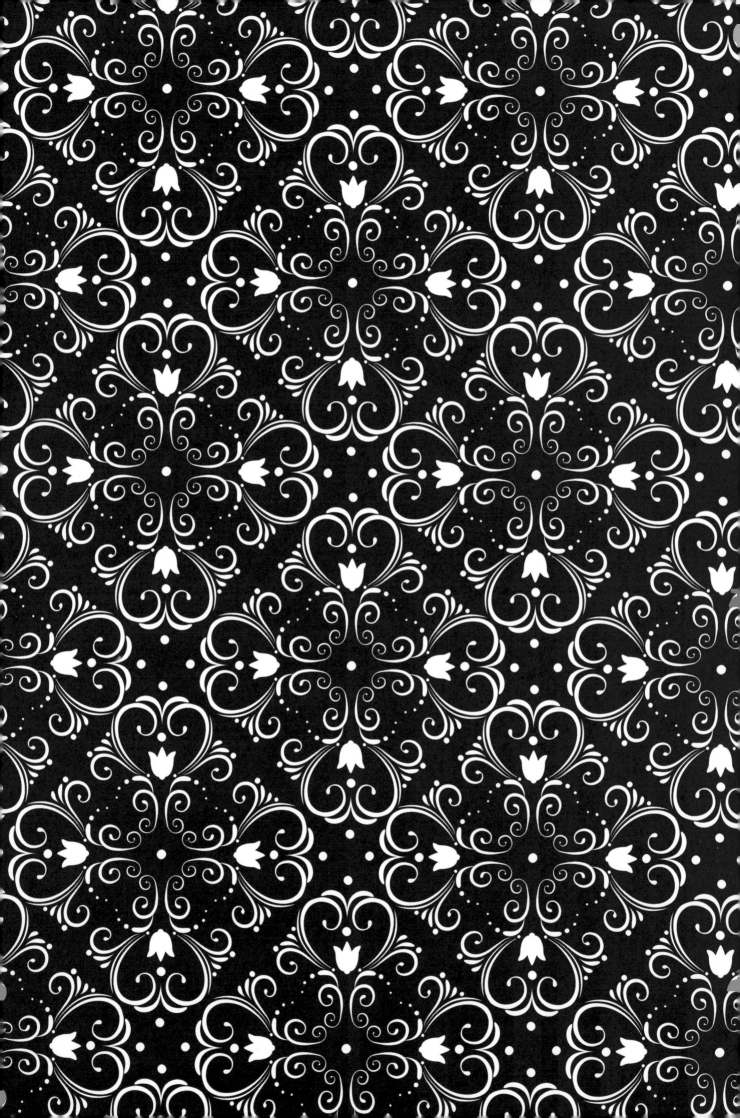

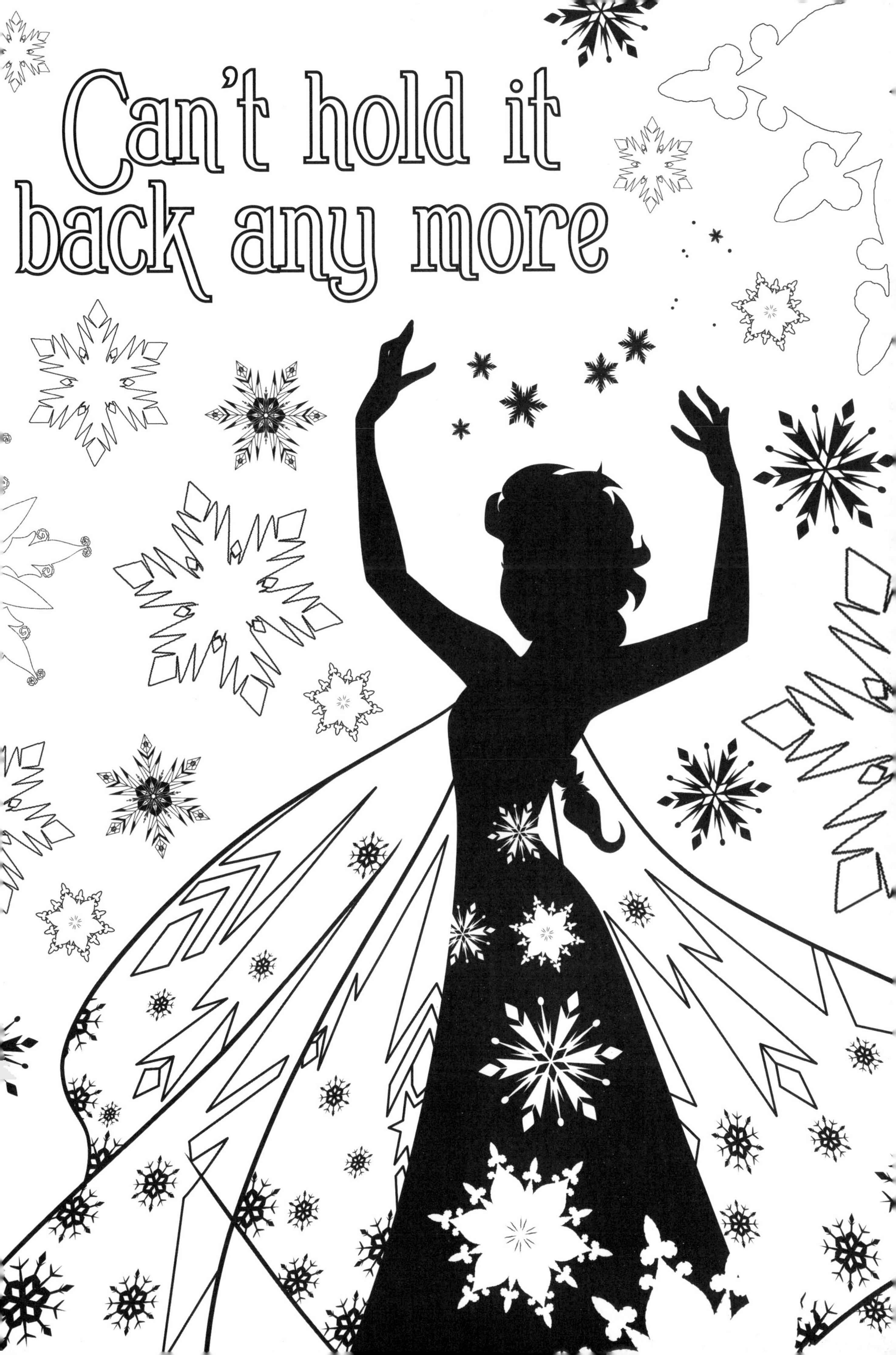
Can't hold it back any more

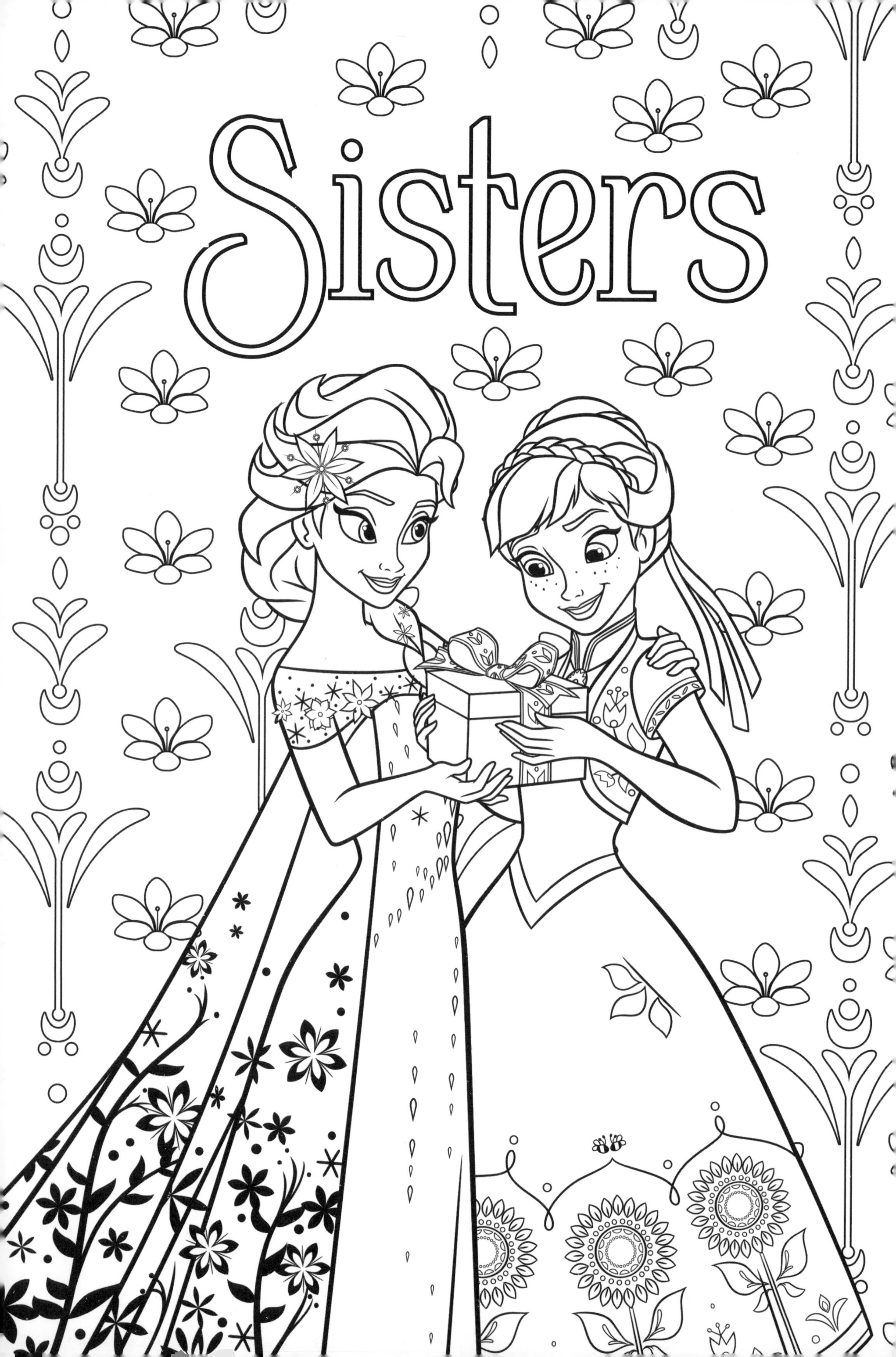
Sisters

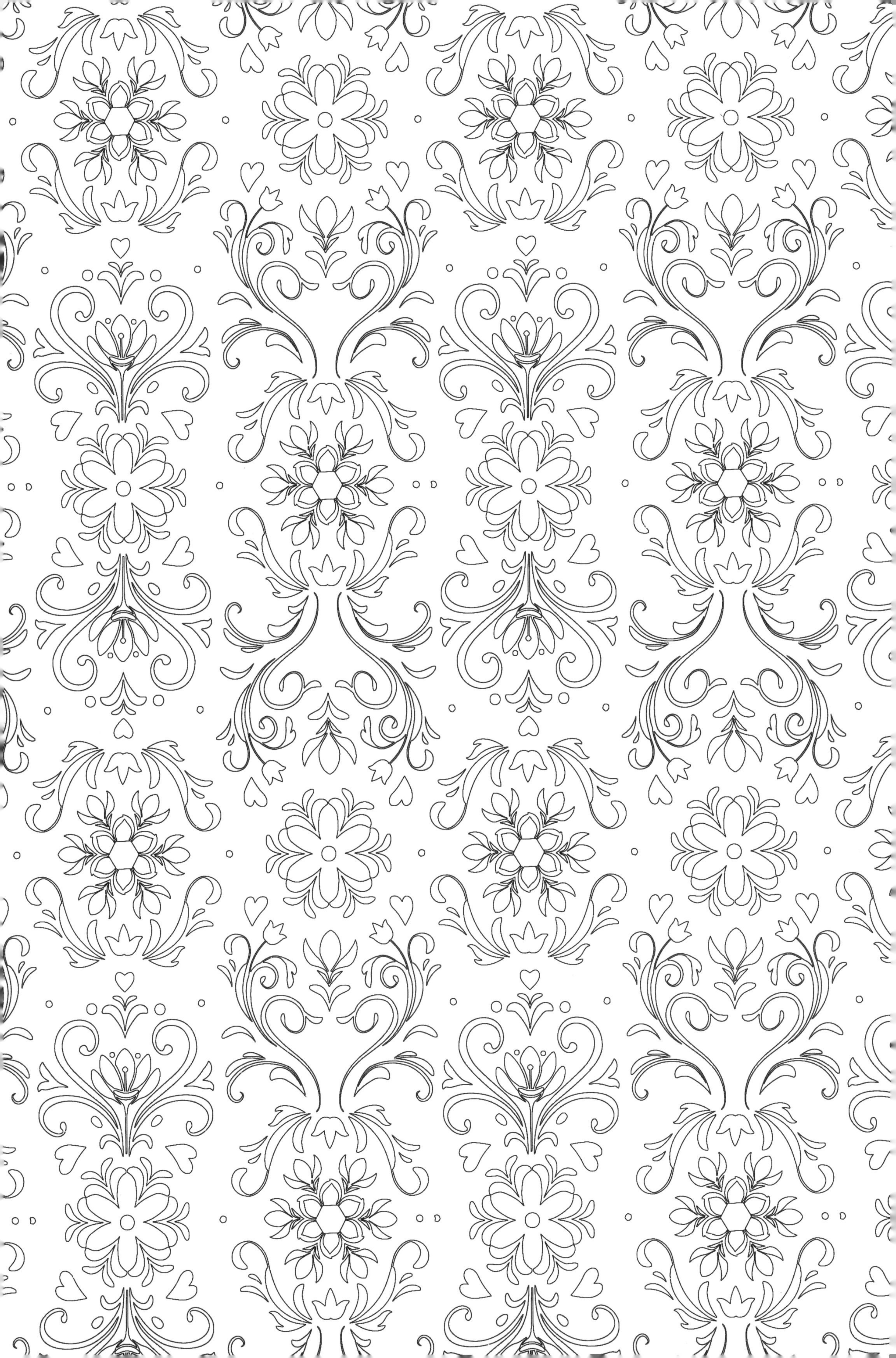

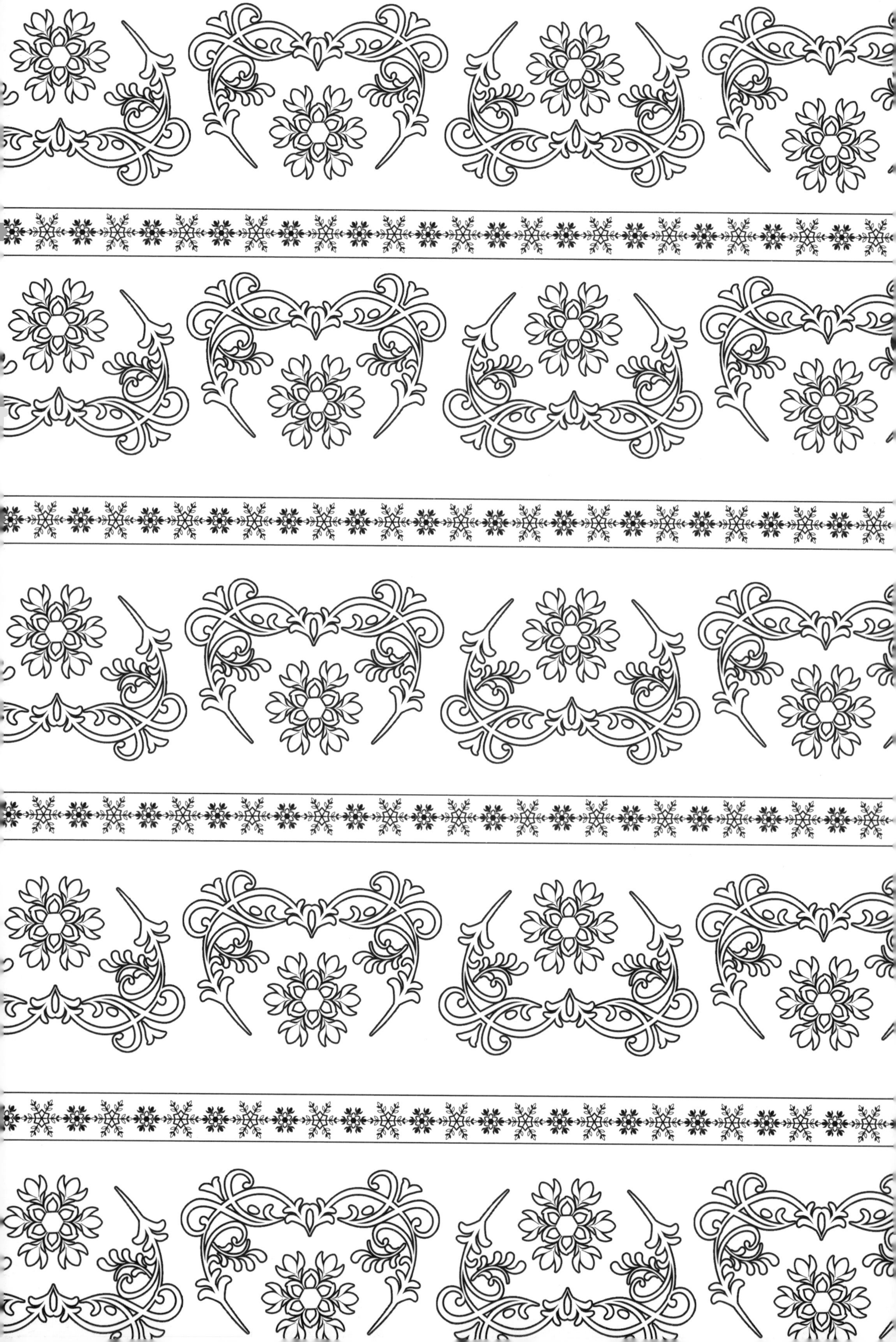

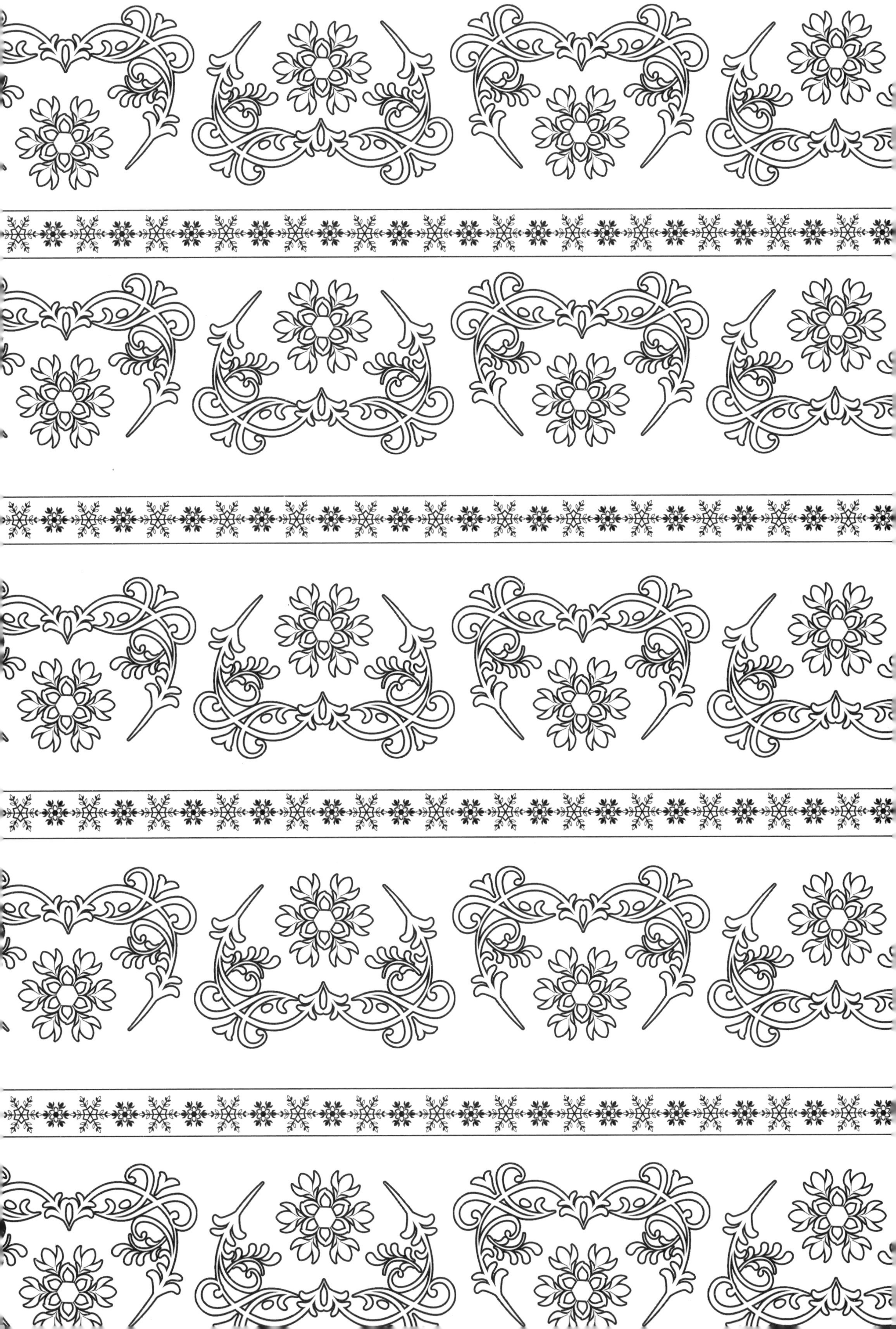

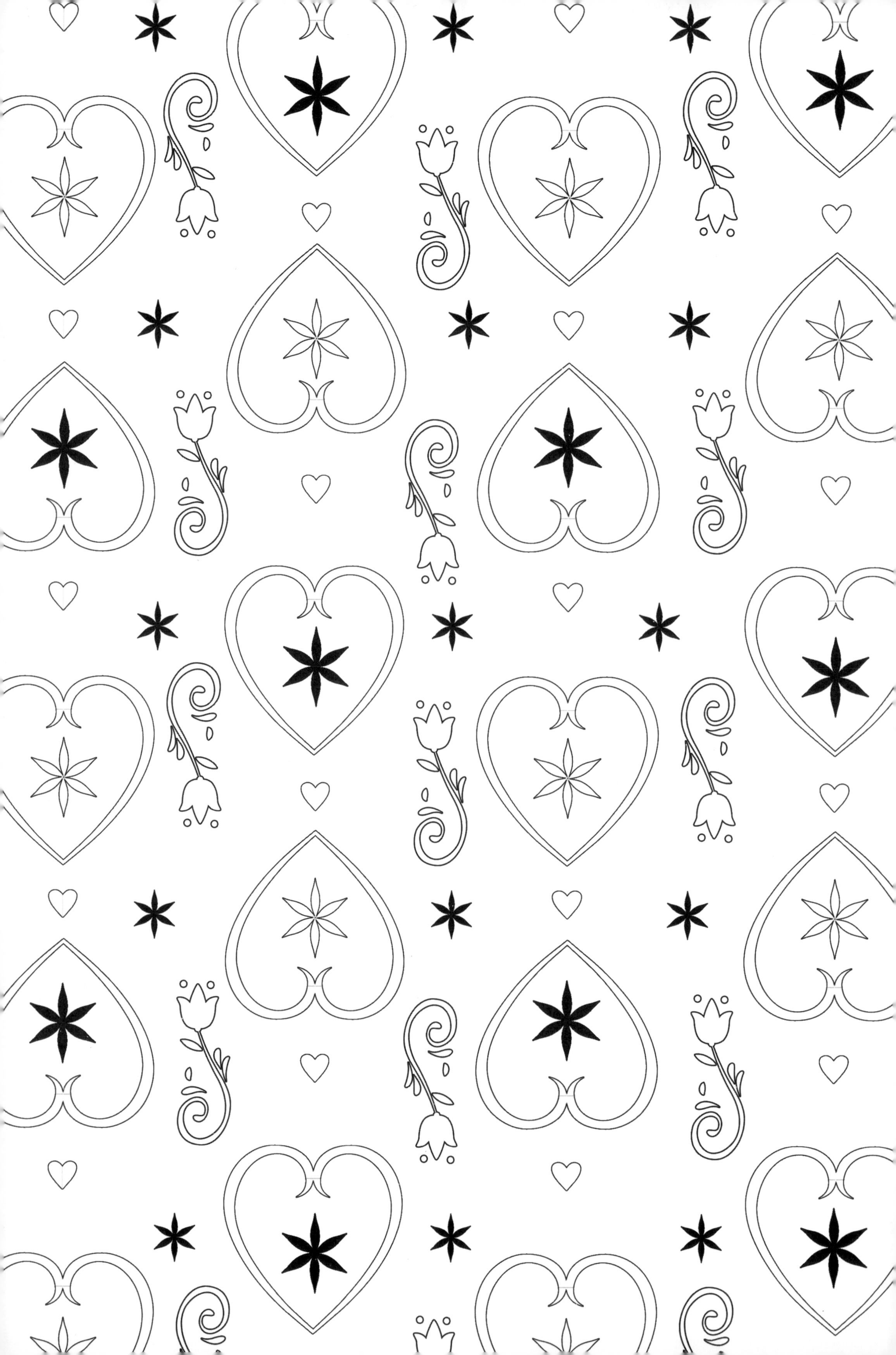

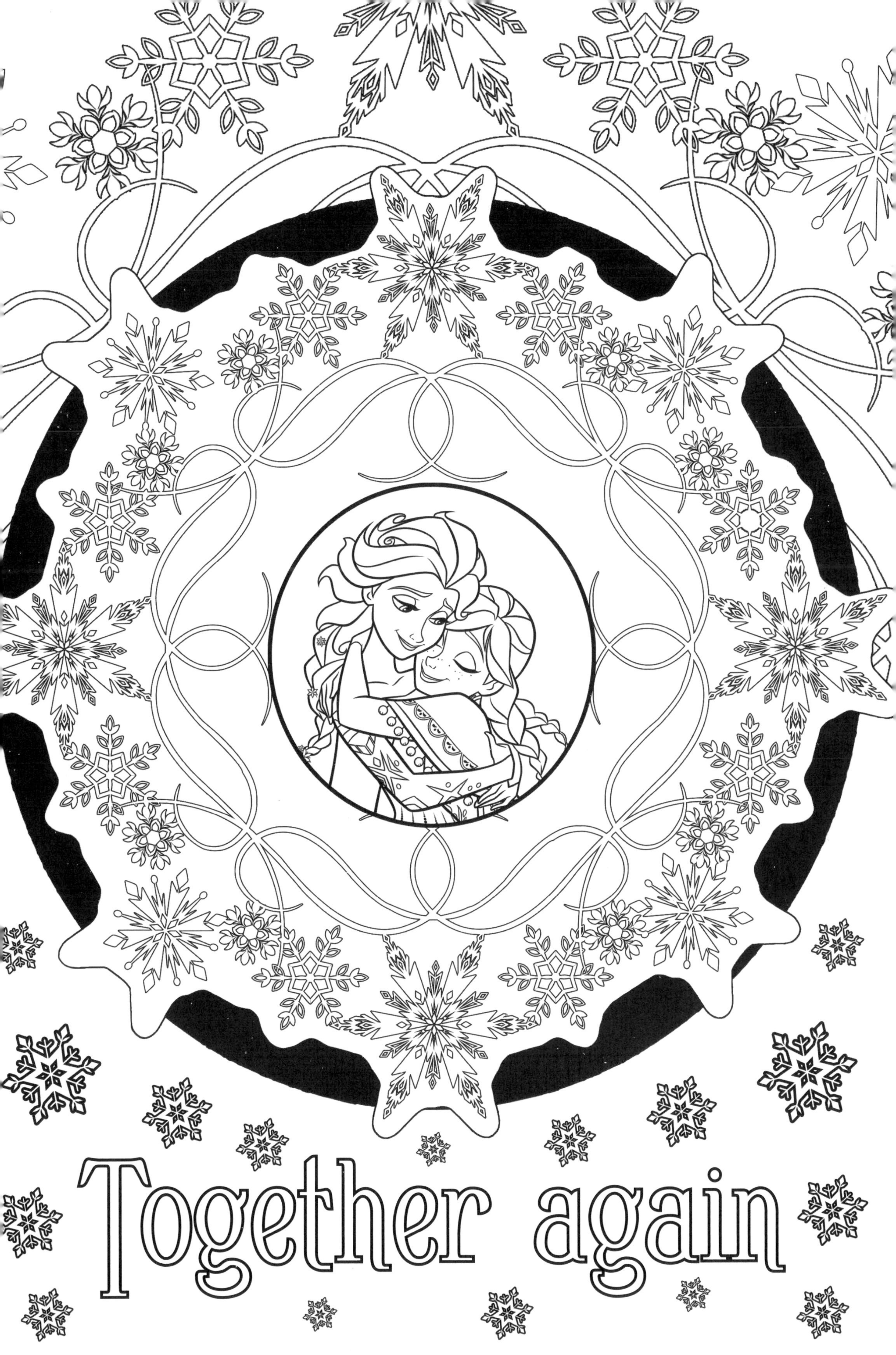
Together again

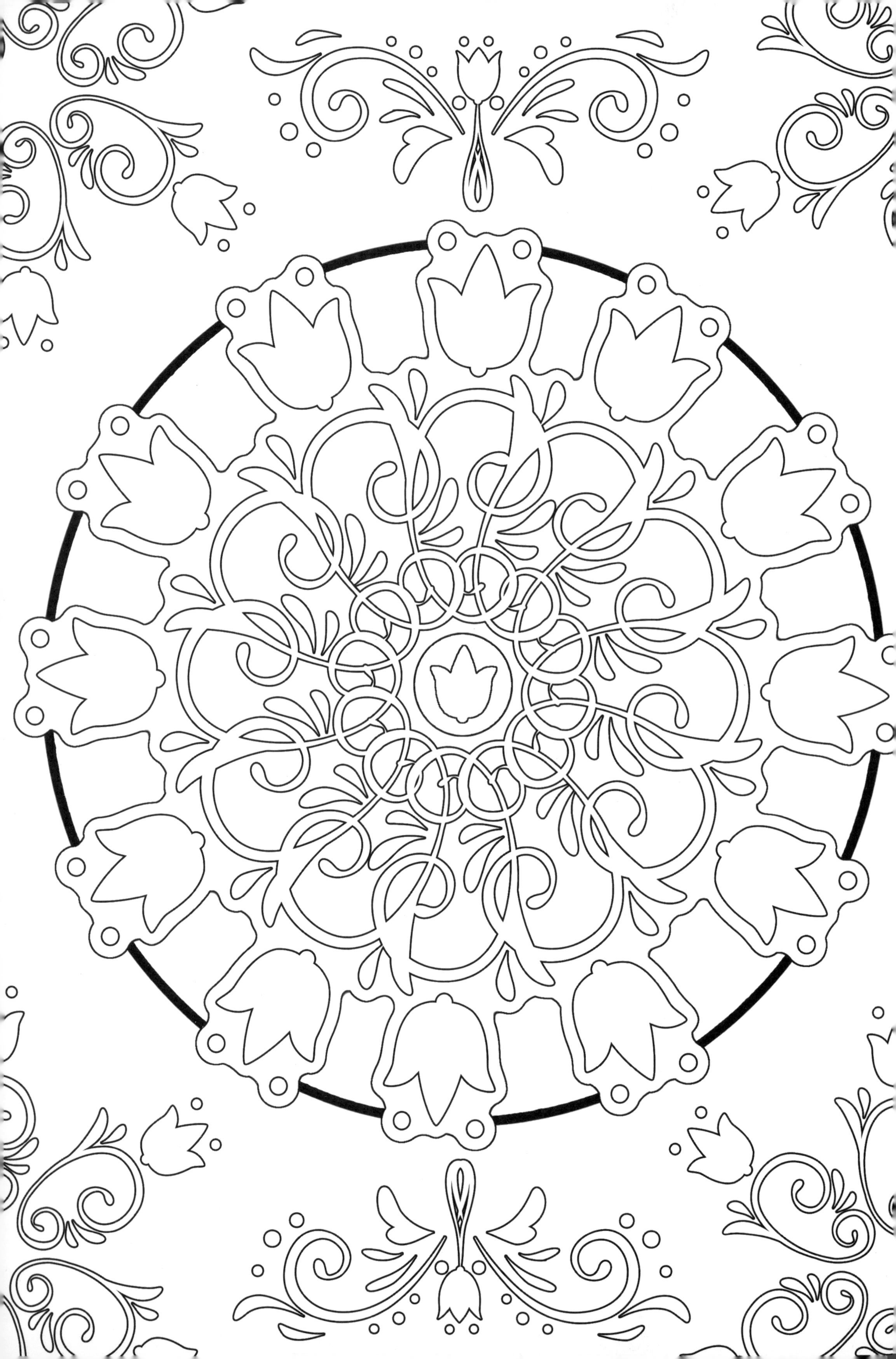

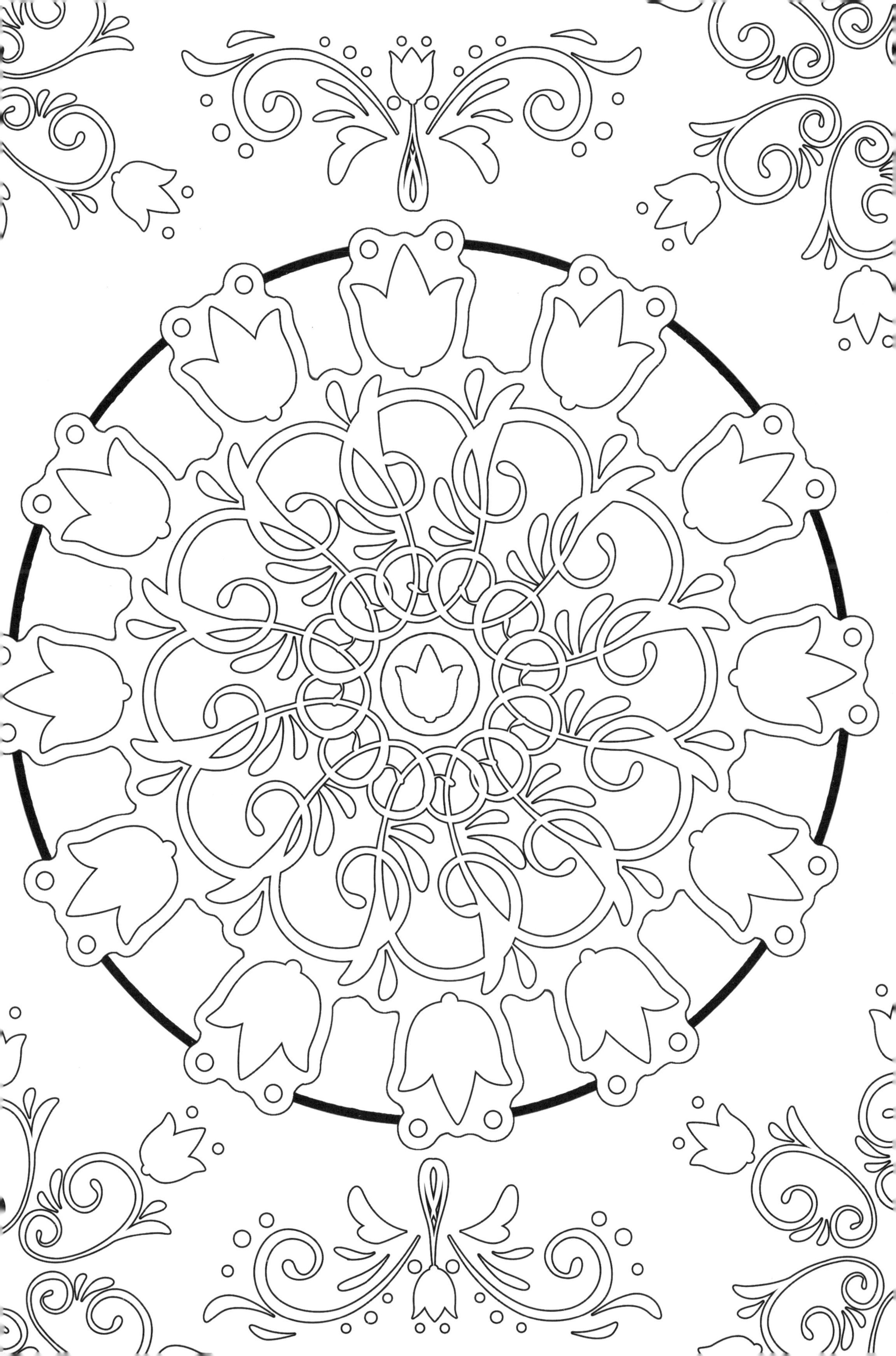

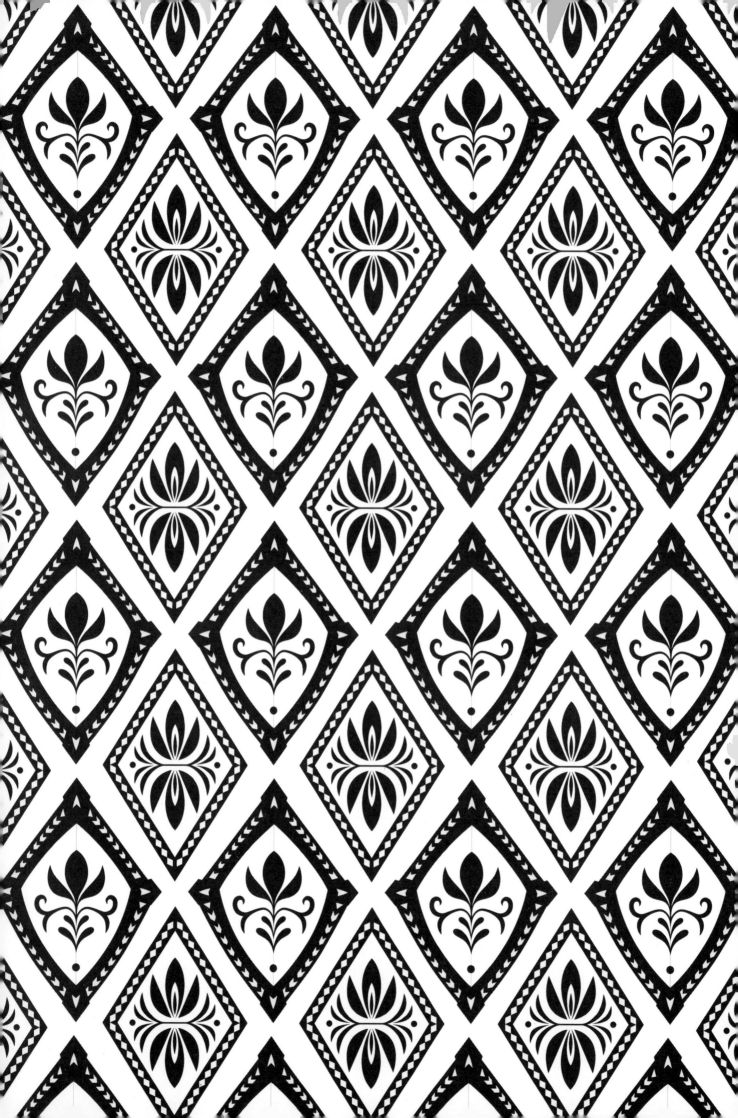

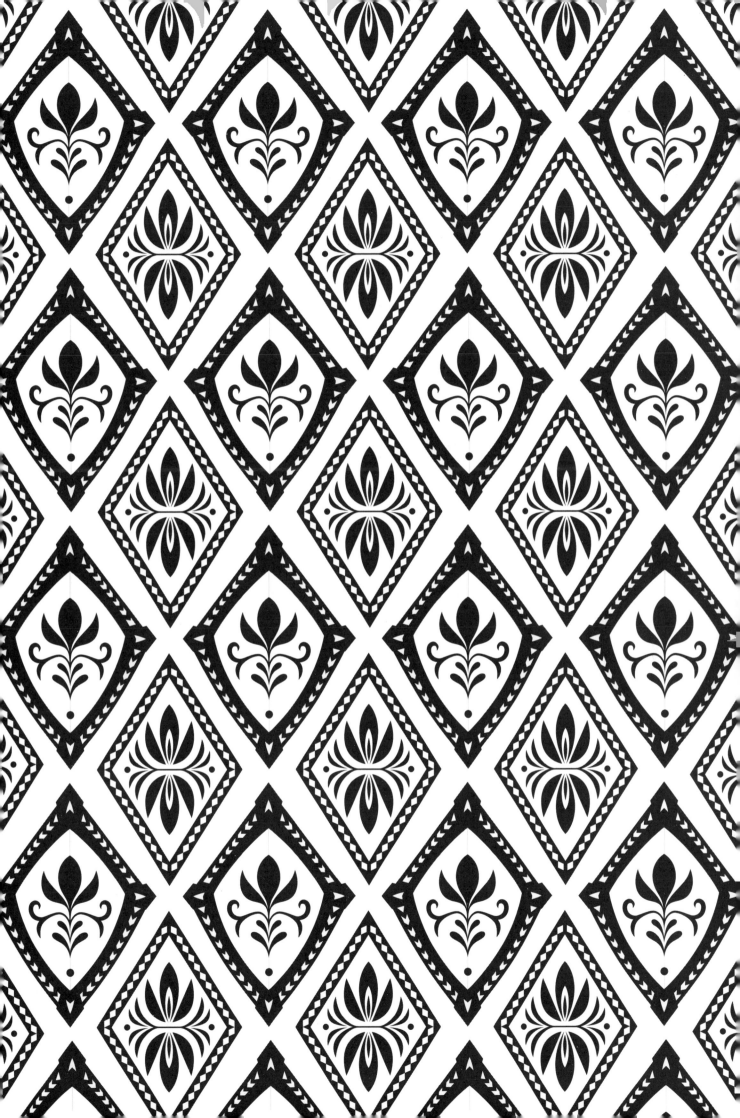

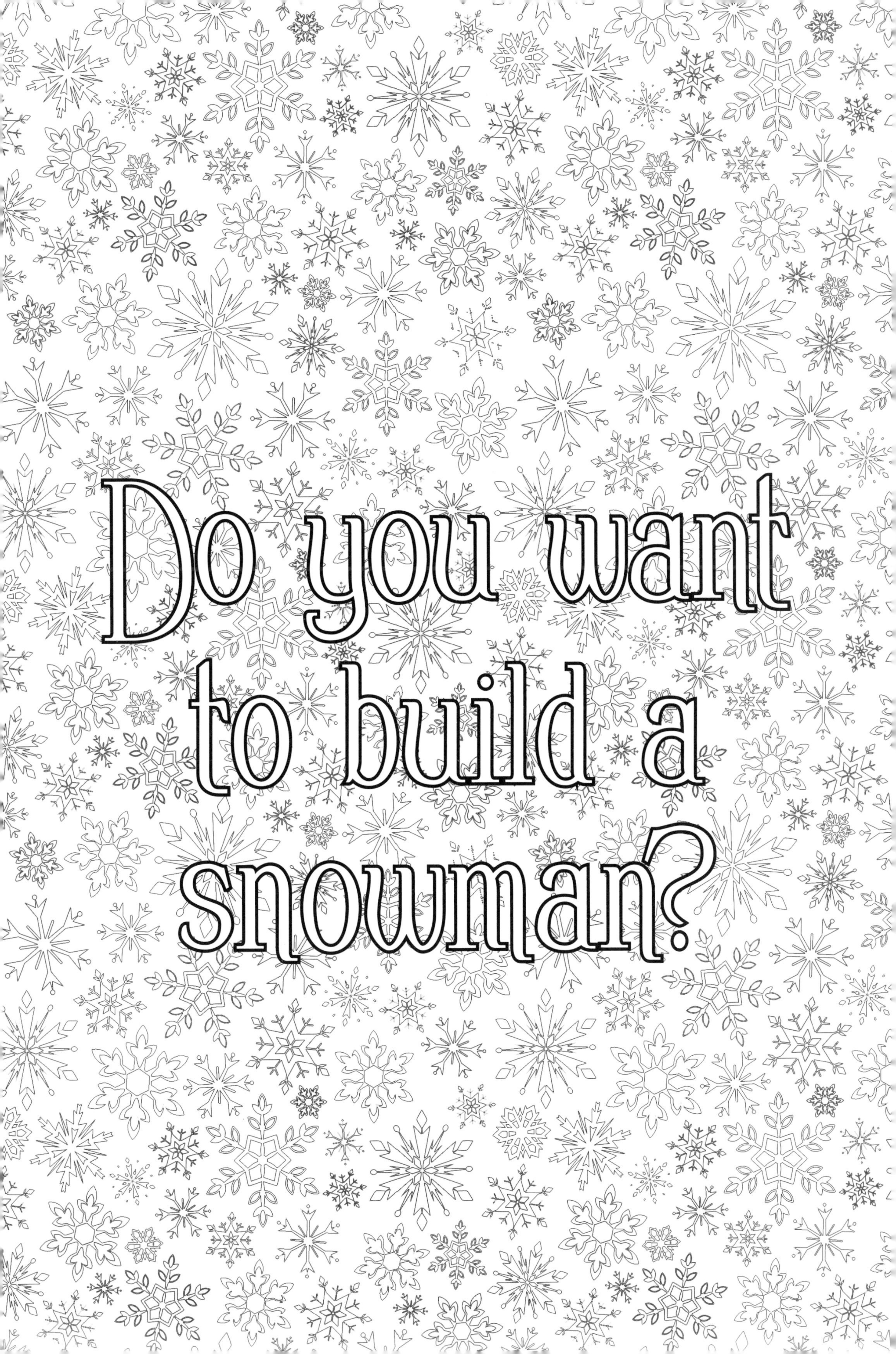
Do you want
to build a
snowman?

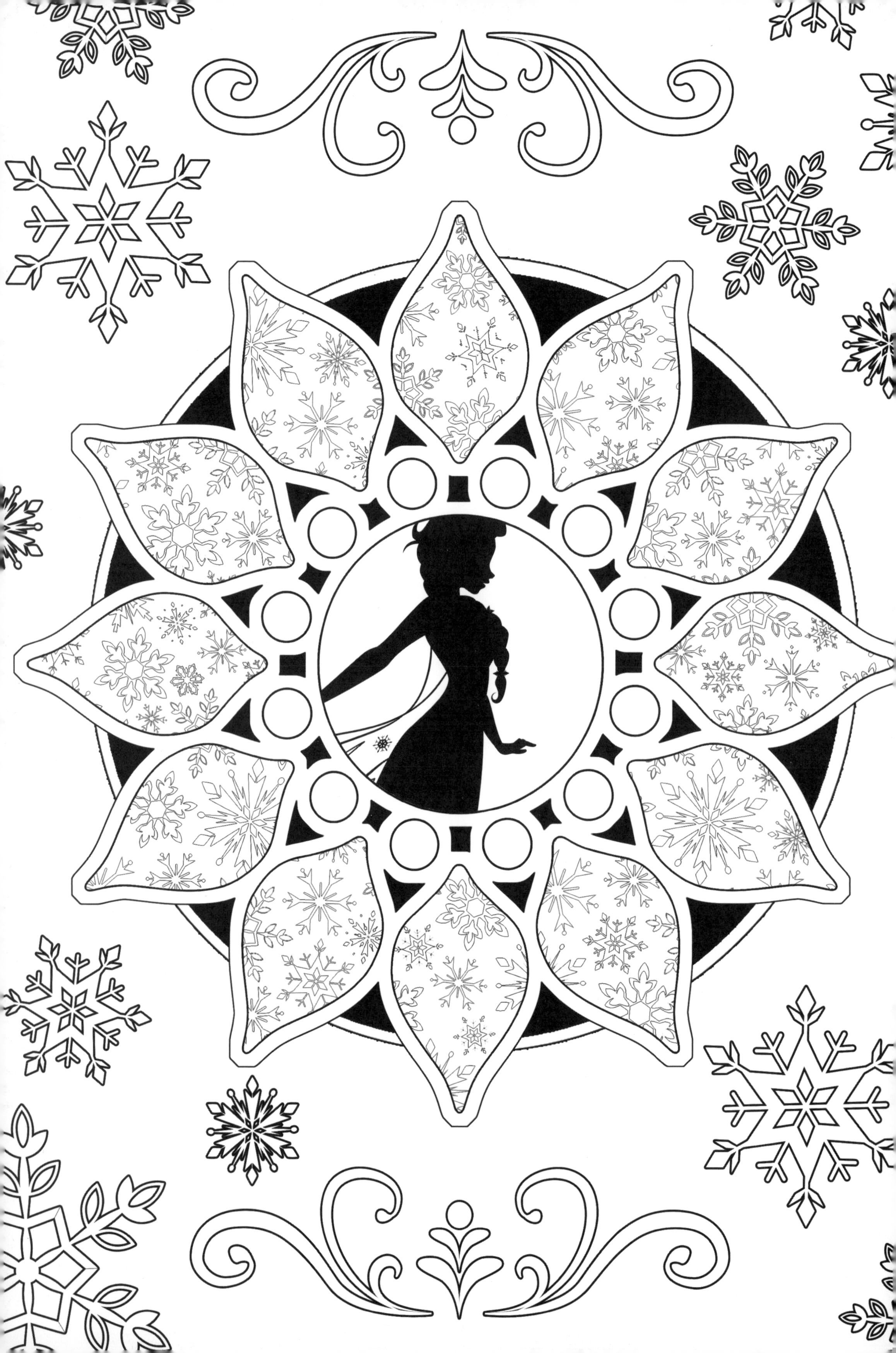

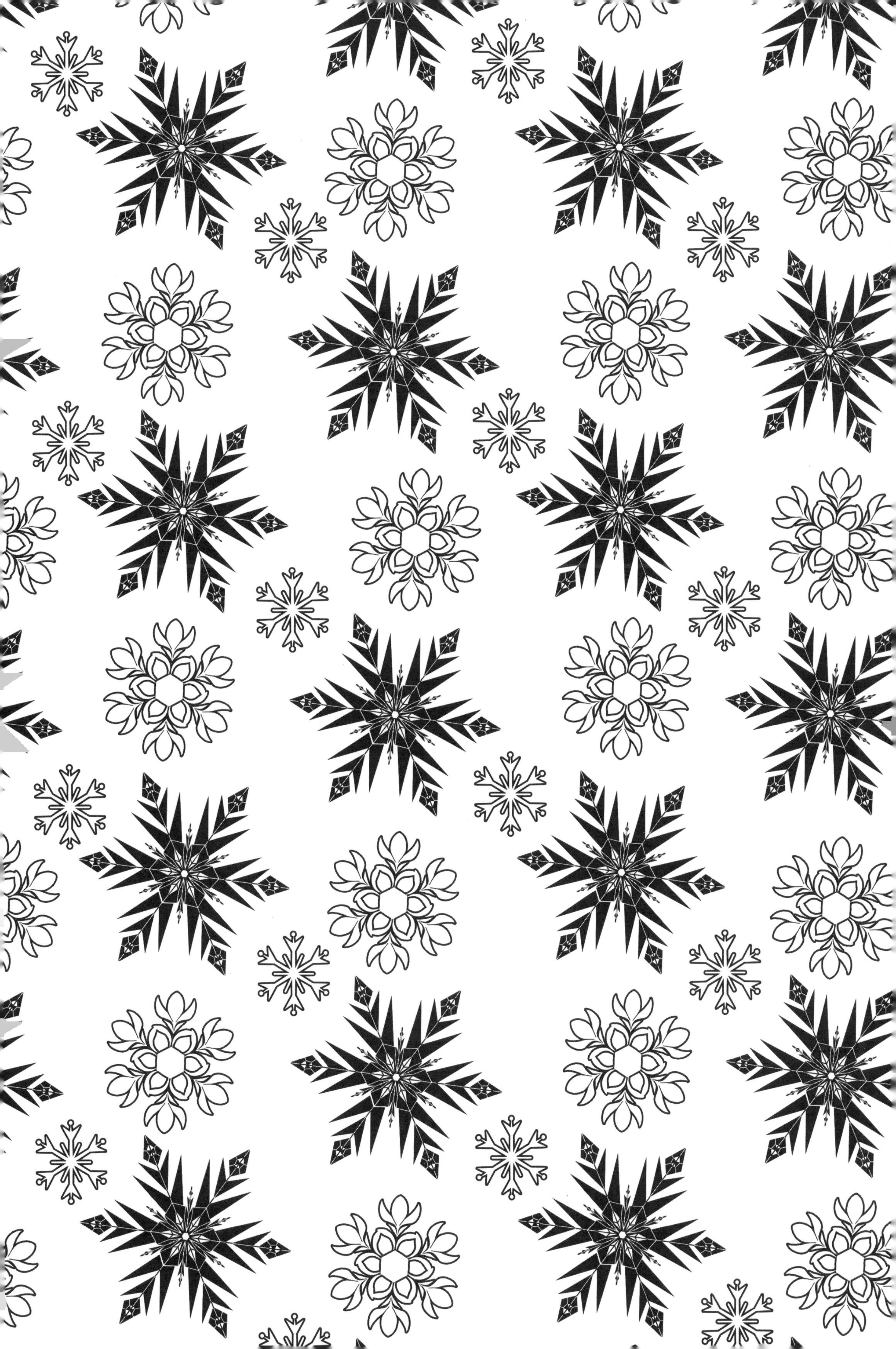

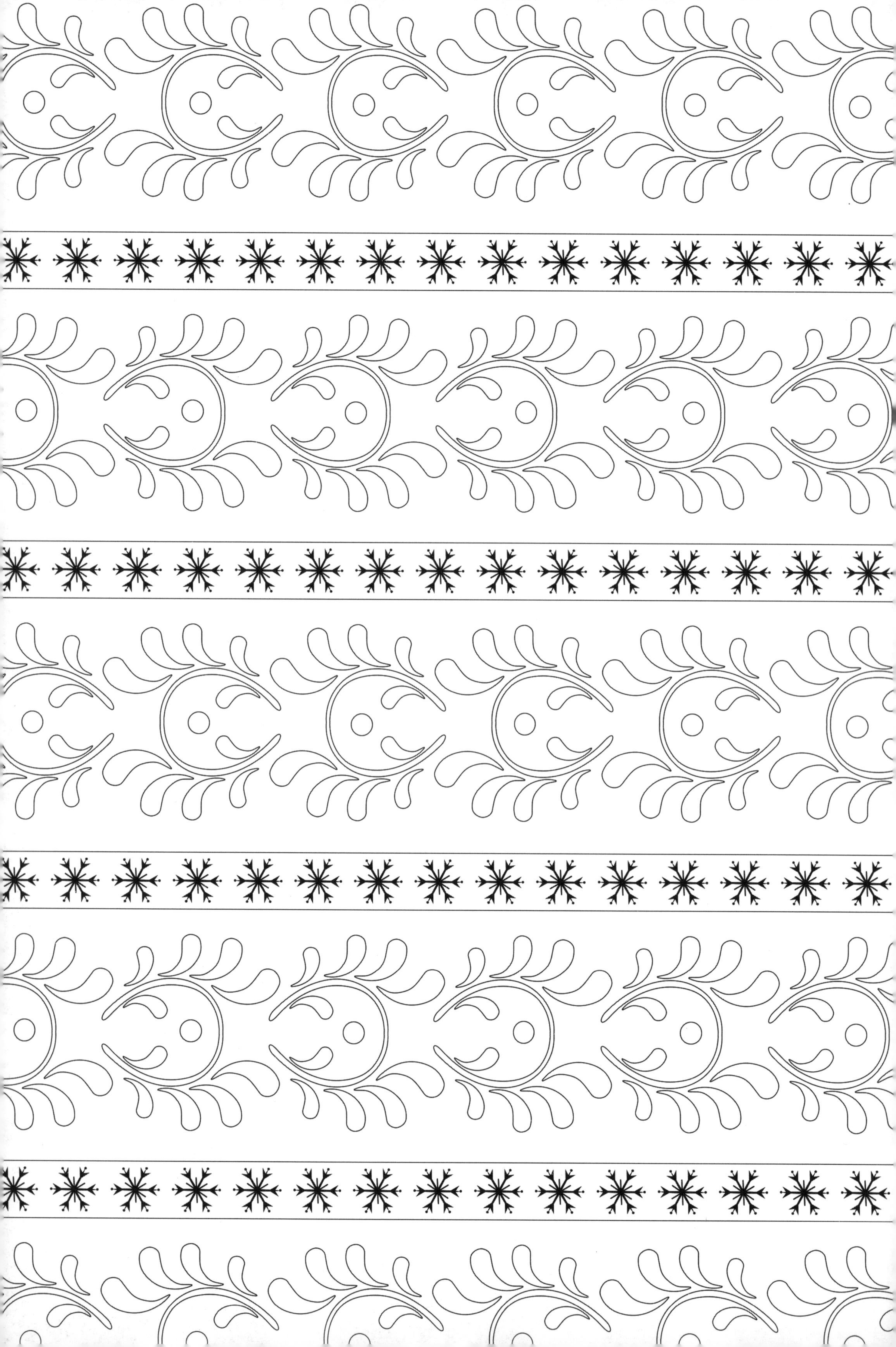

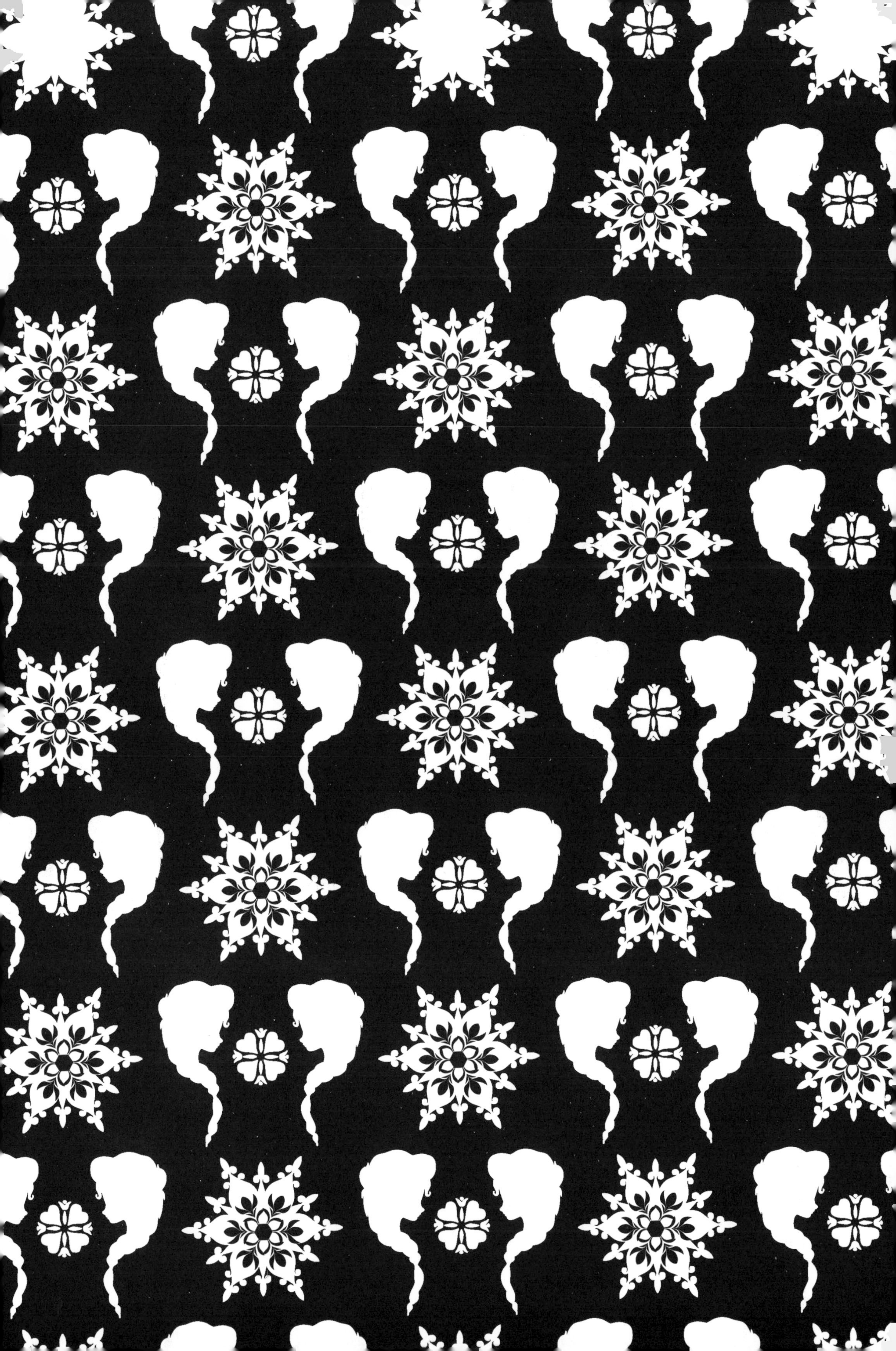

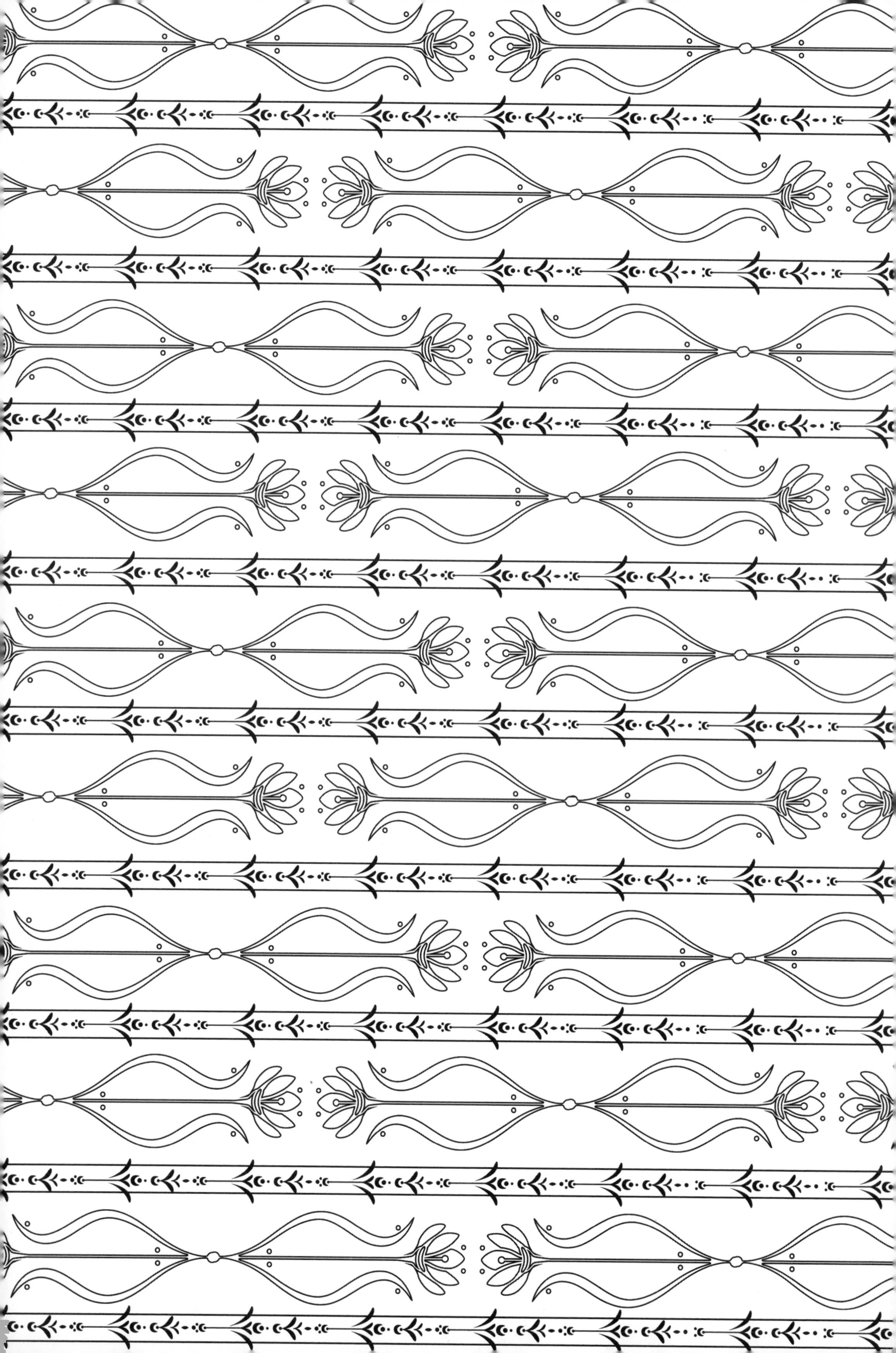

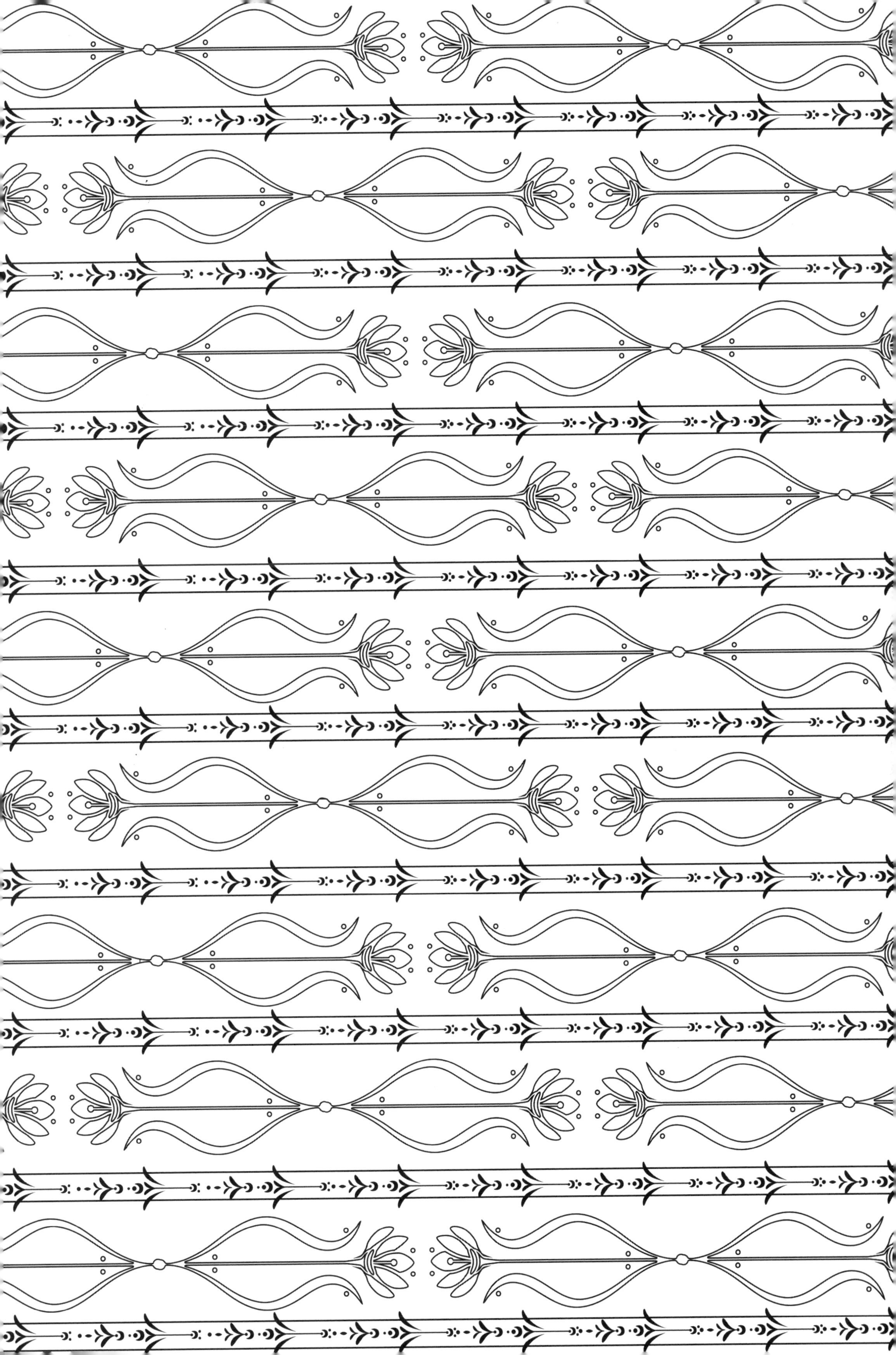

Have courage

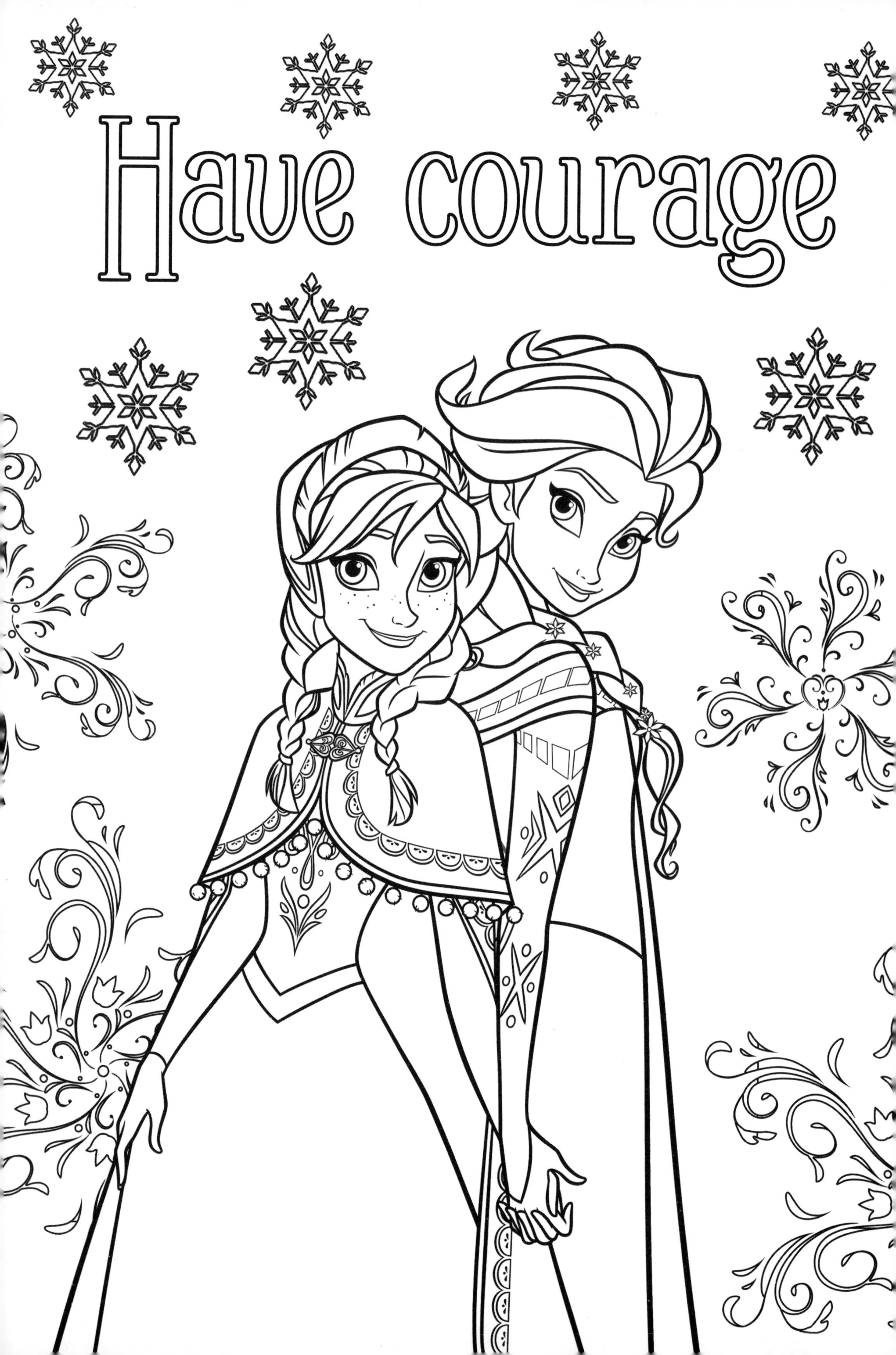

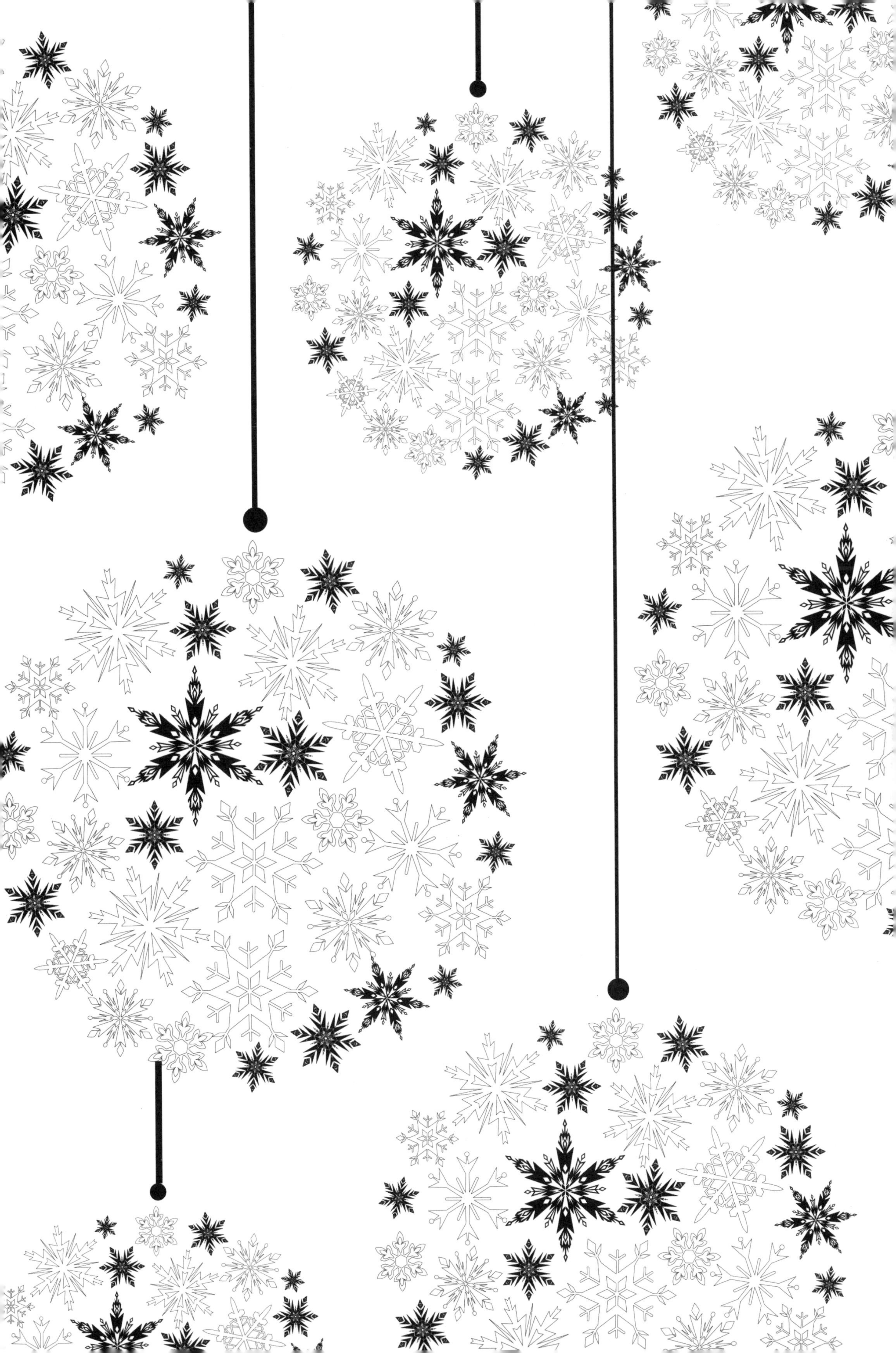

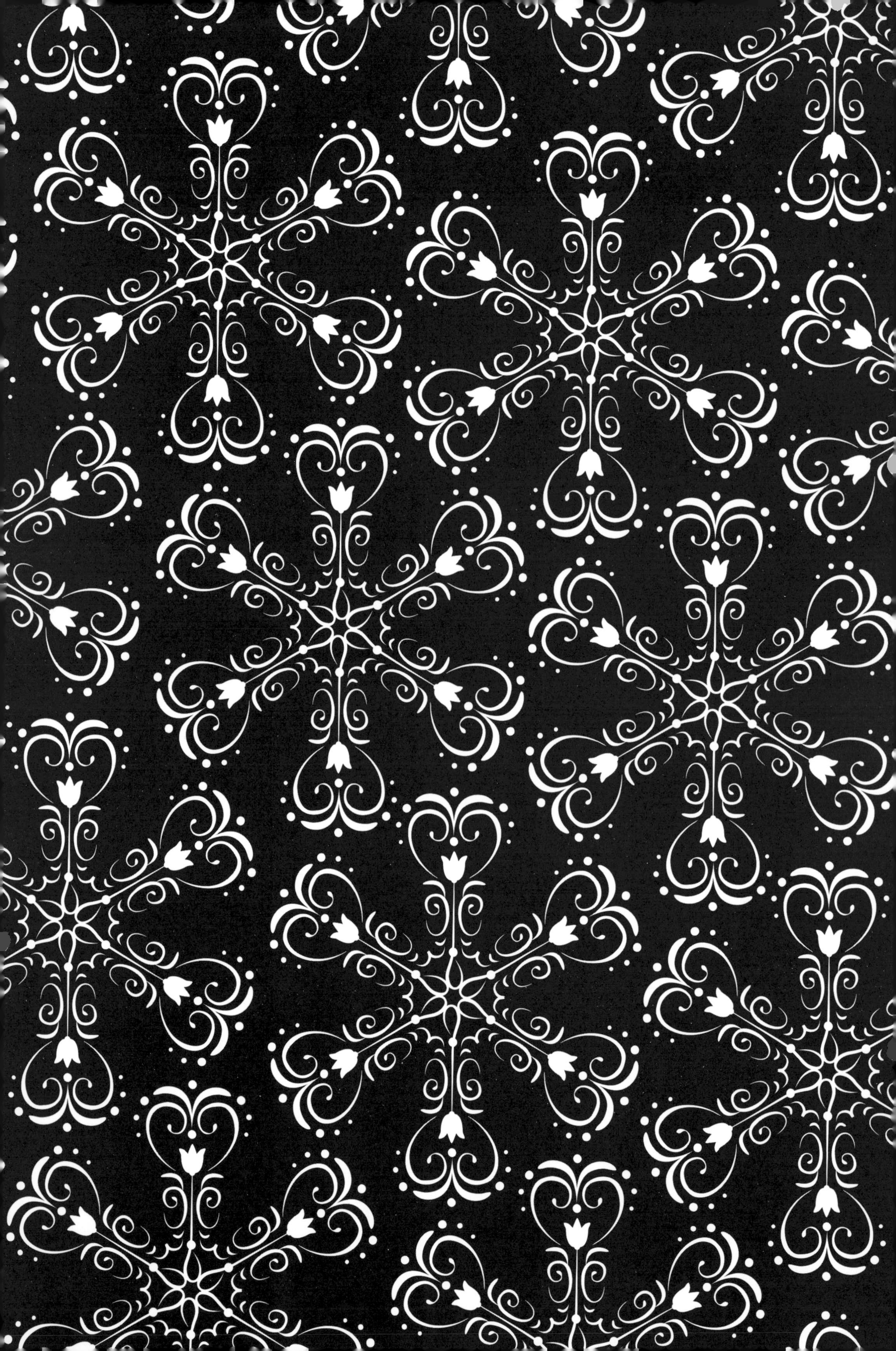

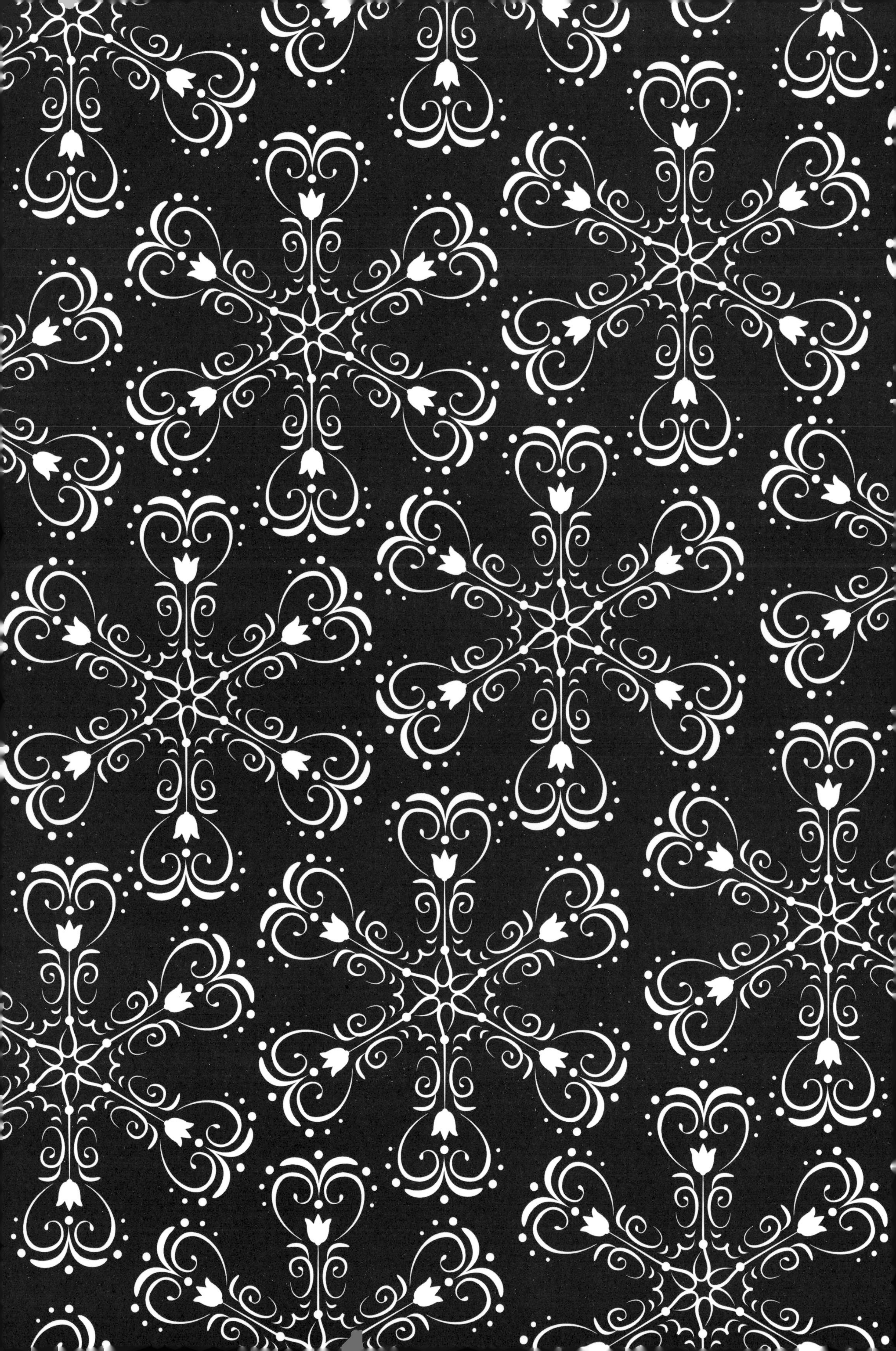

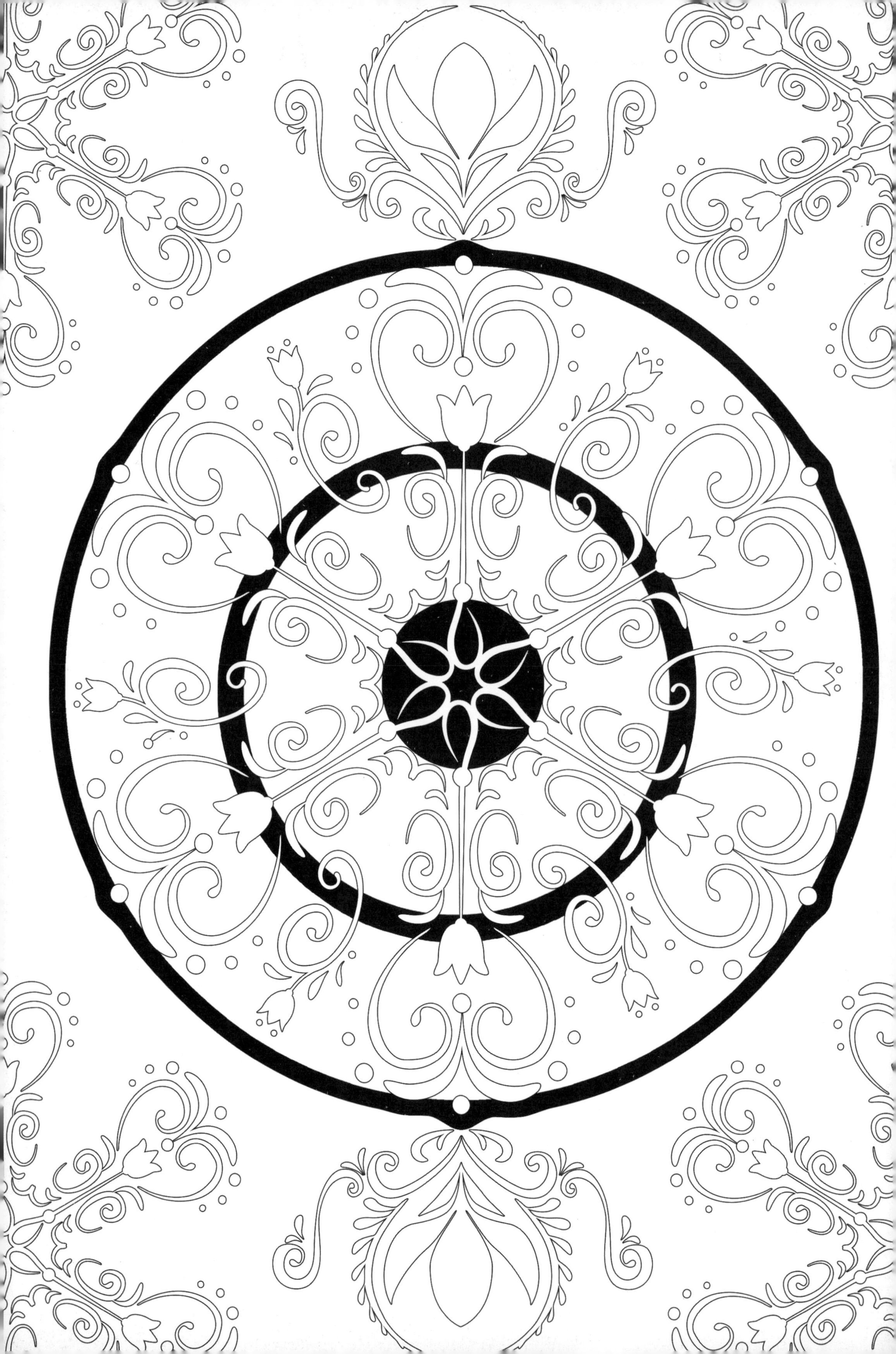

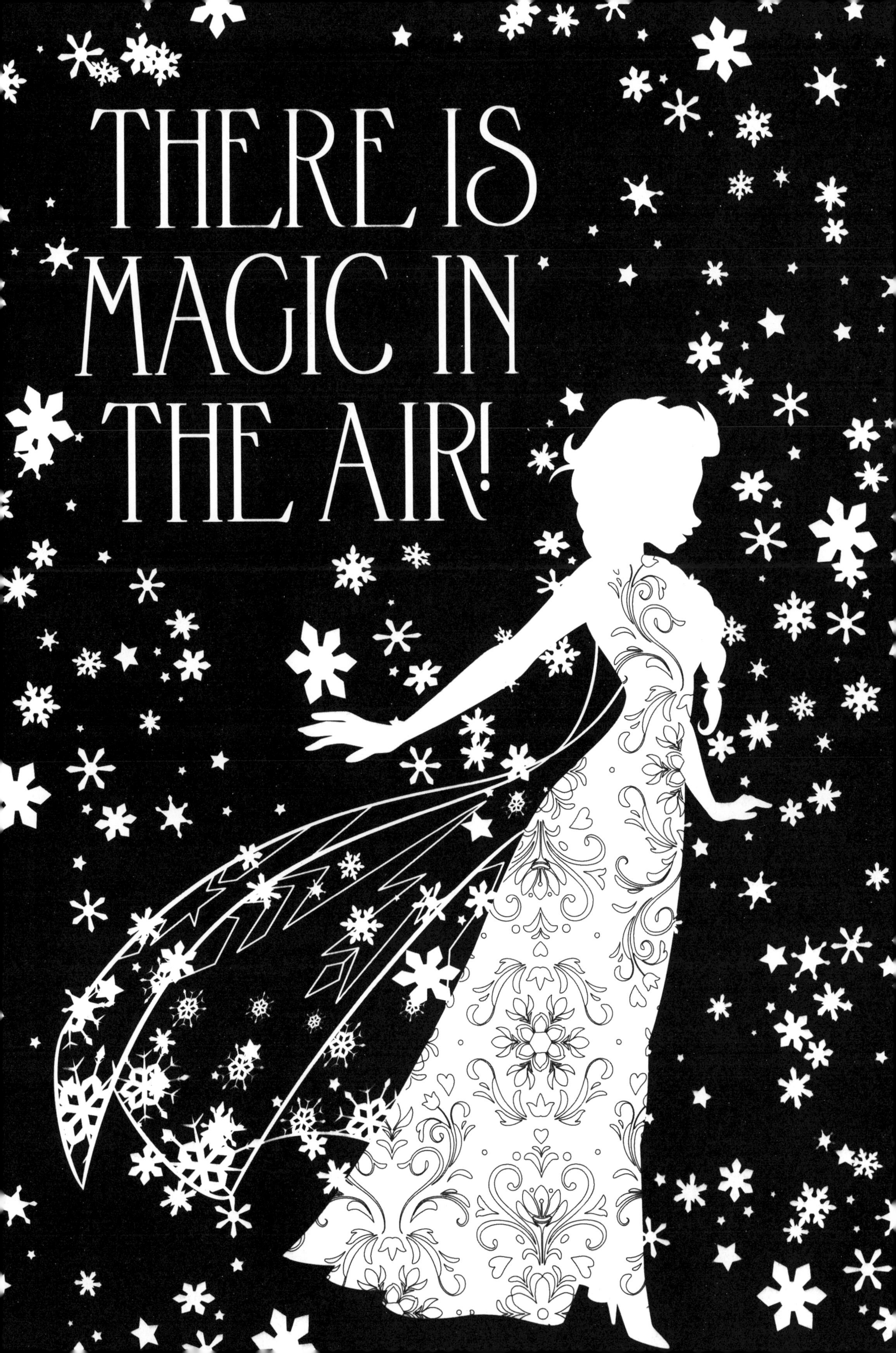
THERE IS
MAGIC IN
THE AIR!

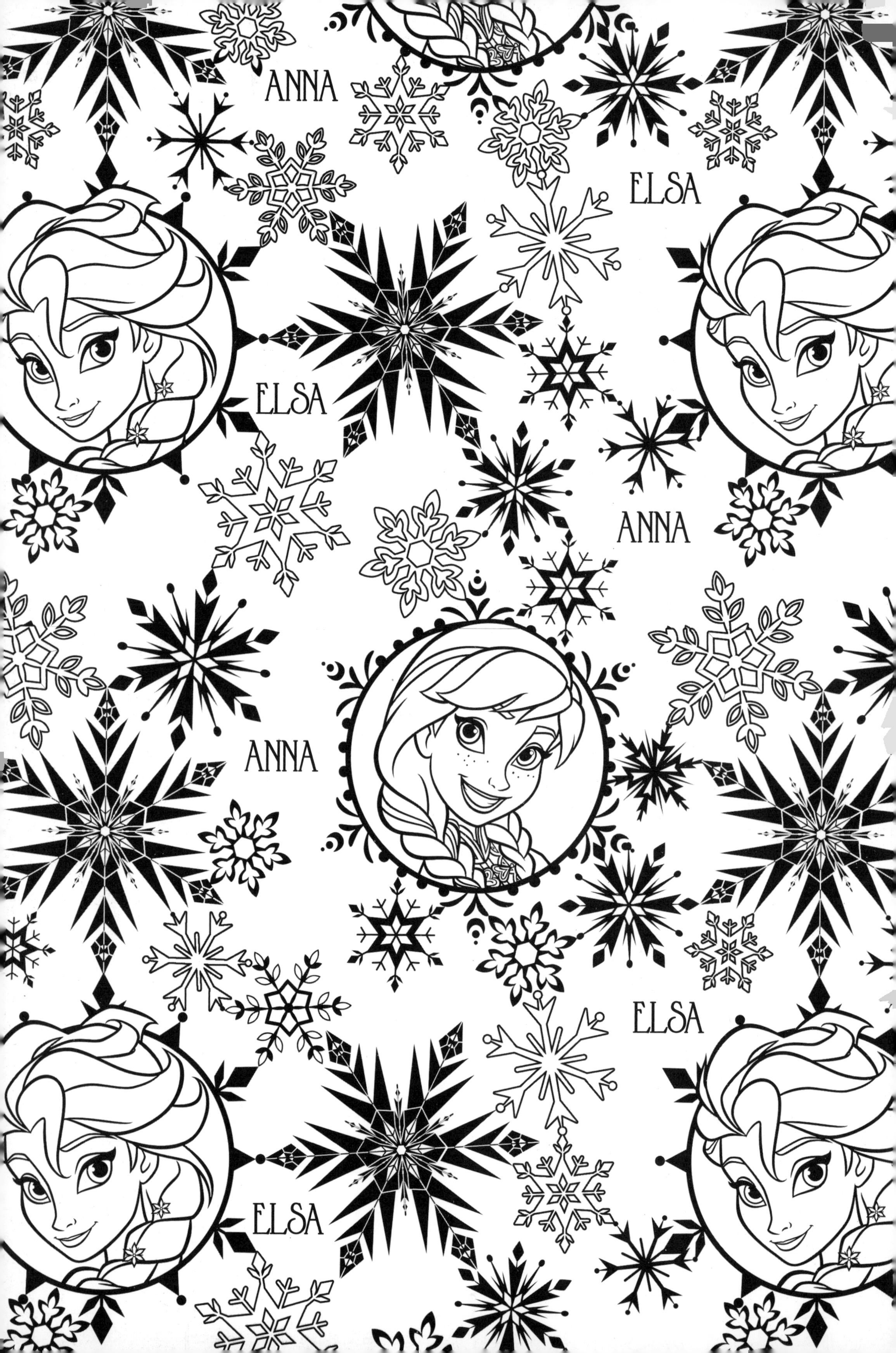
ANNA
ELSA
ELSA
ANNA
ANNA
ELSA
ELSA

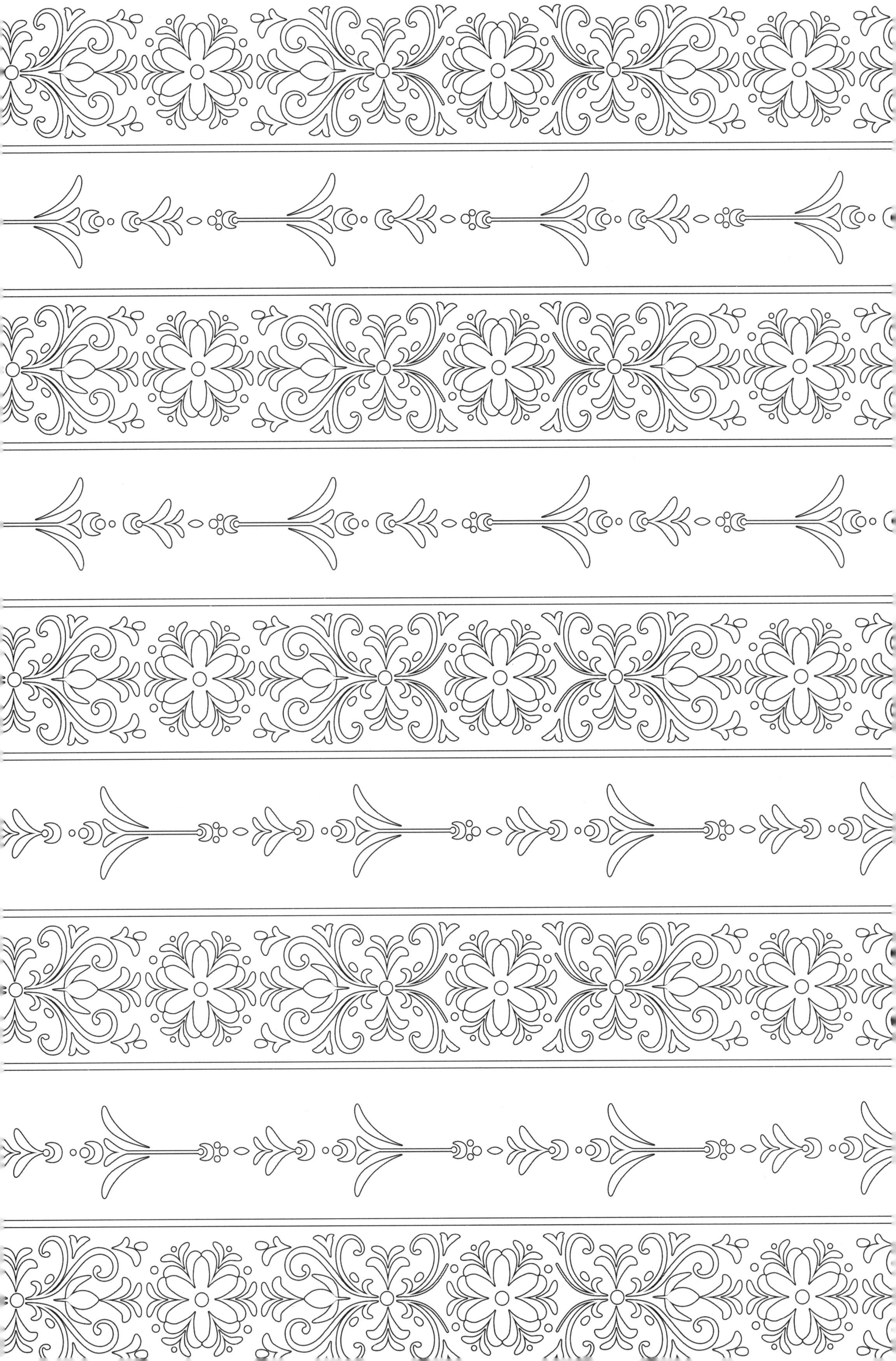

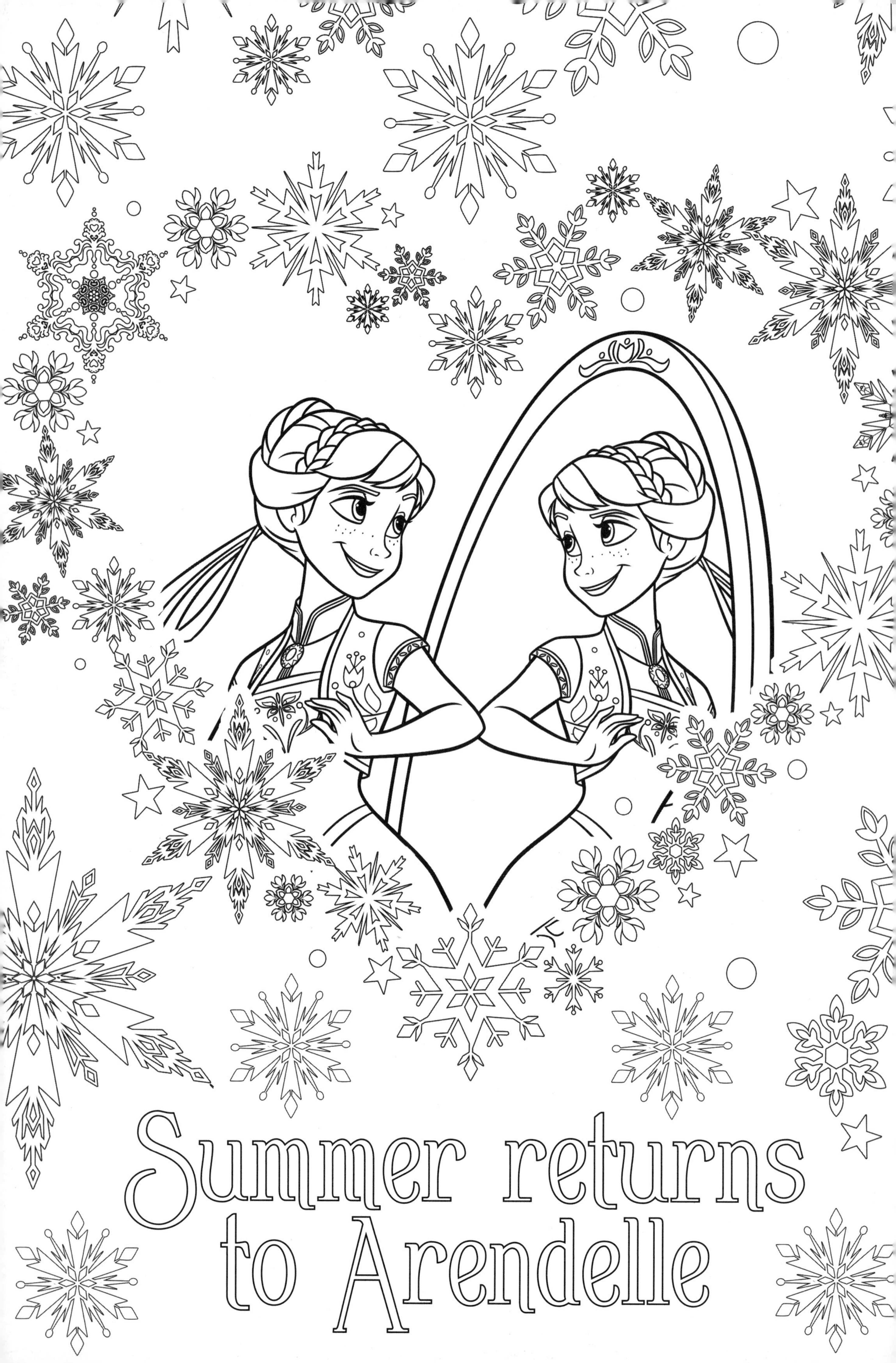
Summer returns
to Arendelle

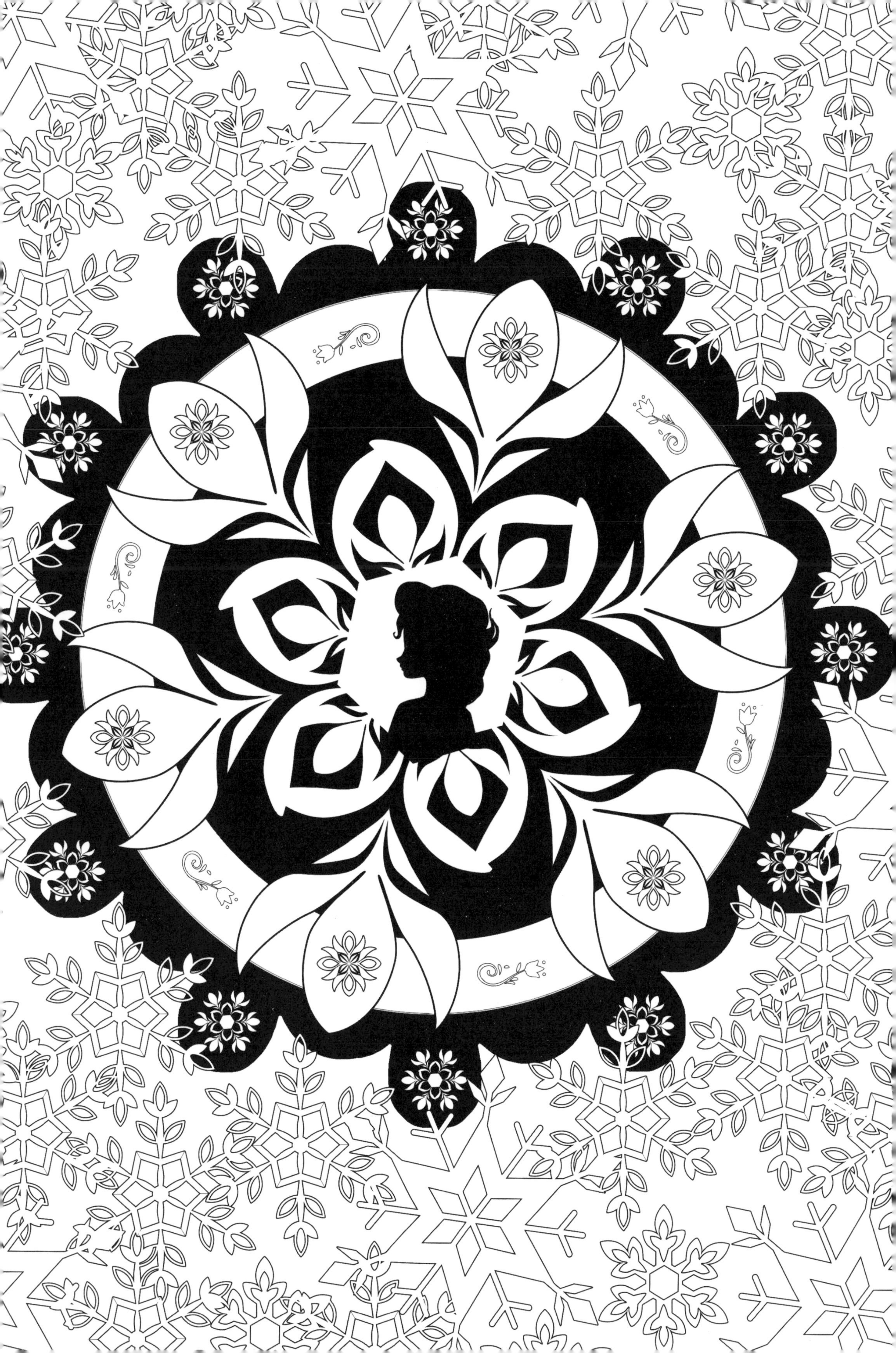

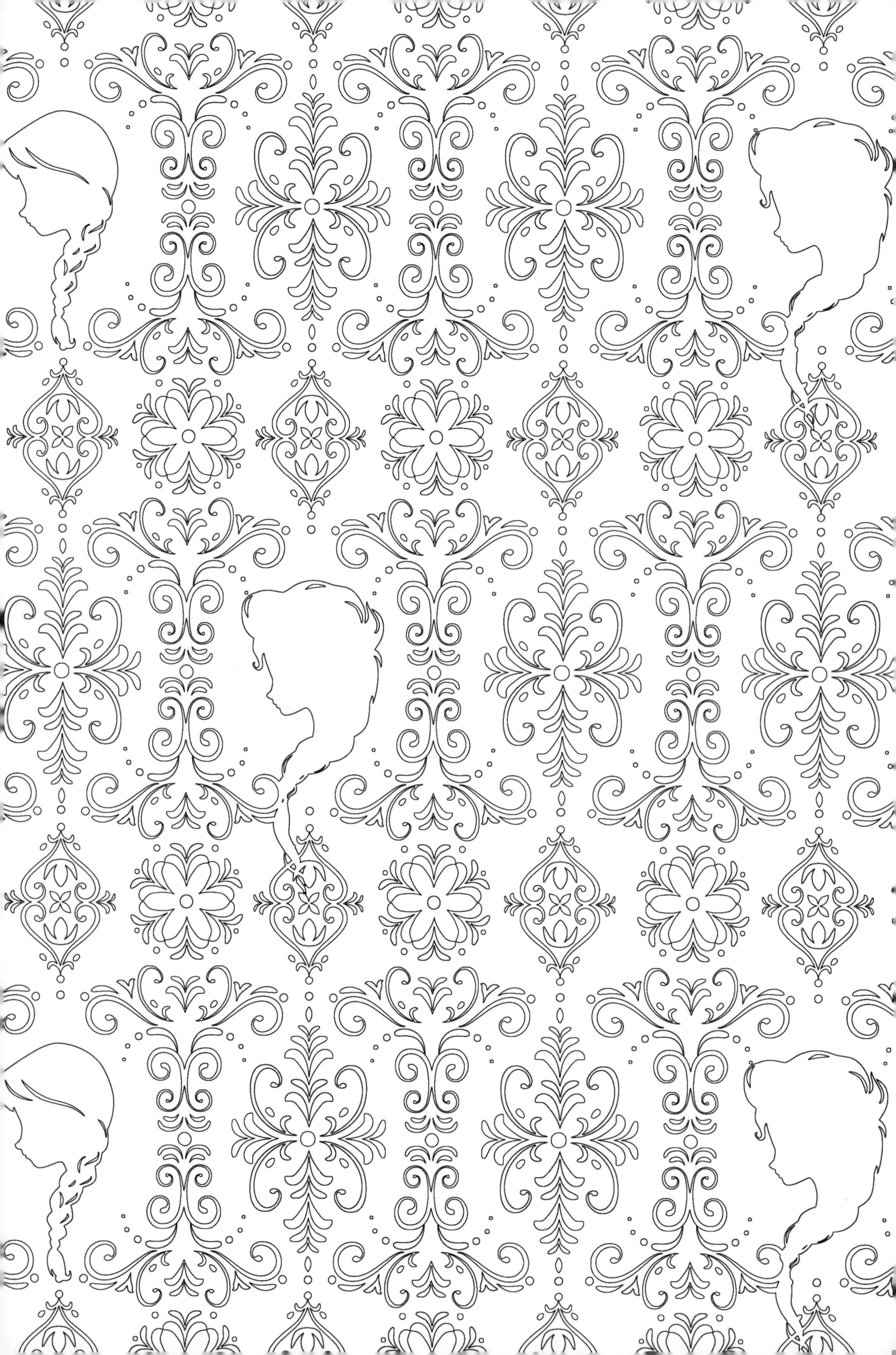

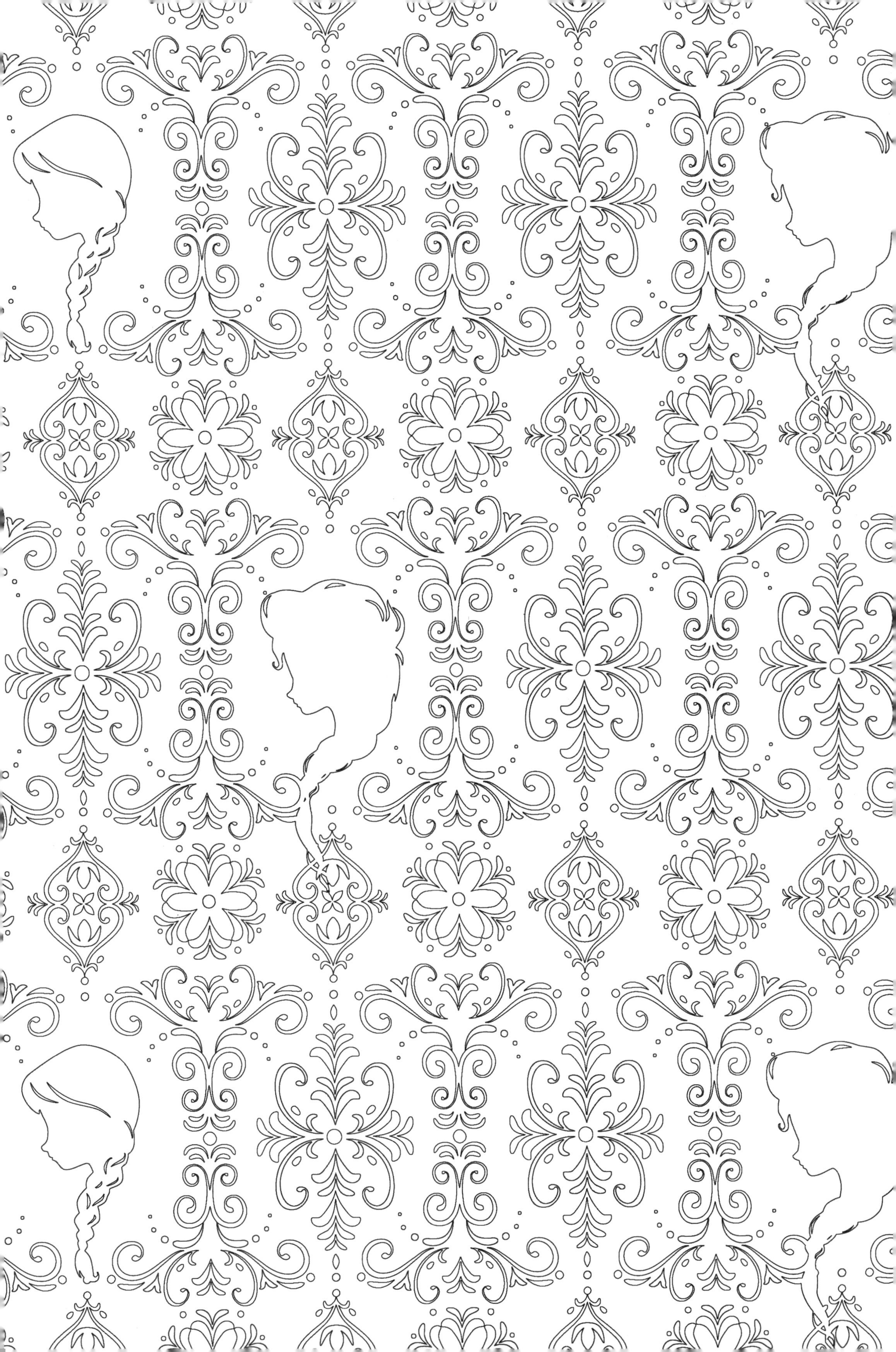

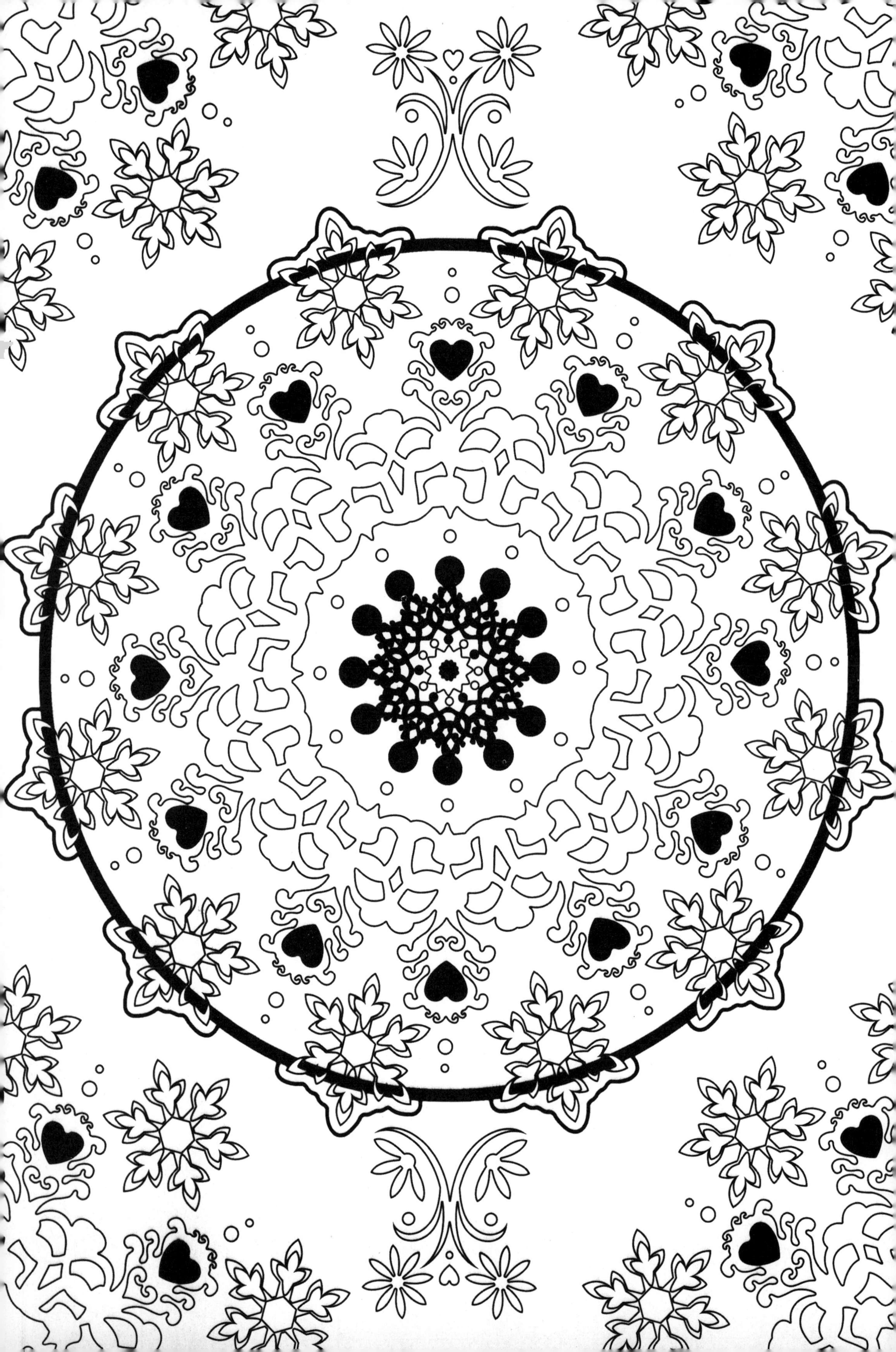

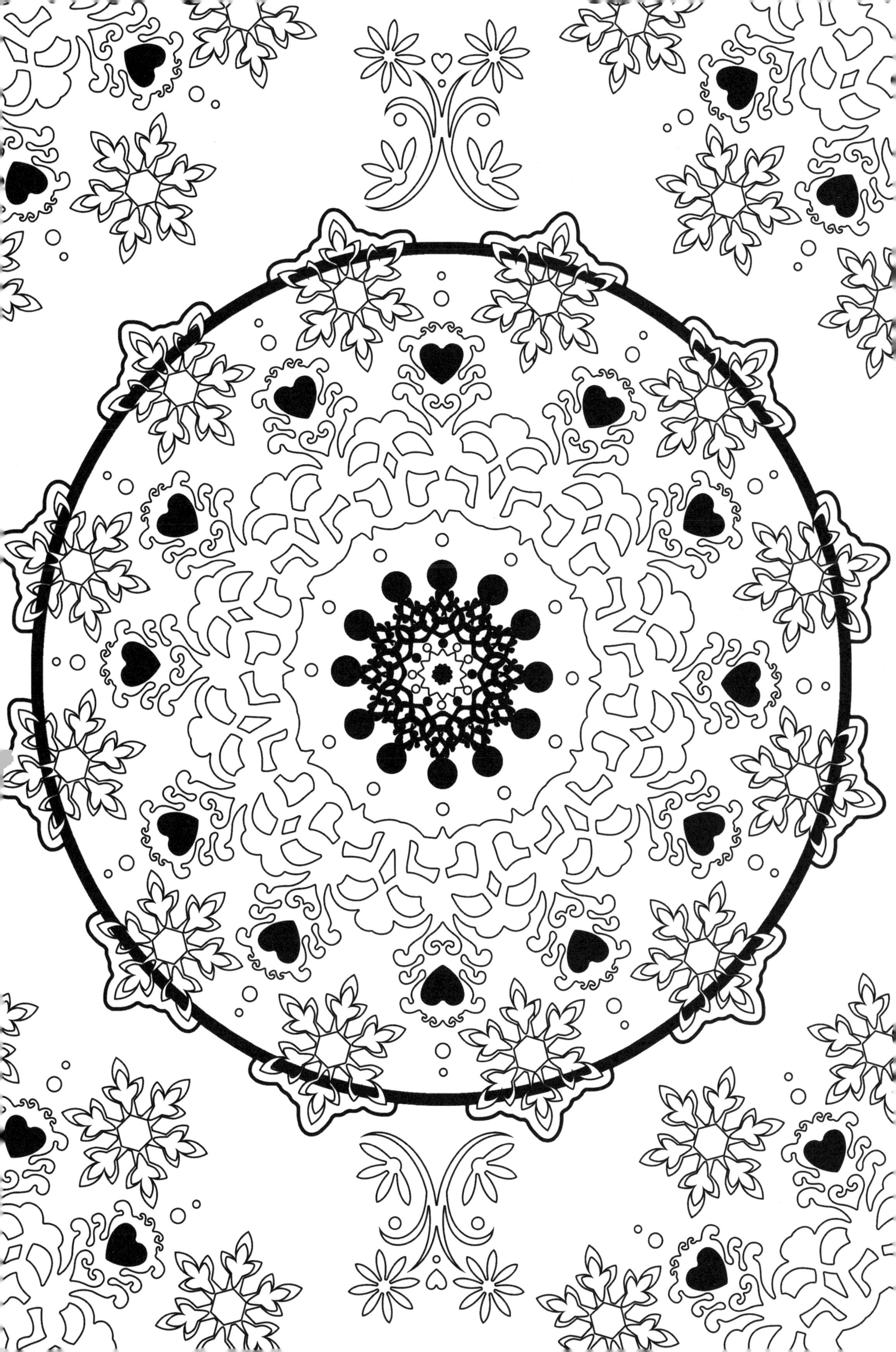

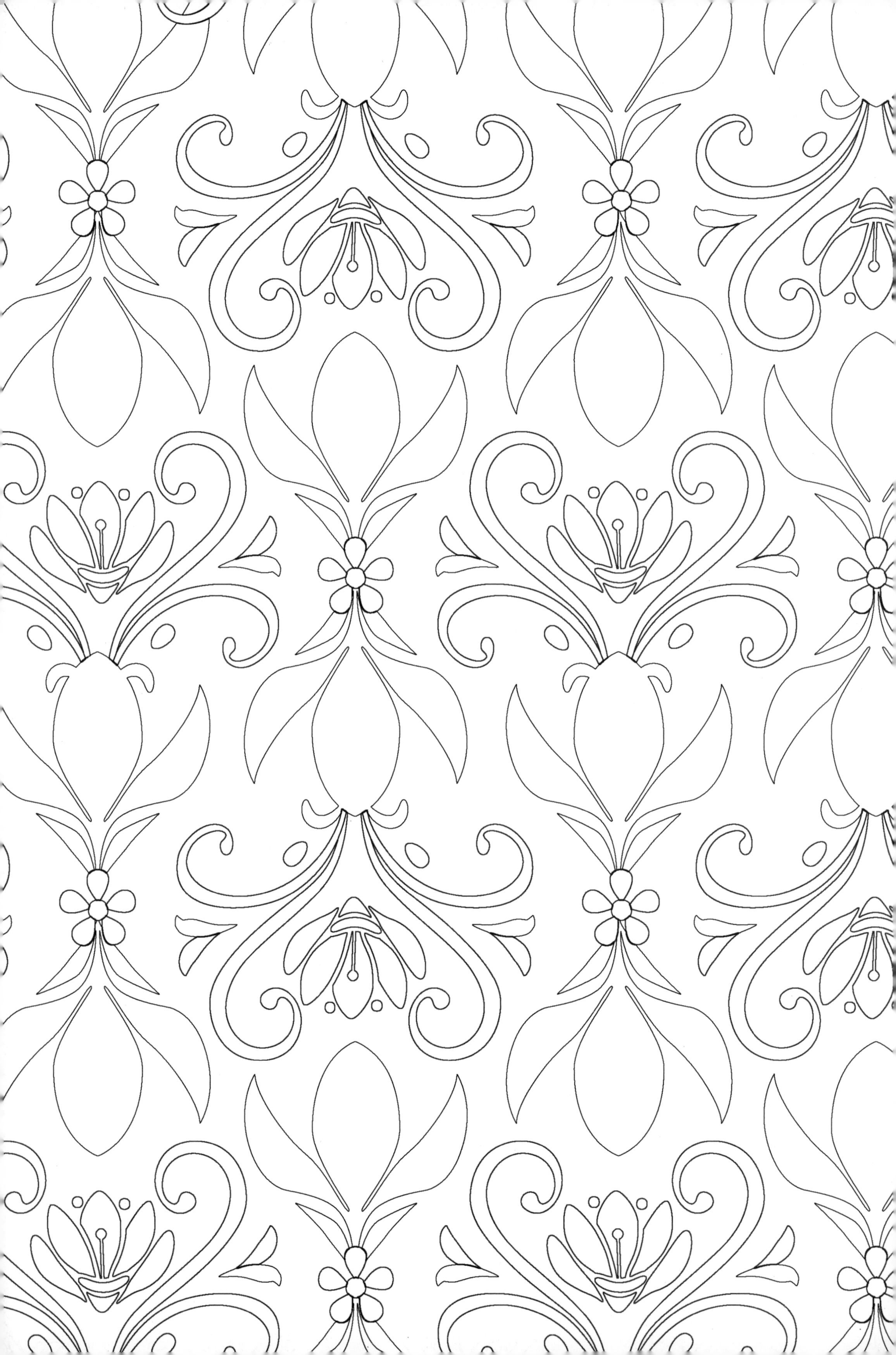

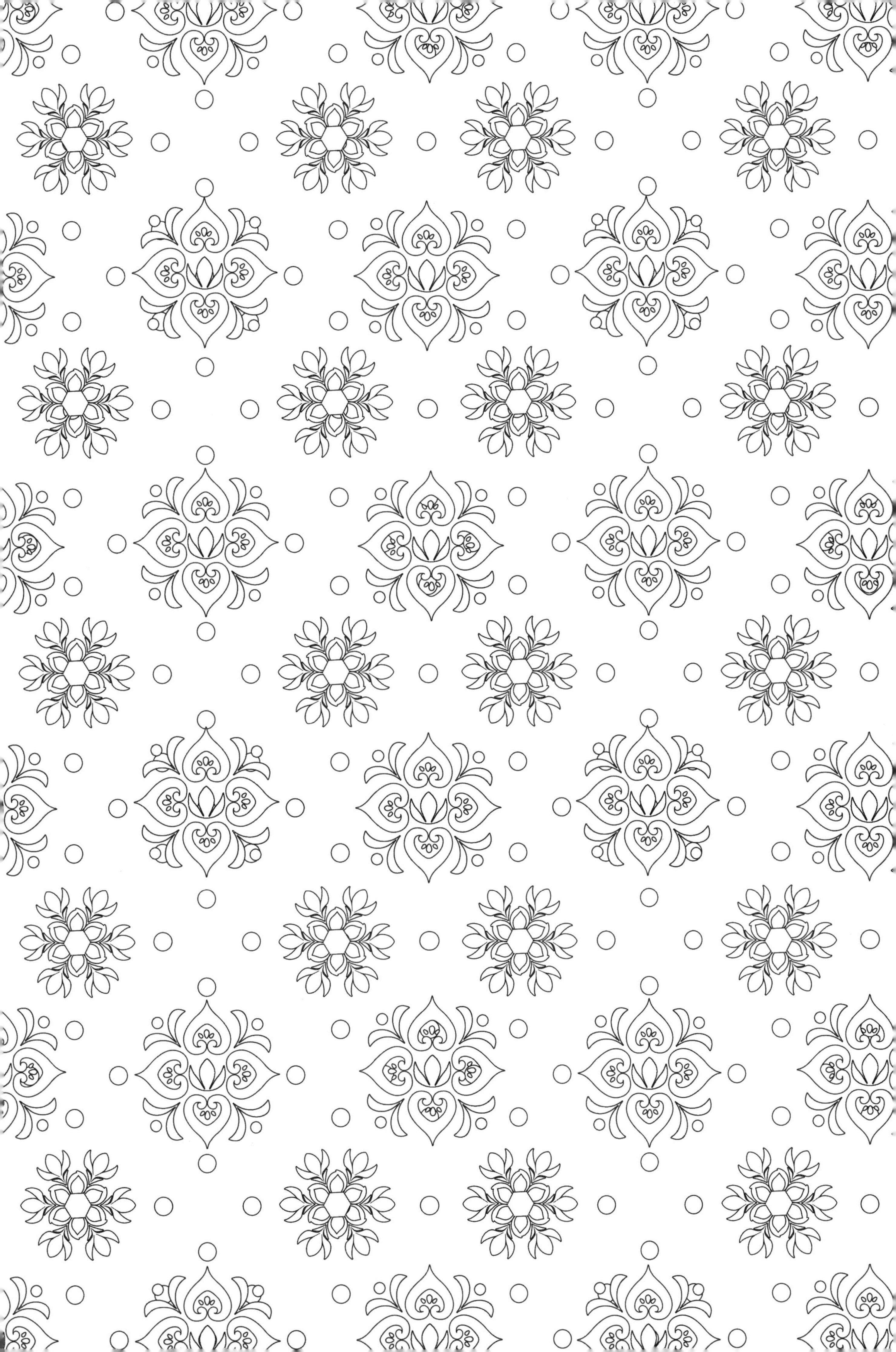

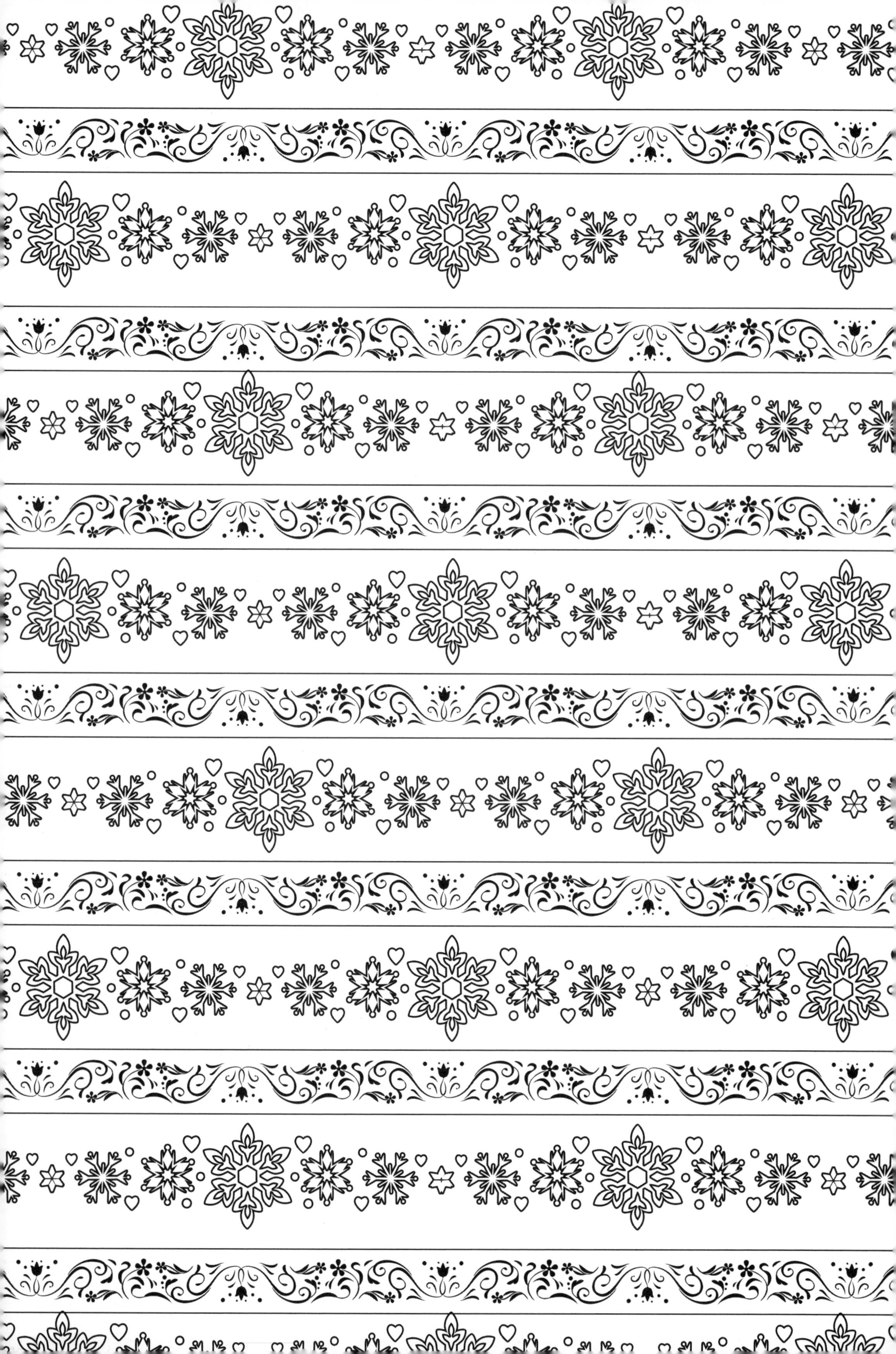

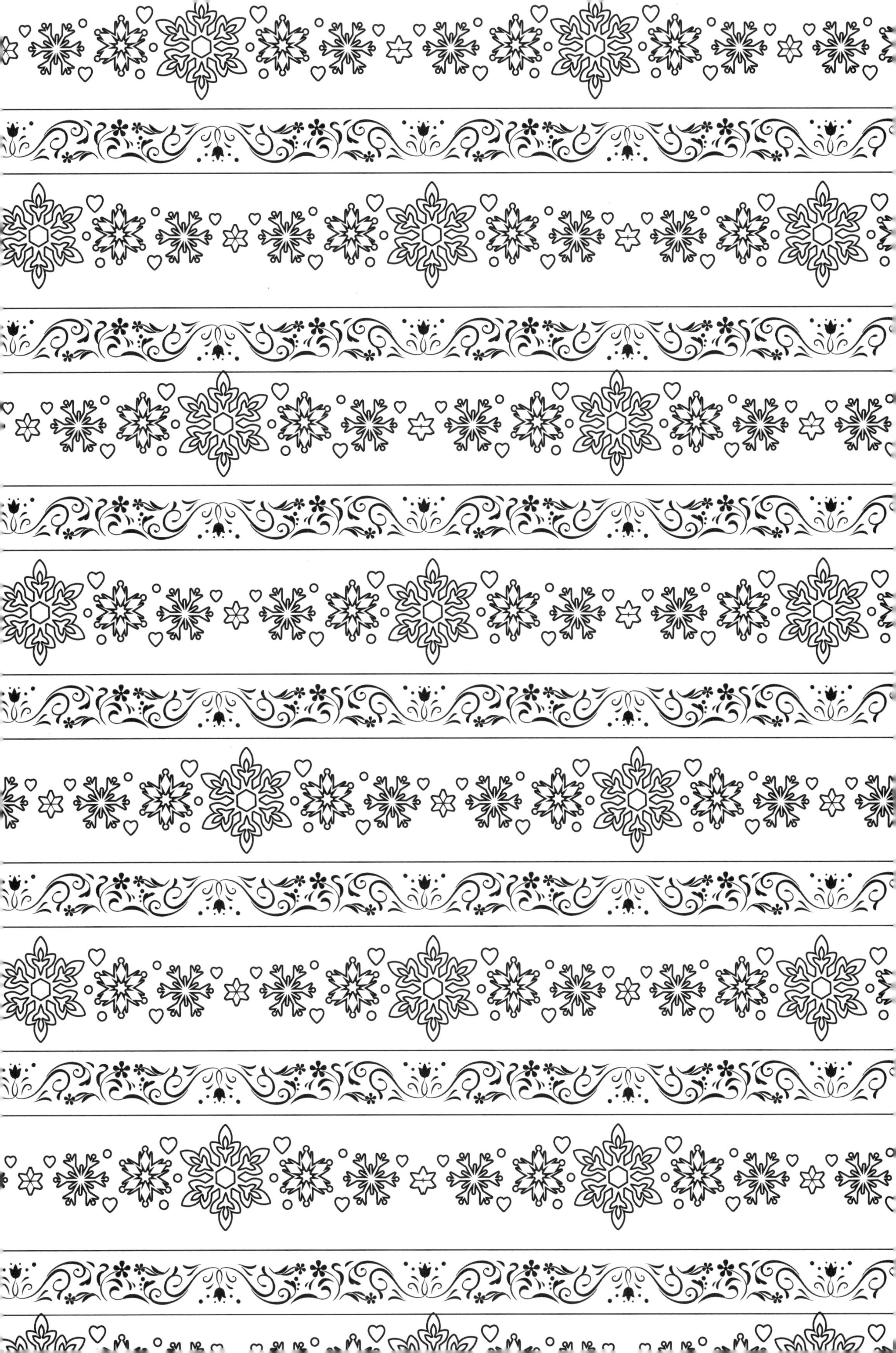

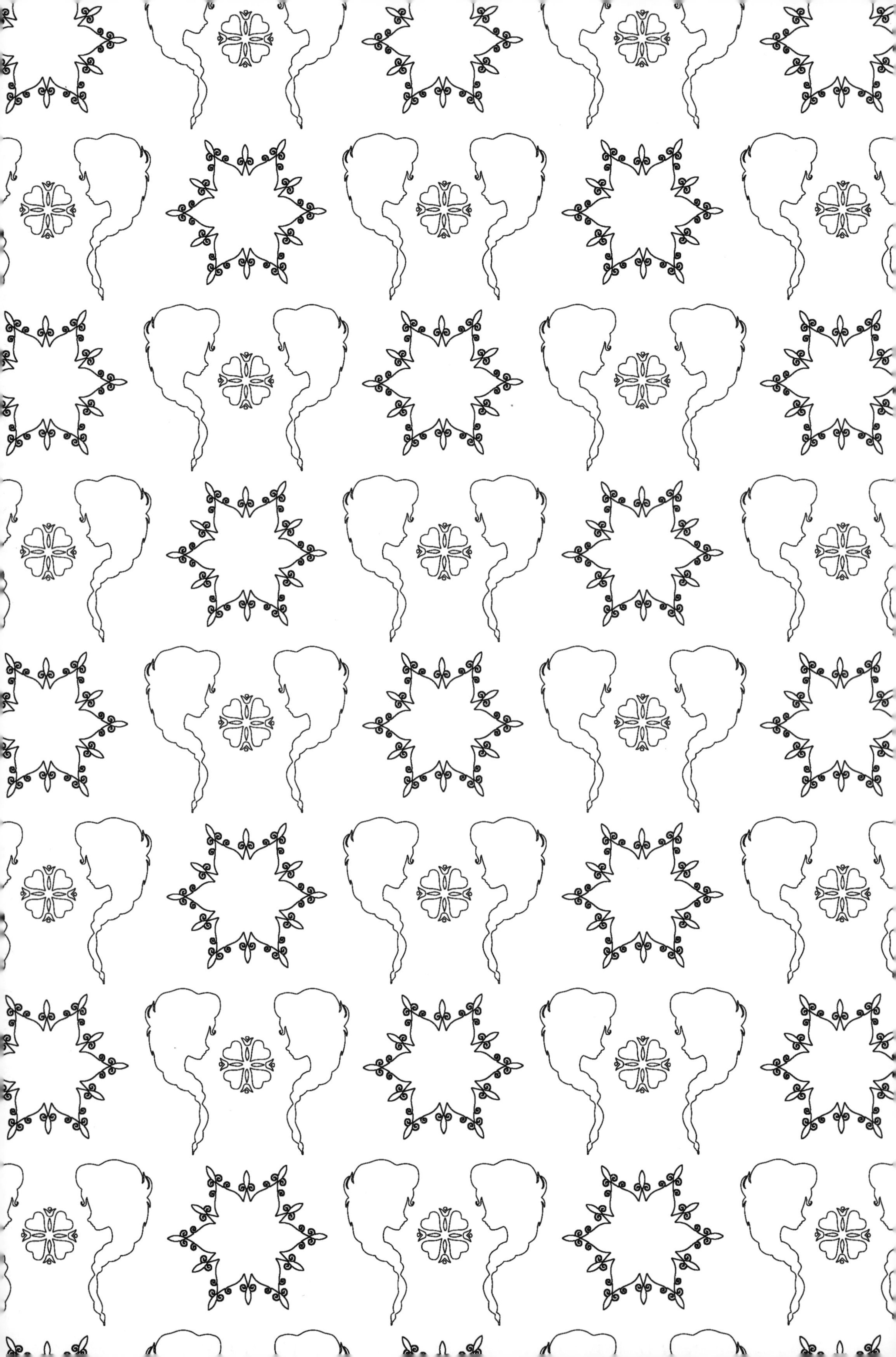

Elsa & Anna

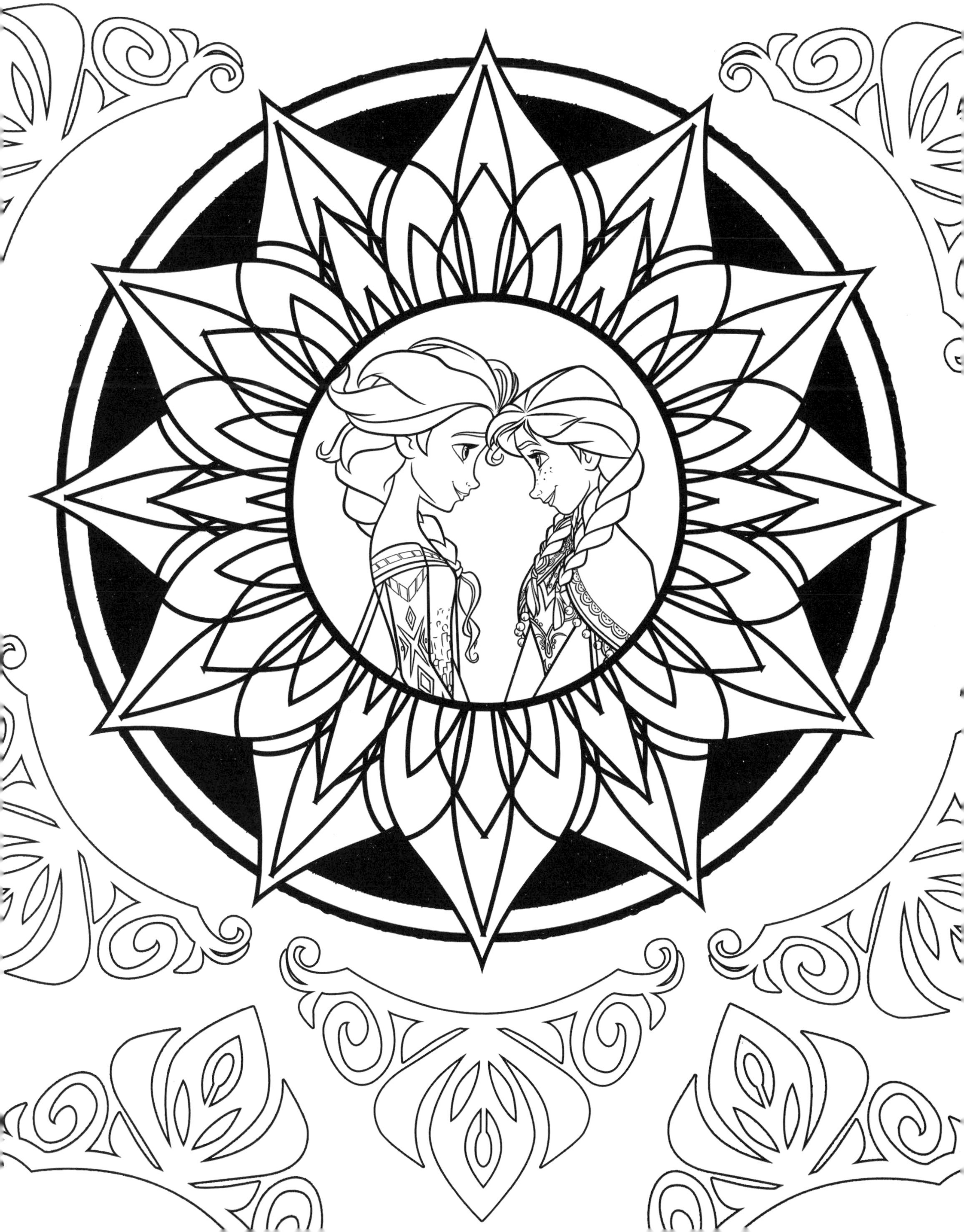

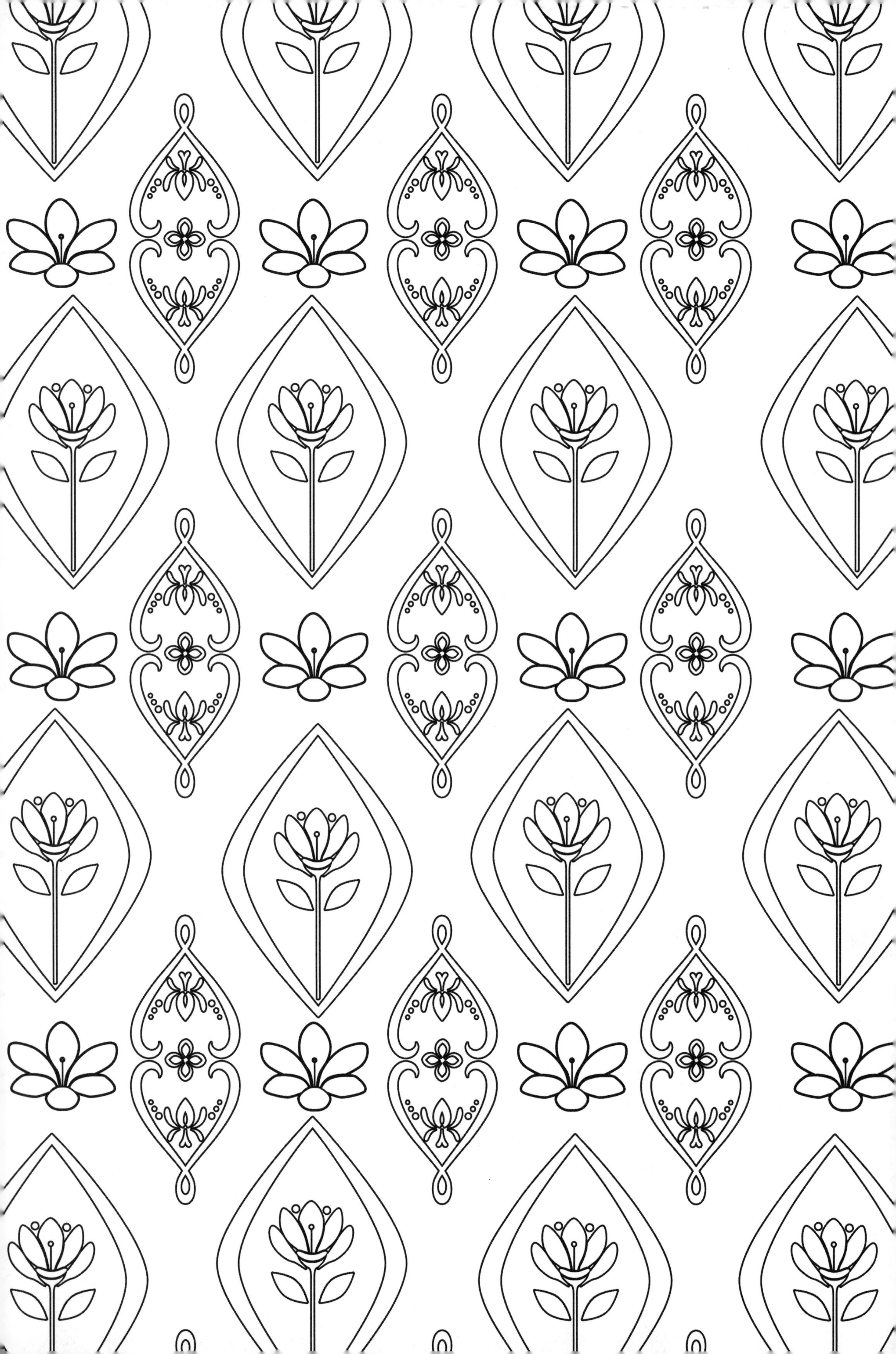

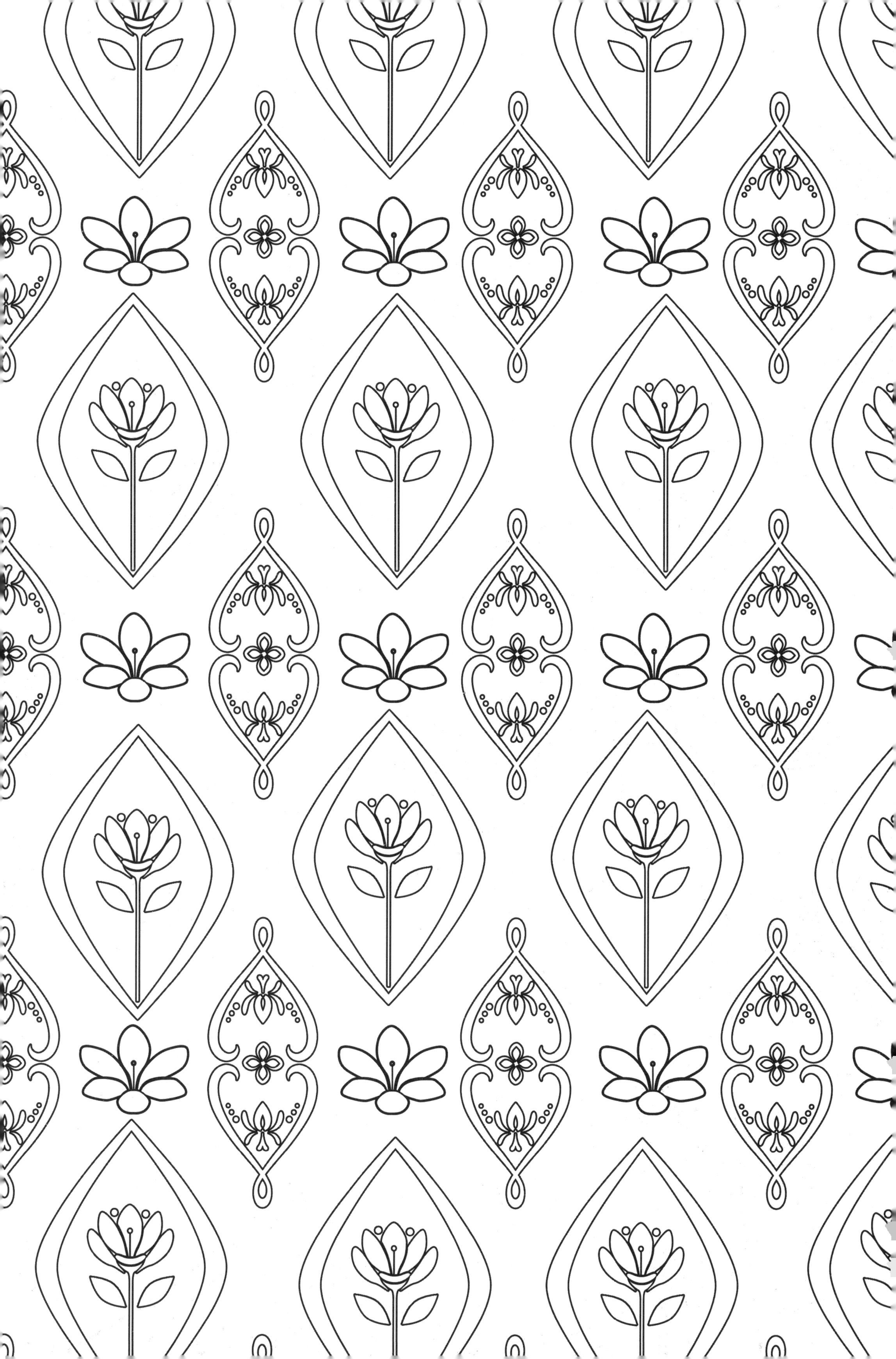

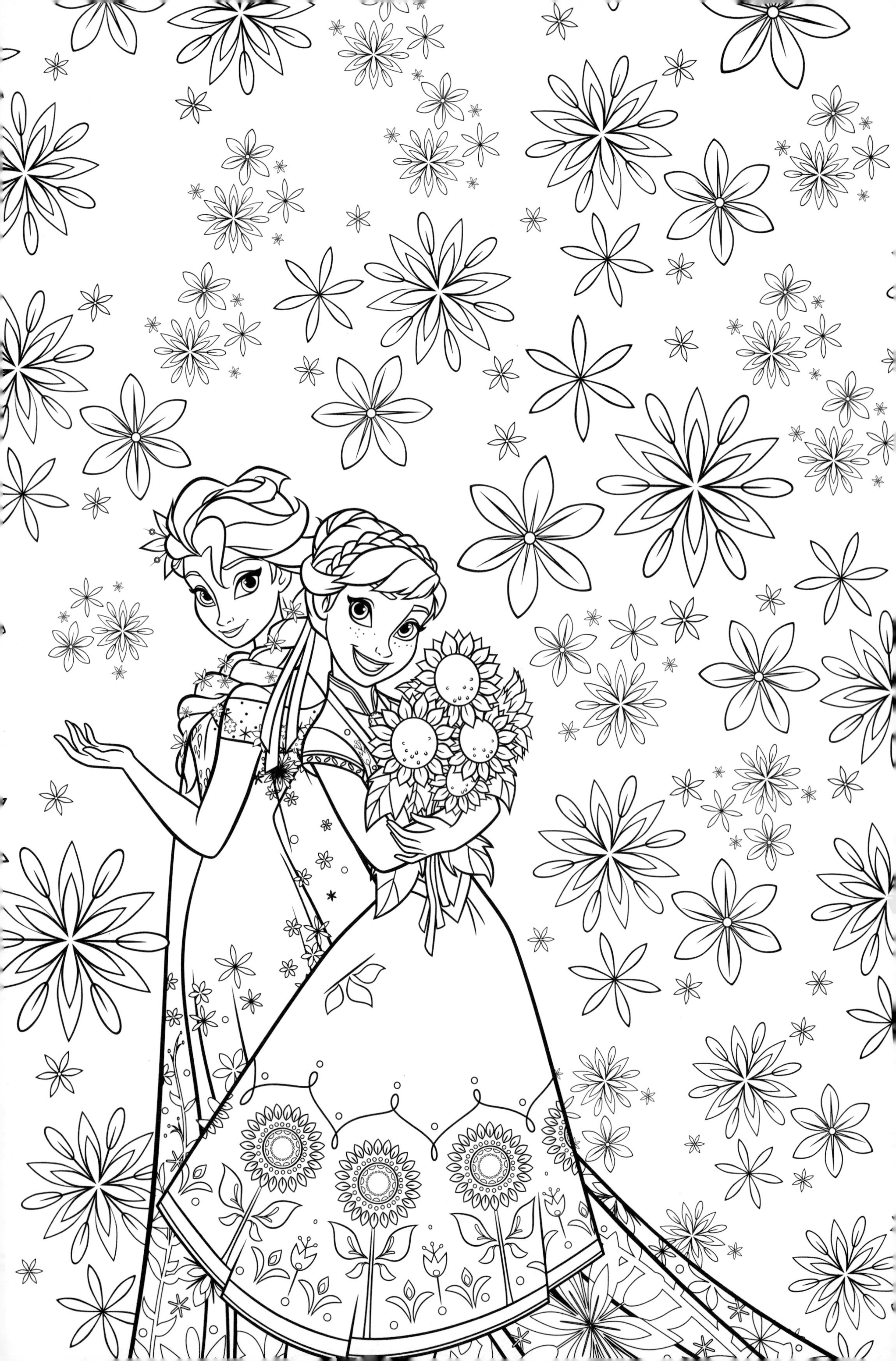

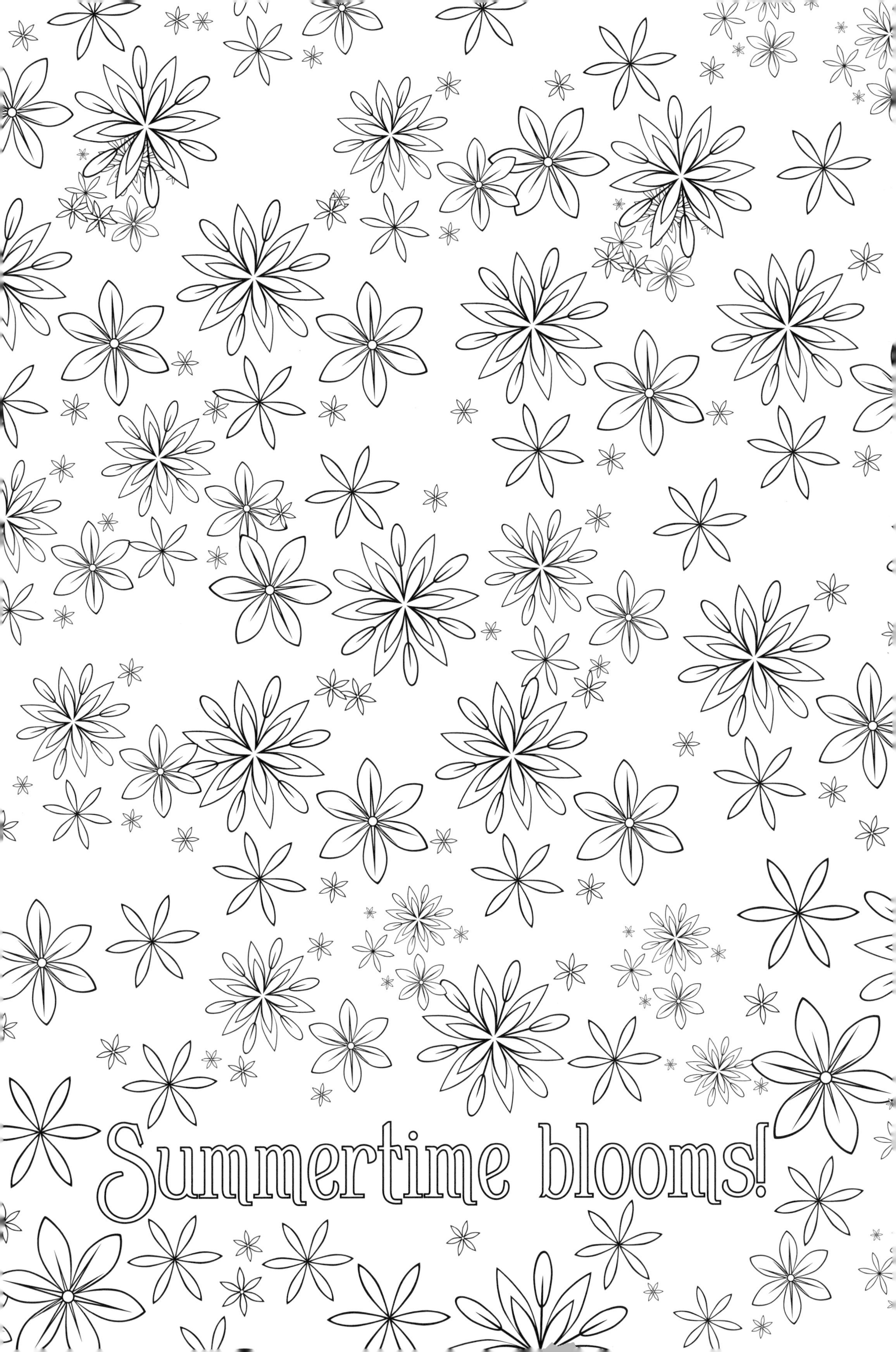
Summertime blooms!

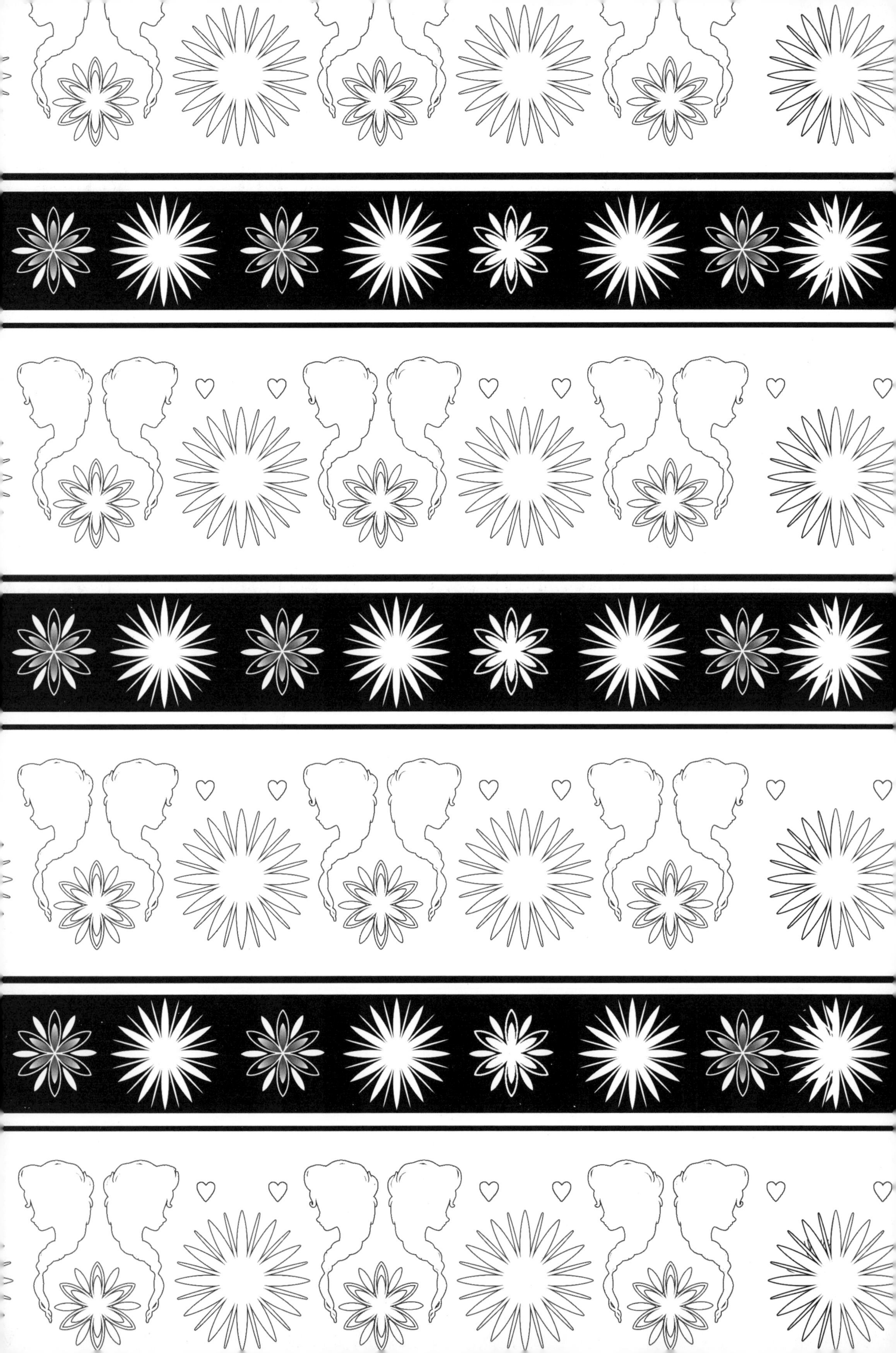

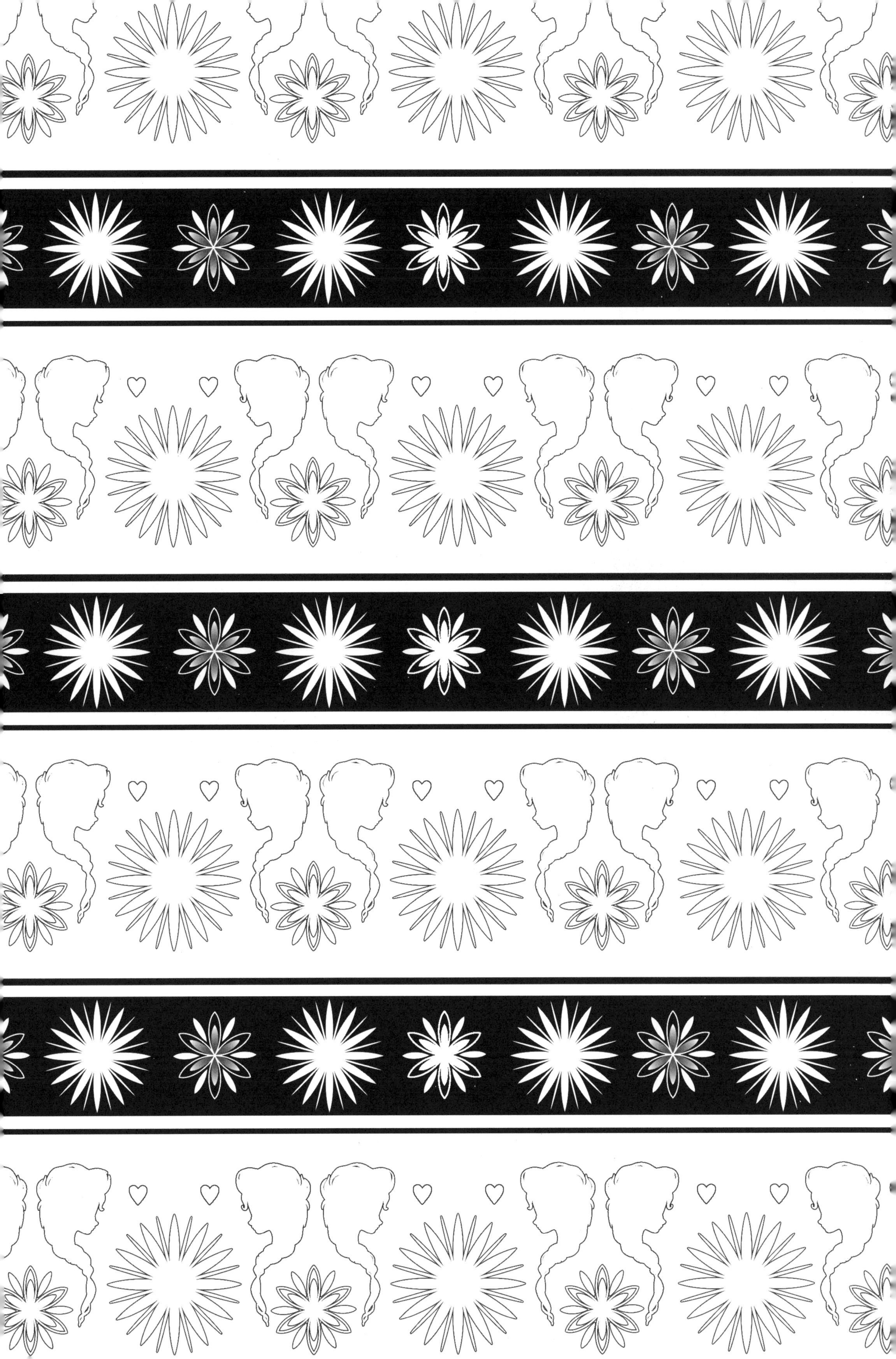

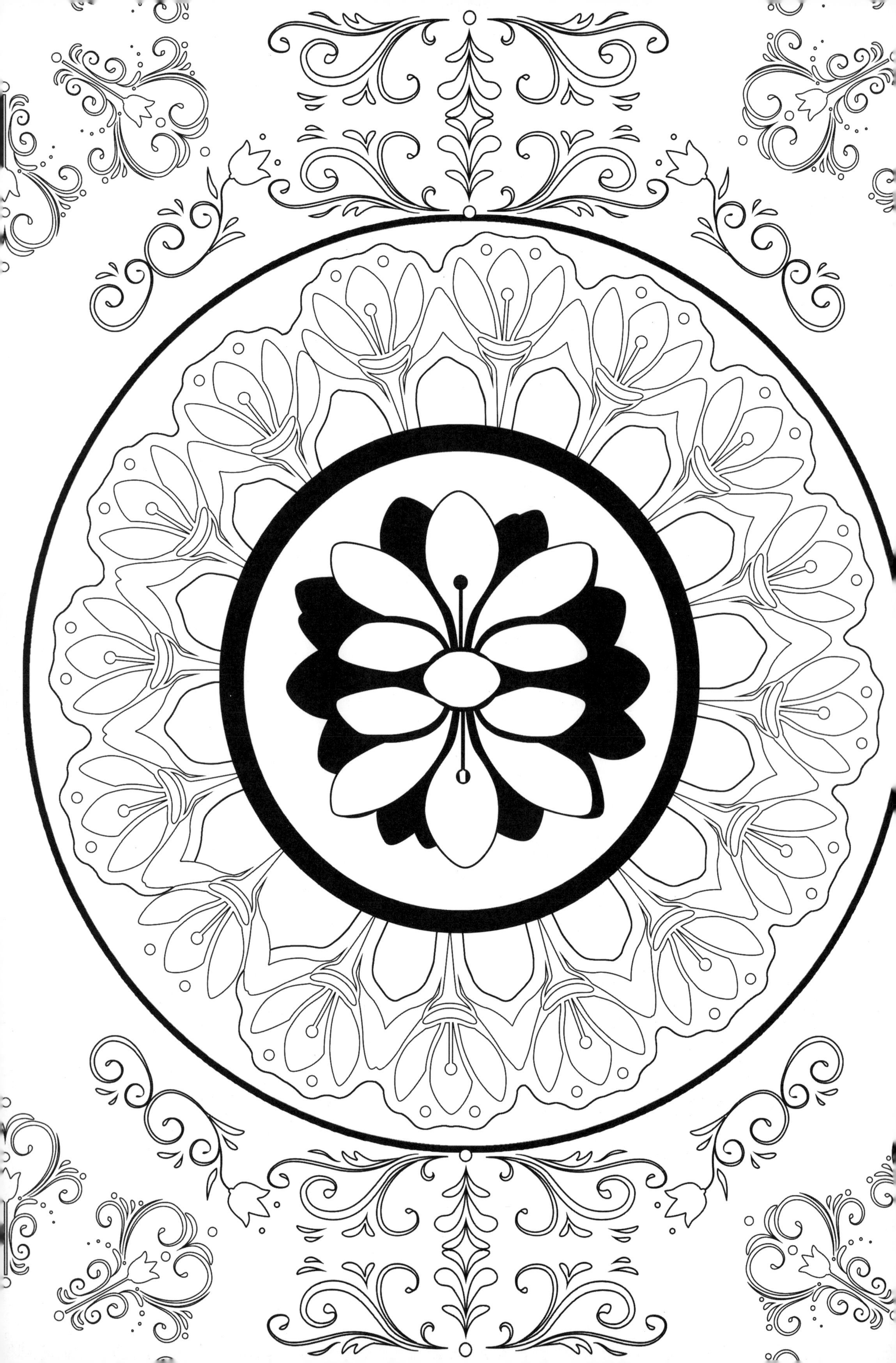

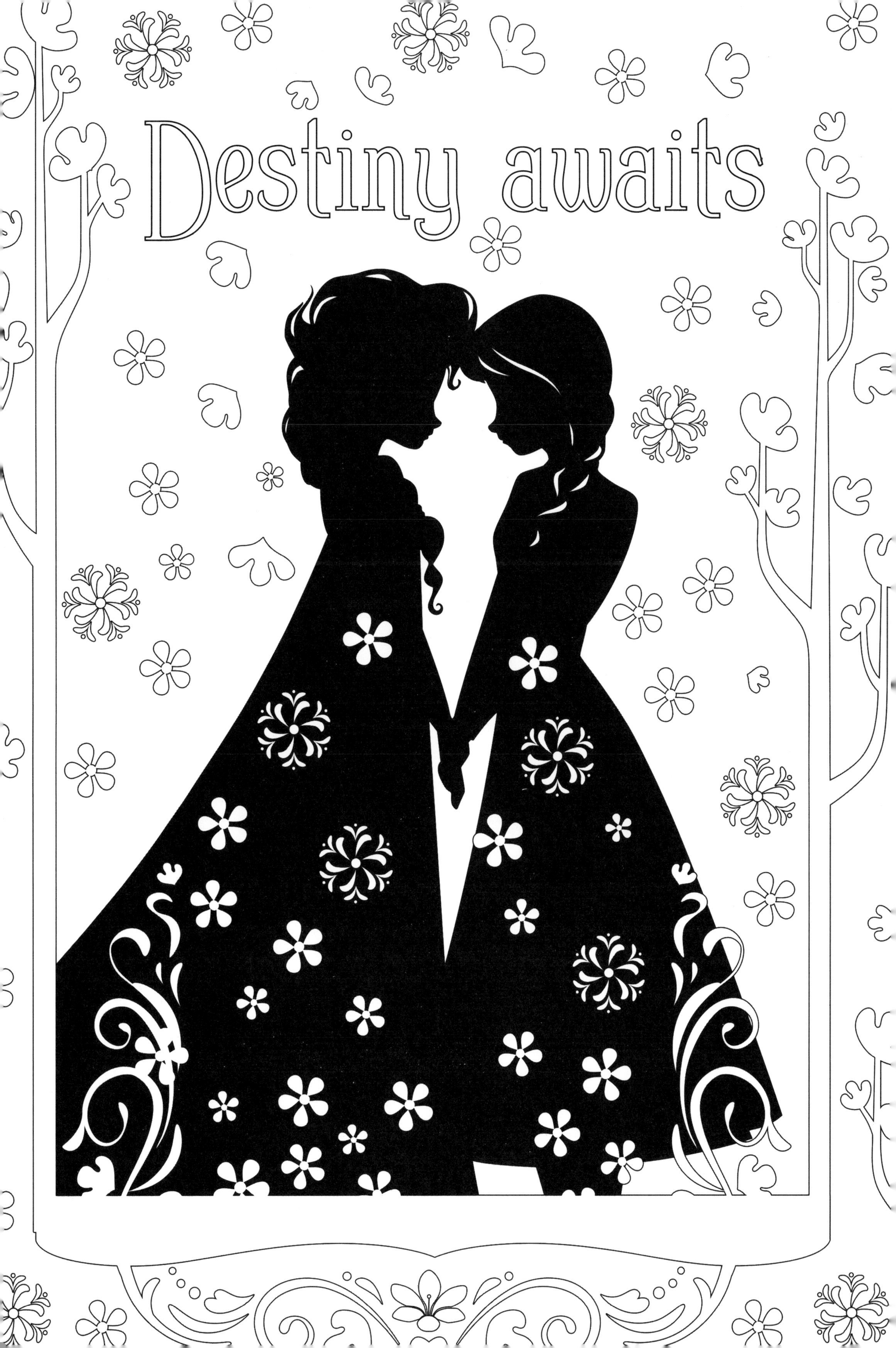
Destiny awaits

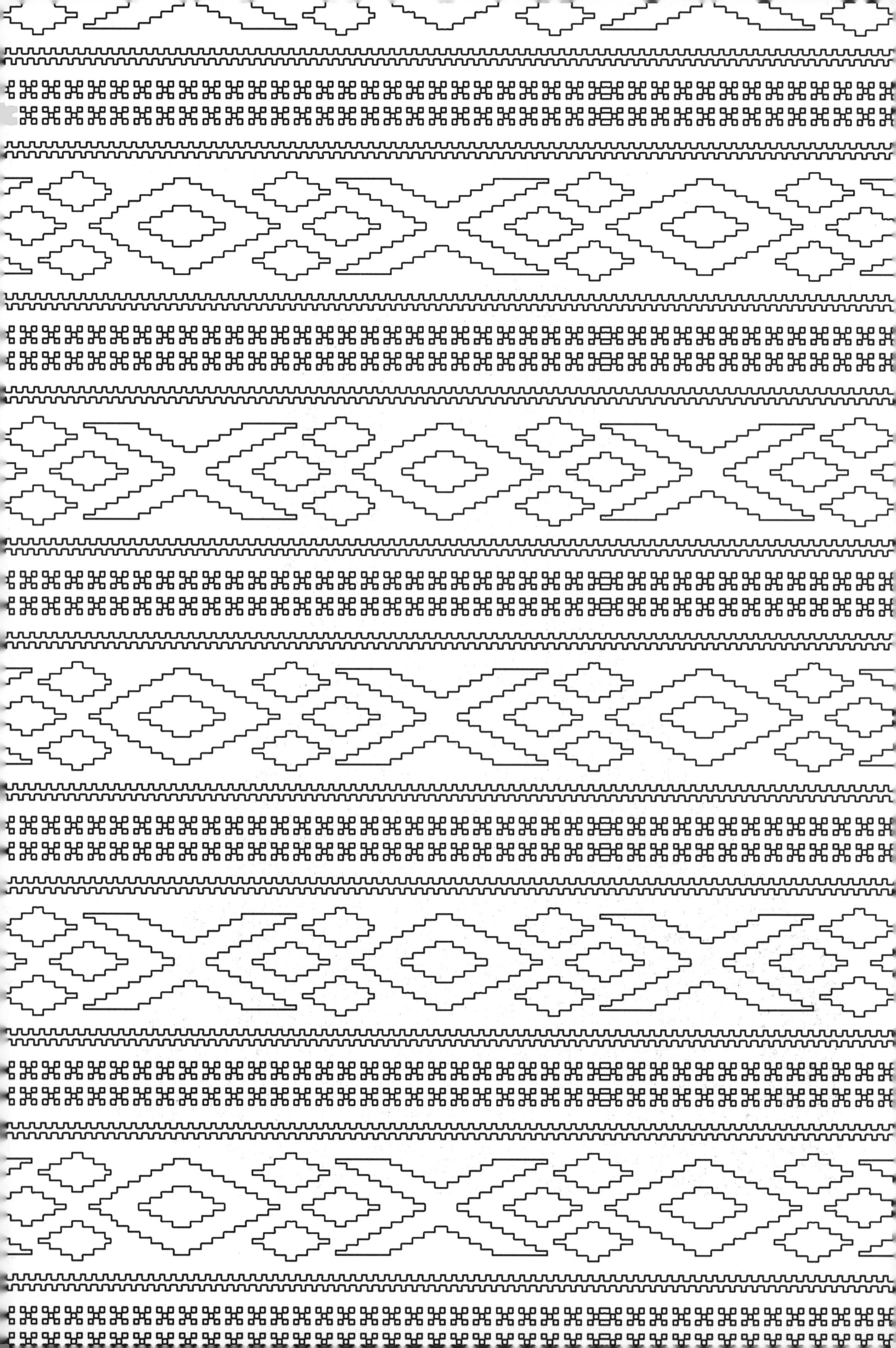

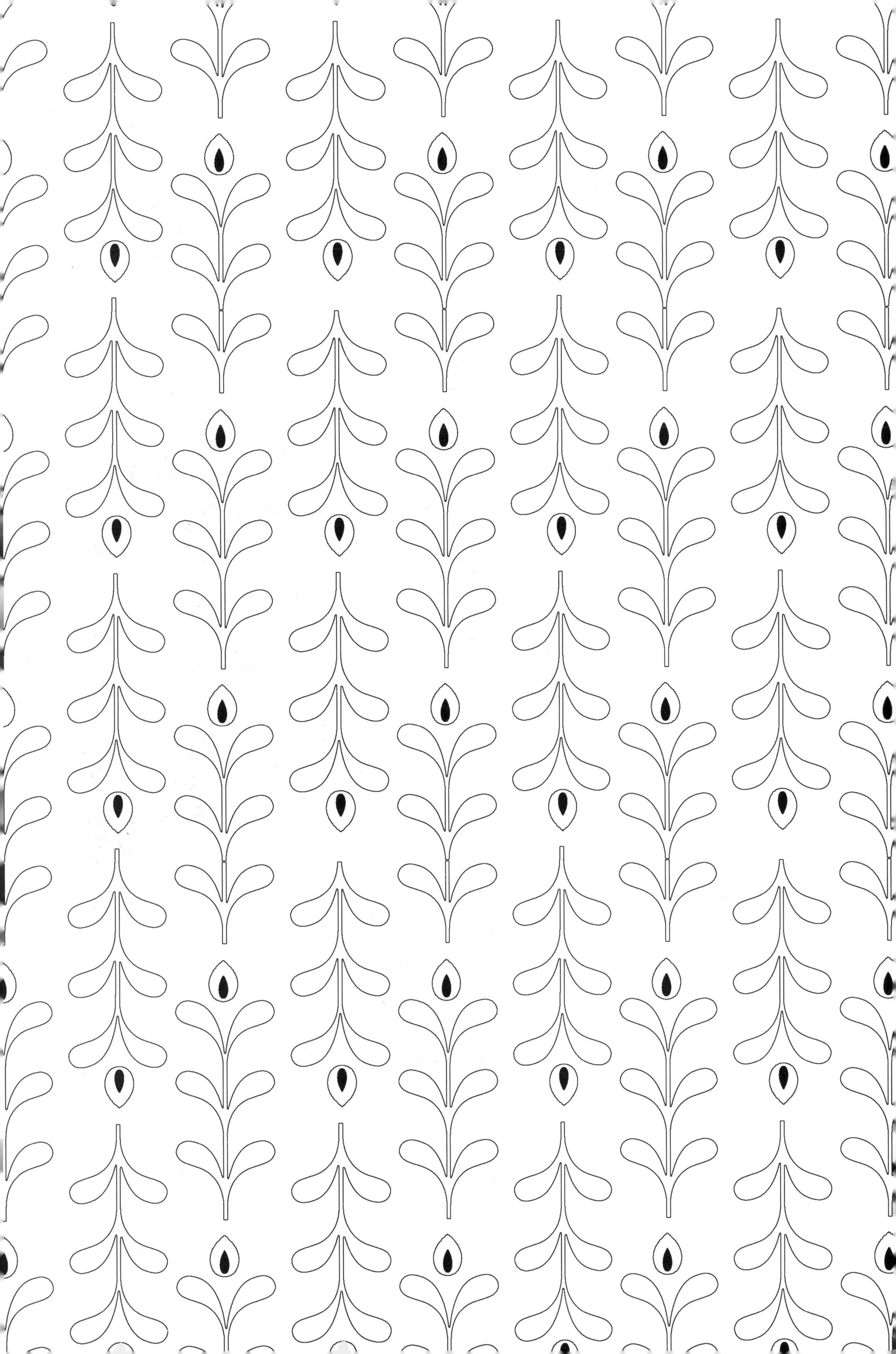

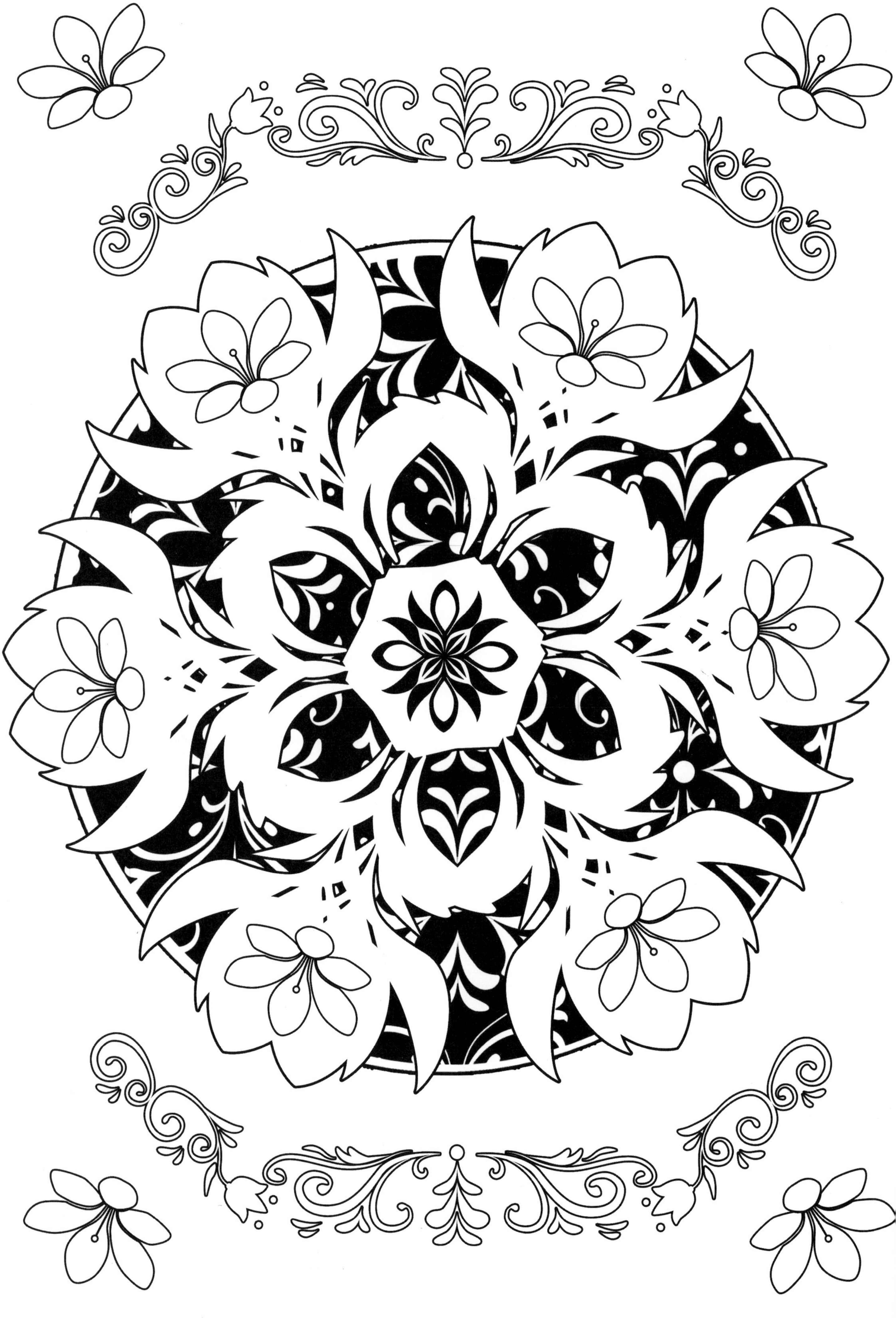

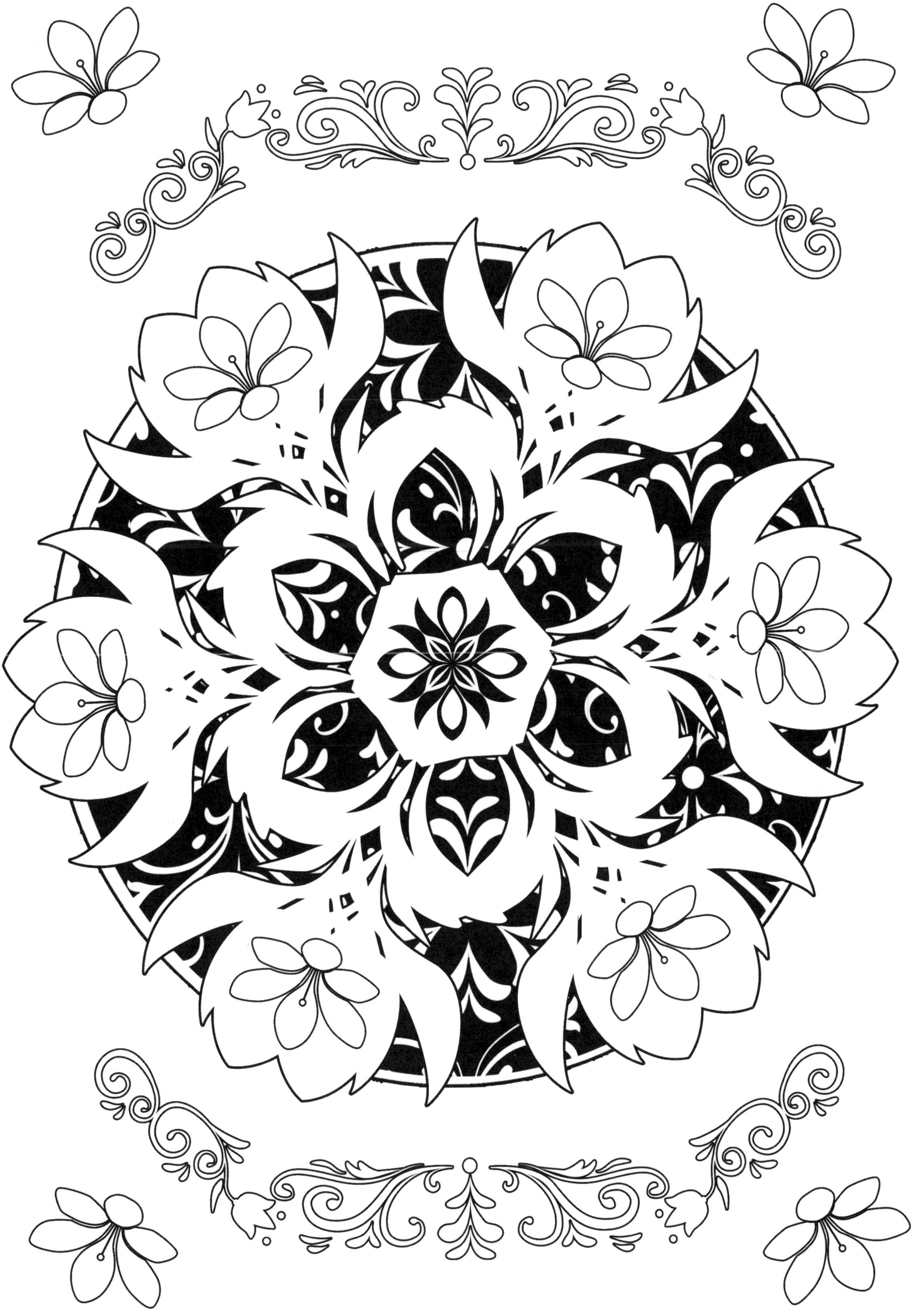

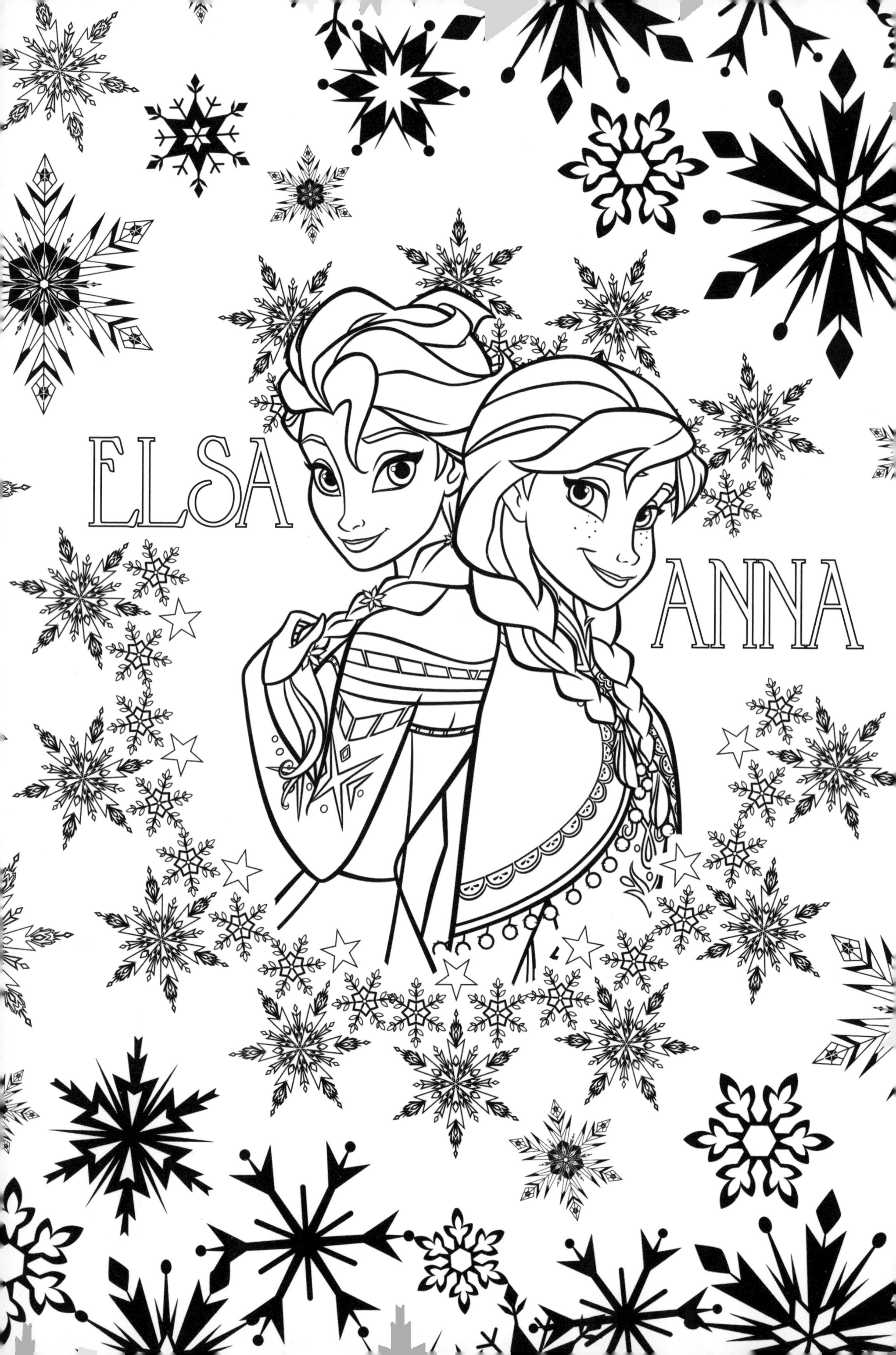
ELSA
ANNA

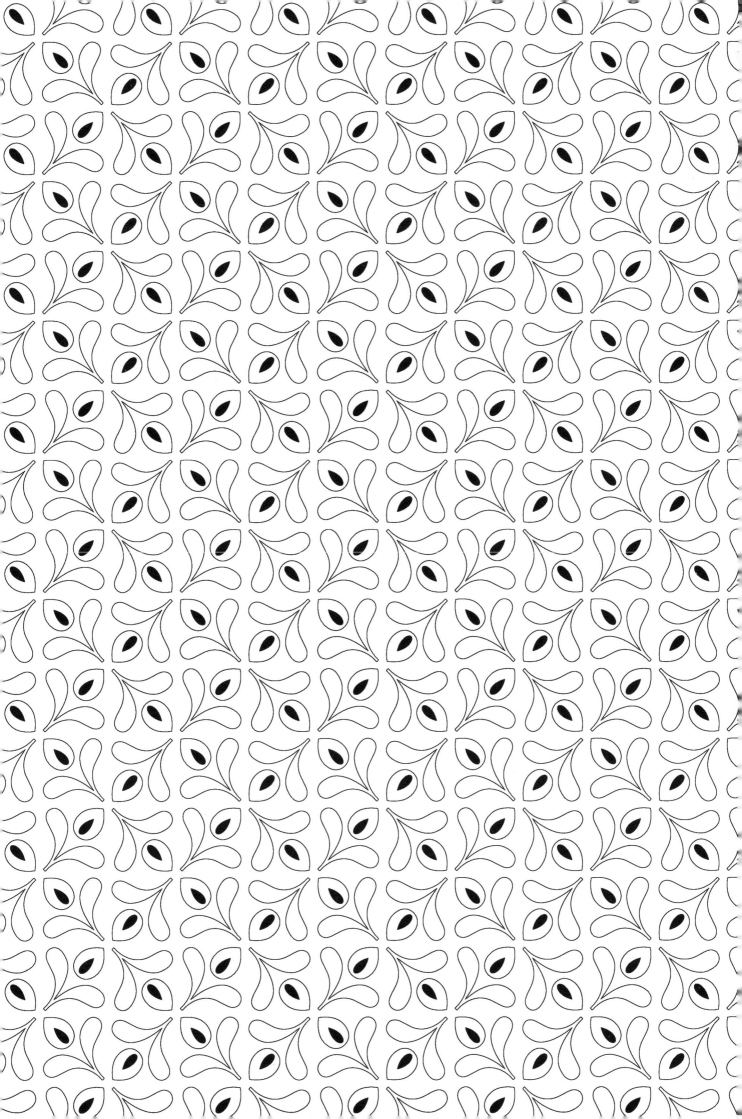

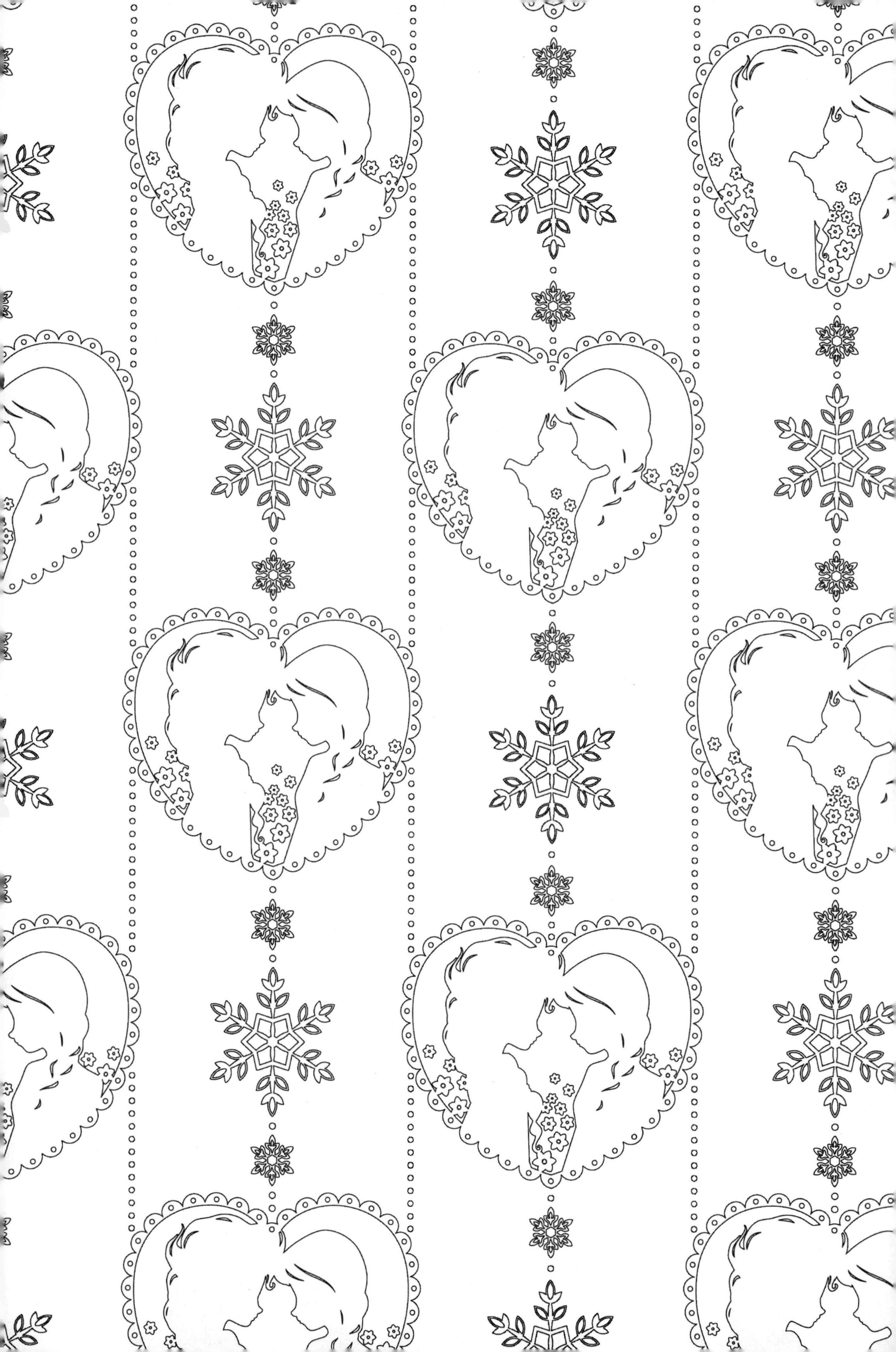

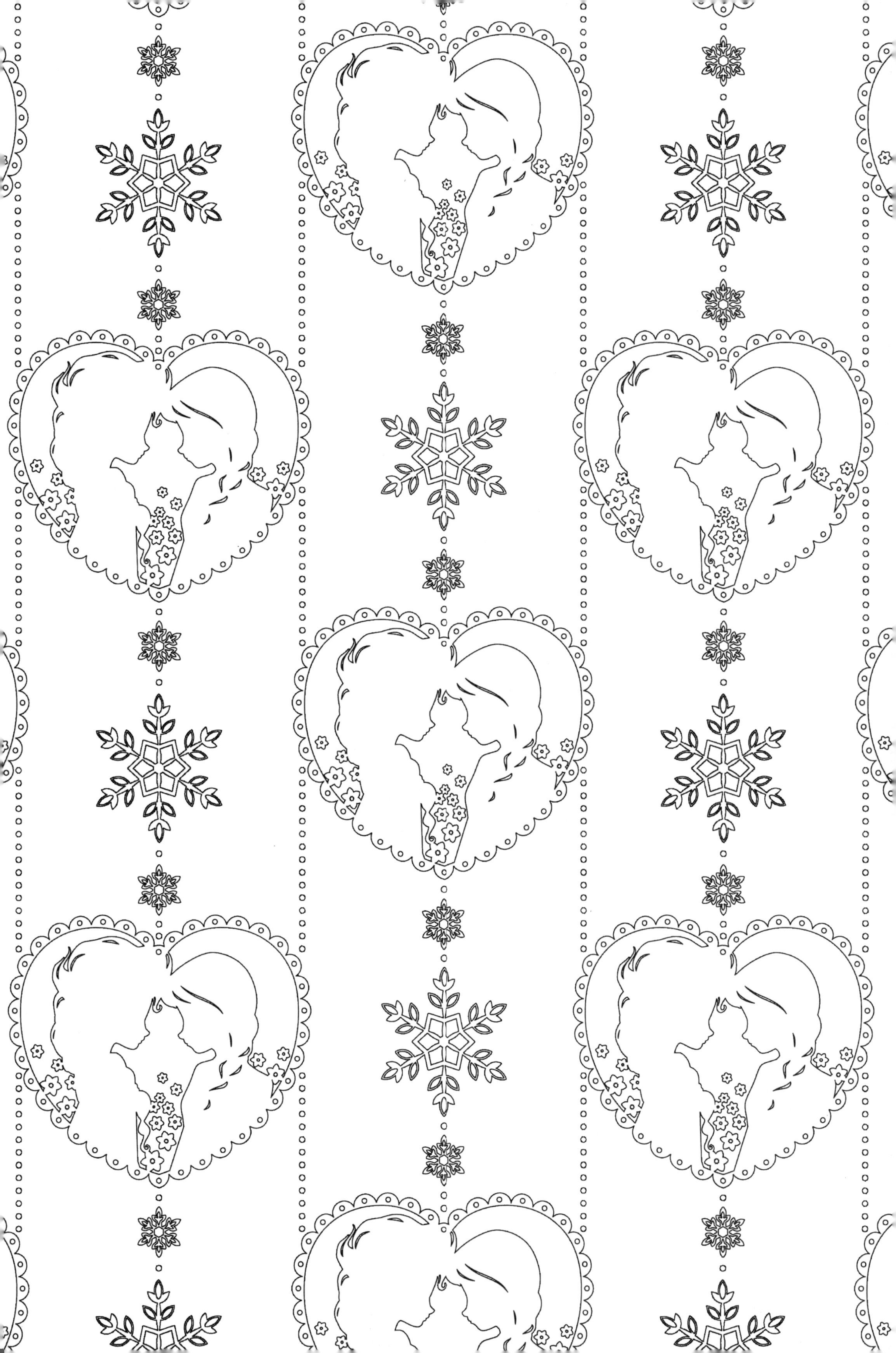

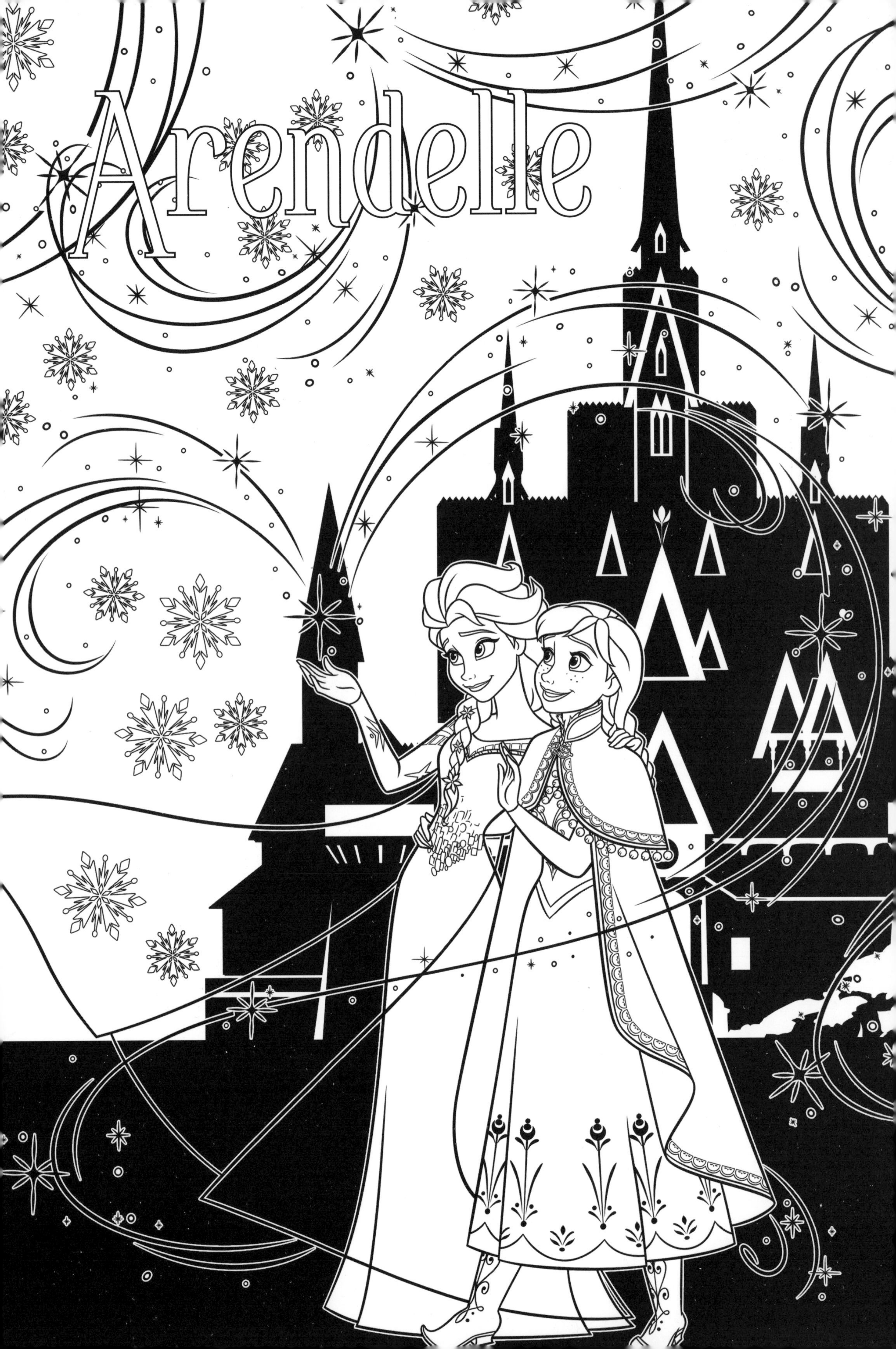
Arendelle

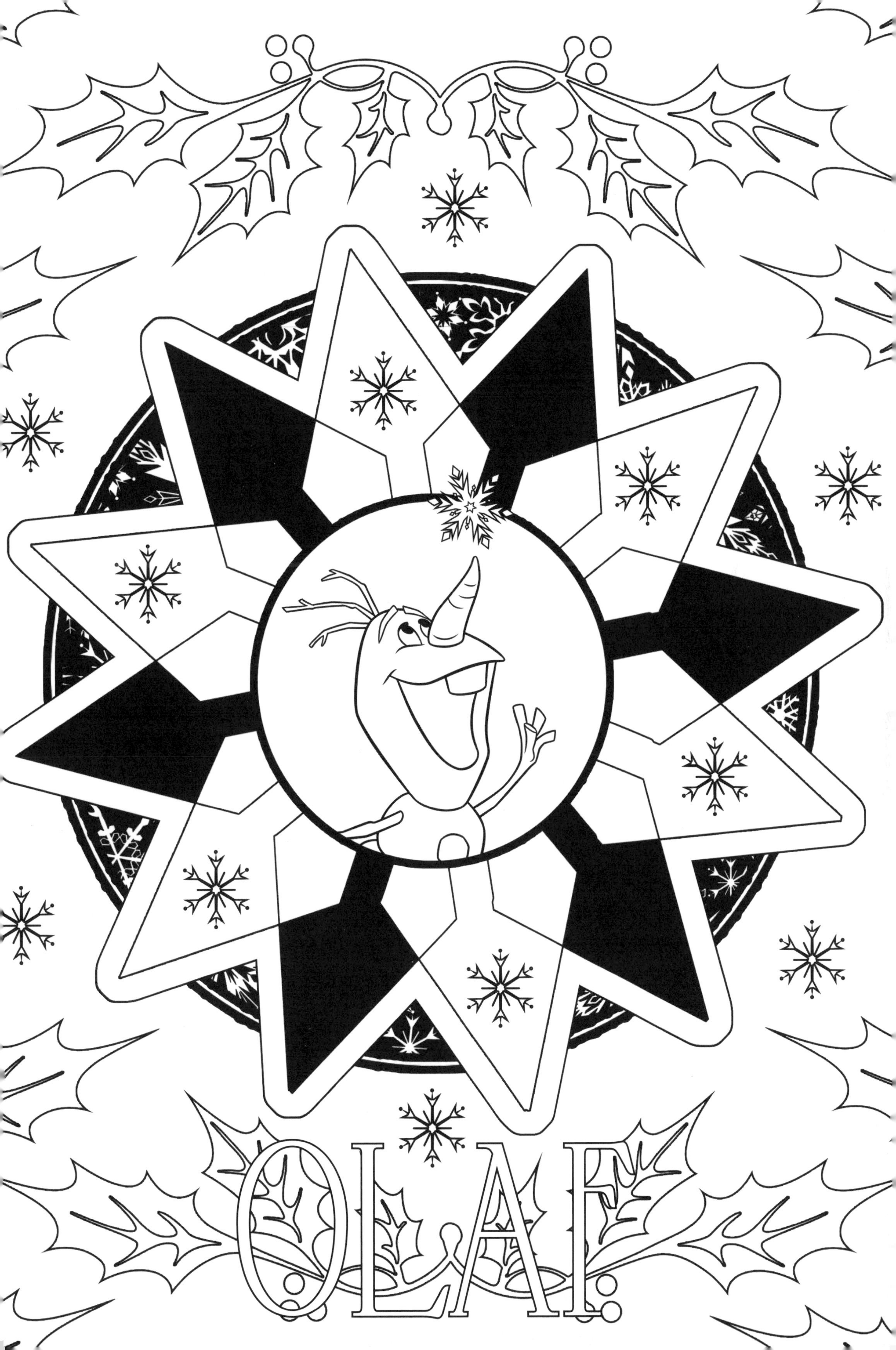
OLAF

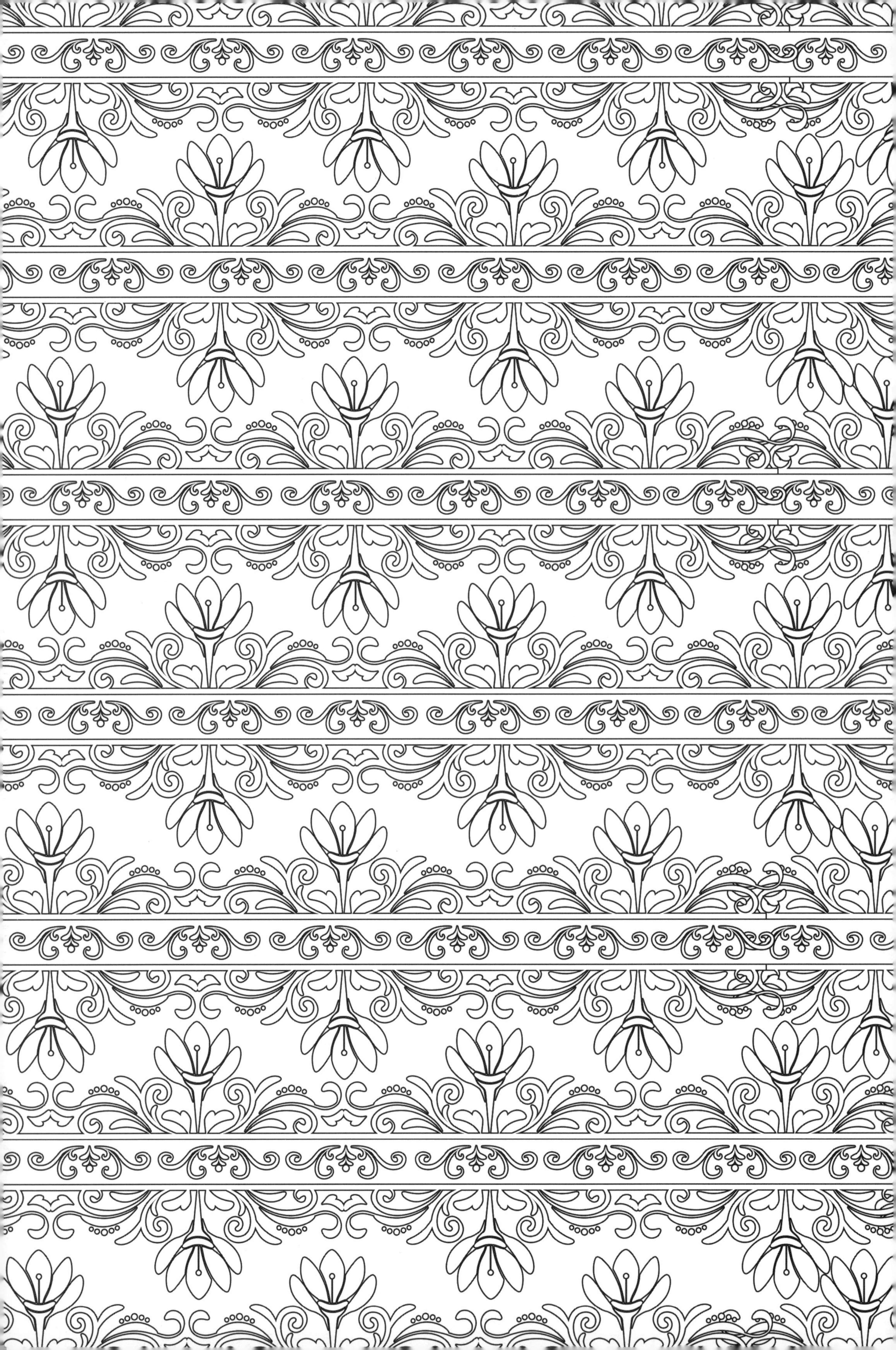

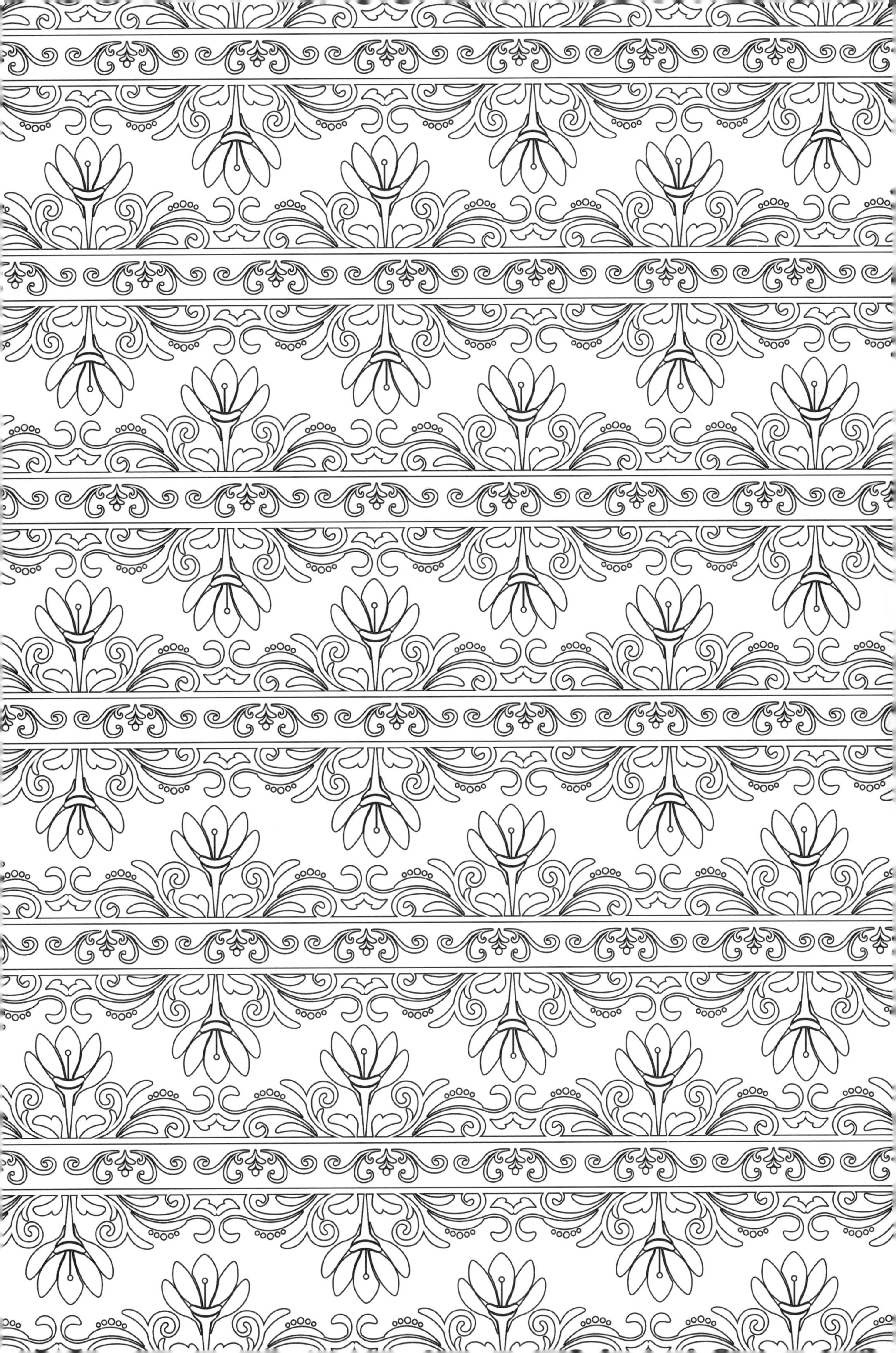

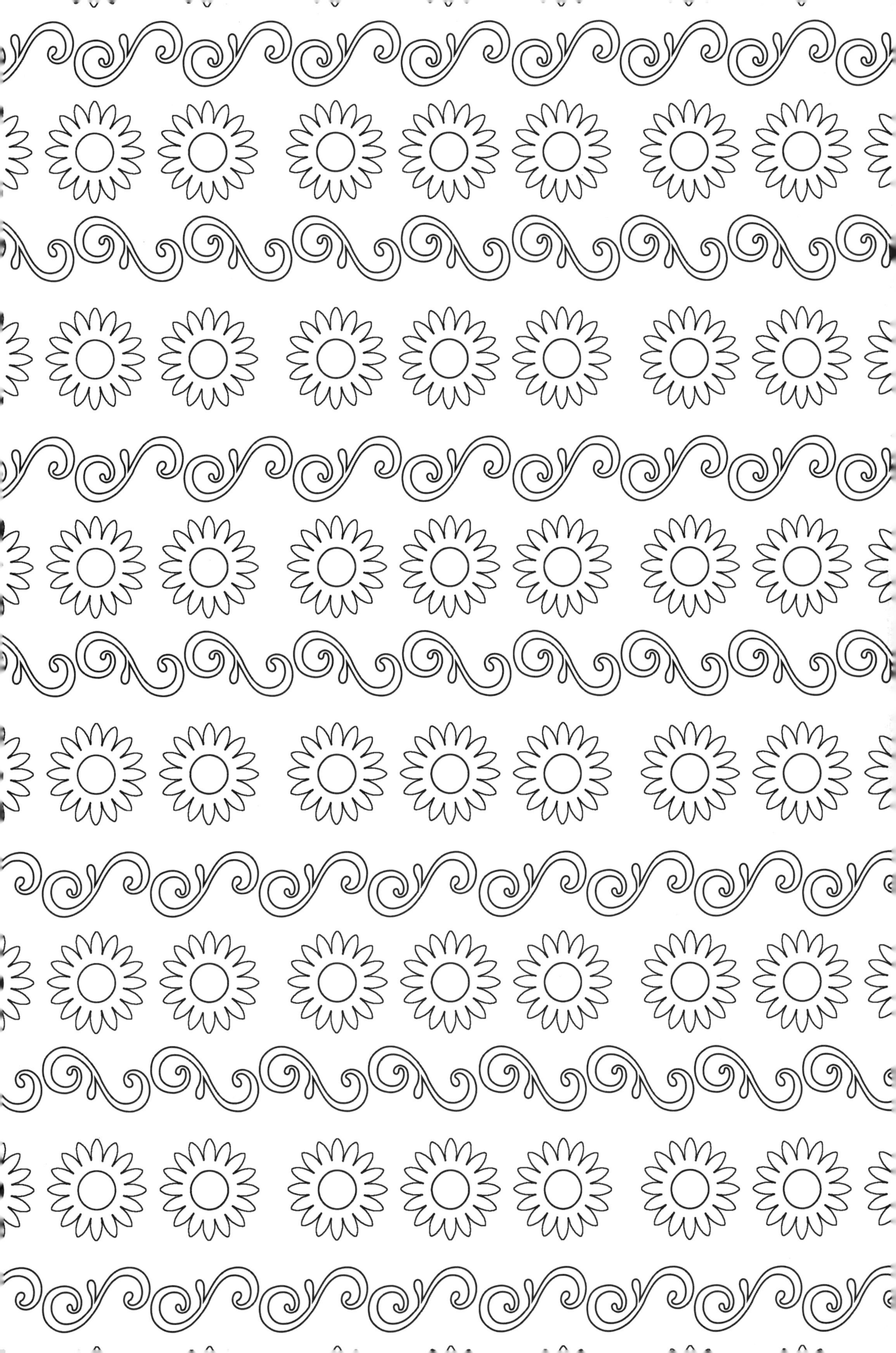

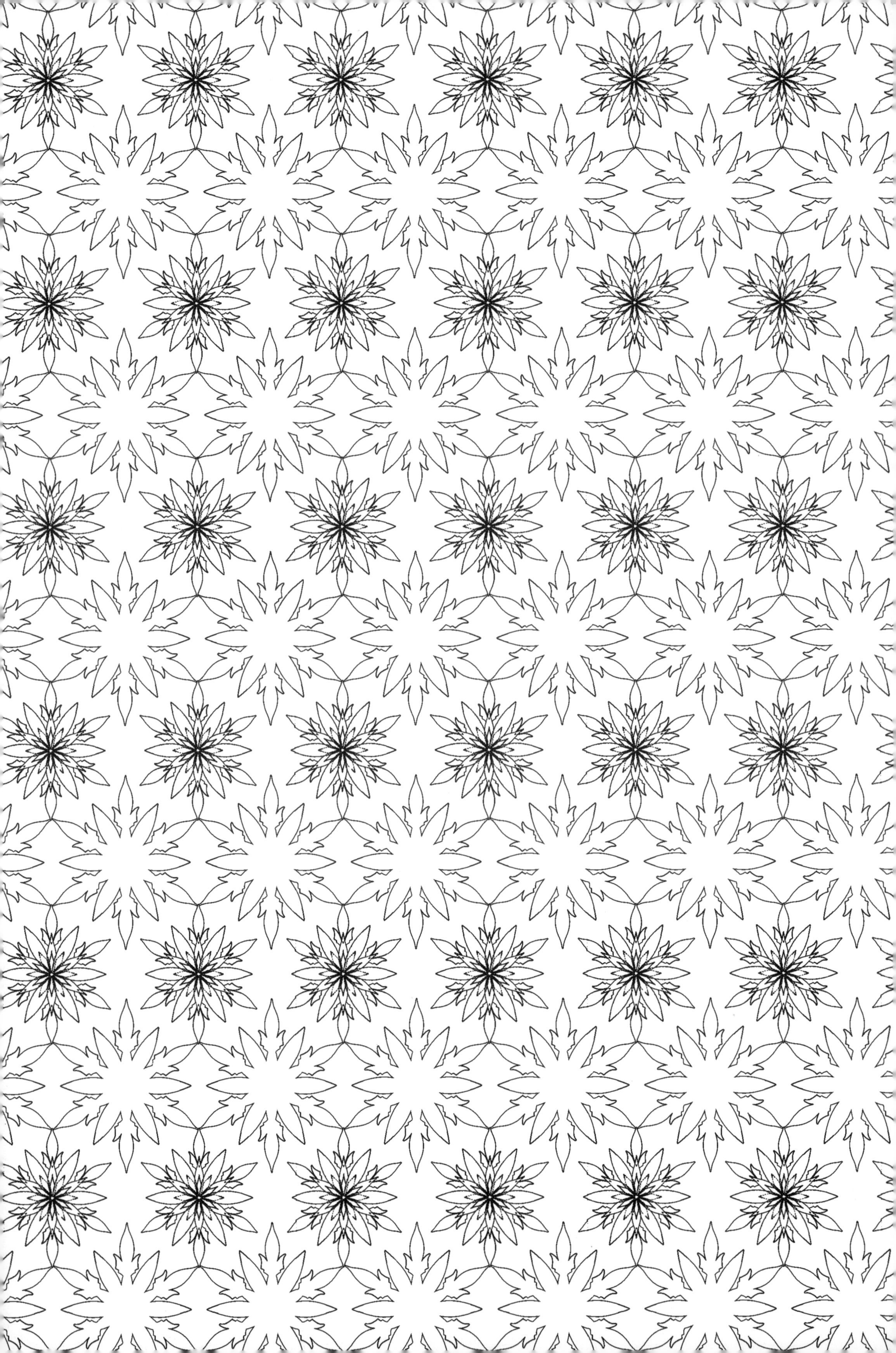

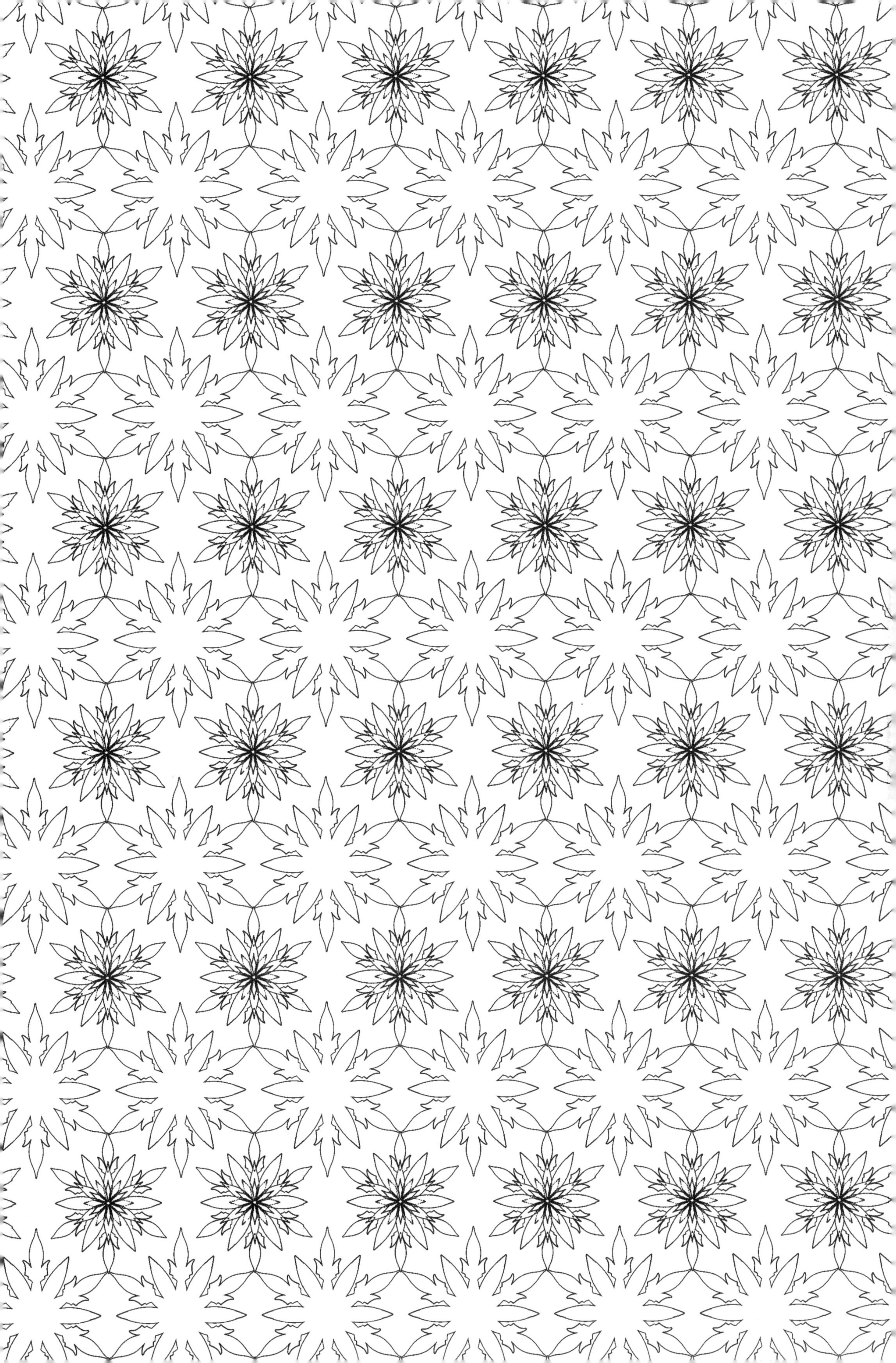

Love is putting someone else's needs before yours.

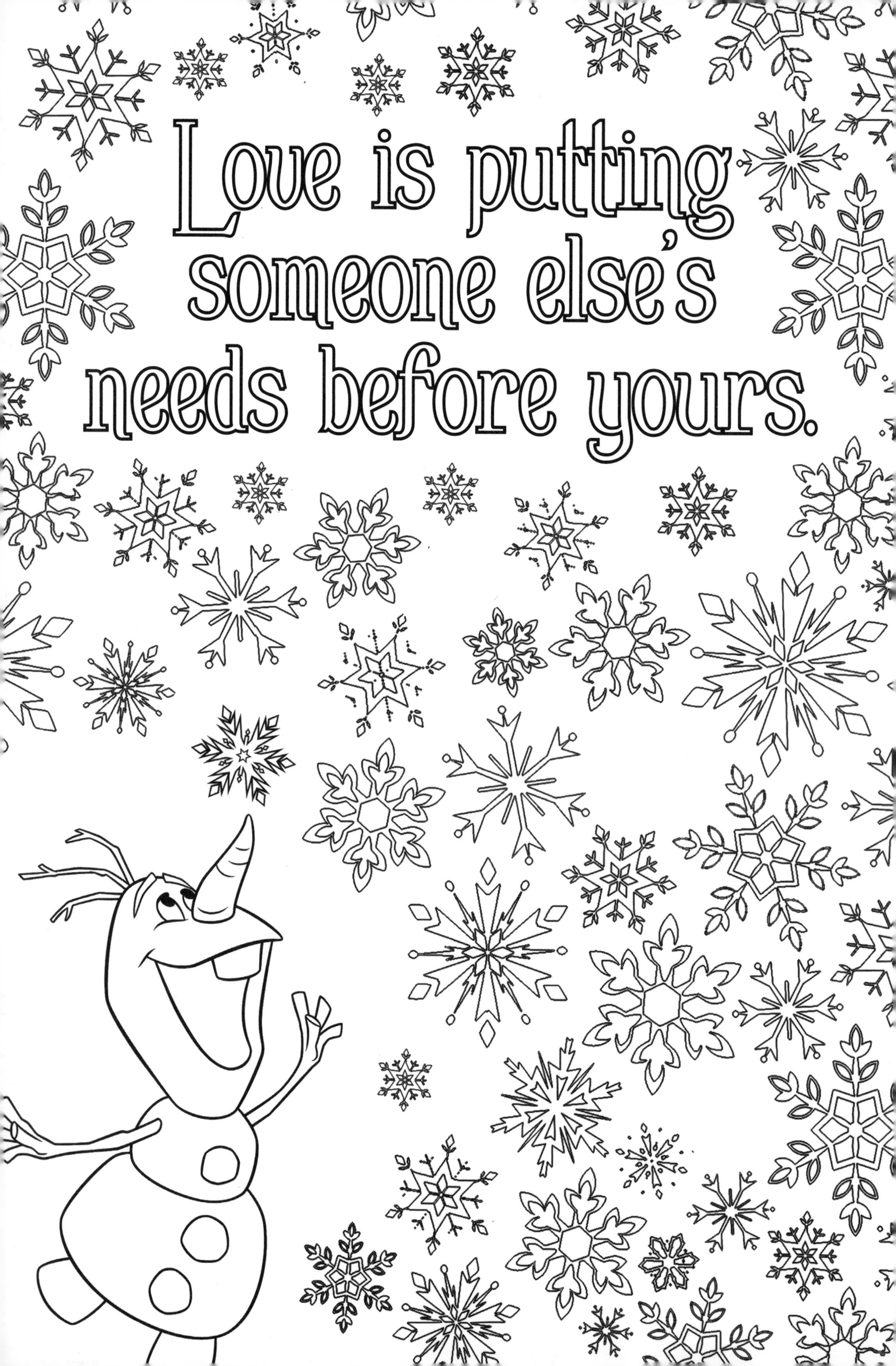

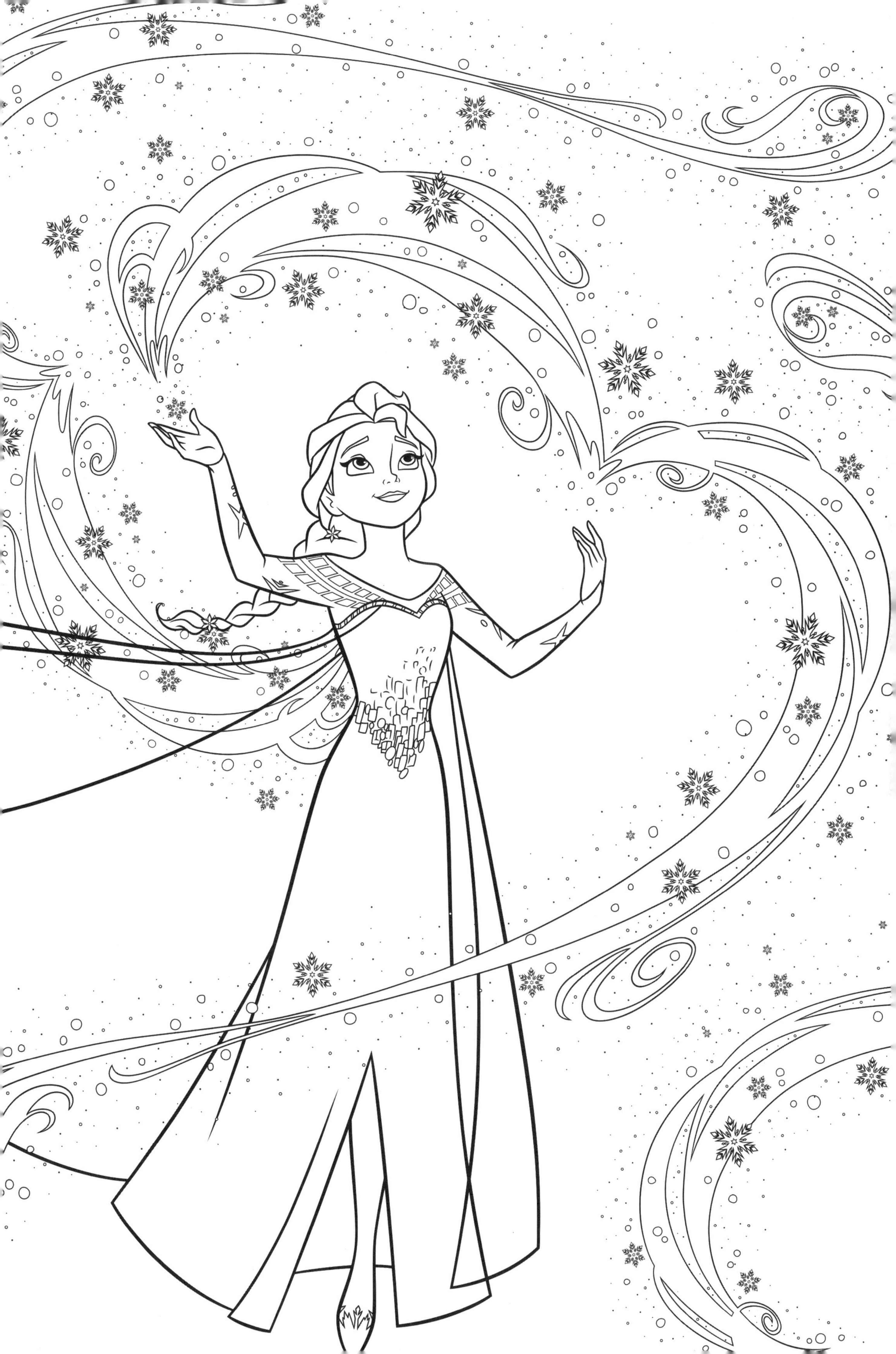

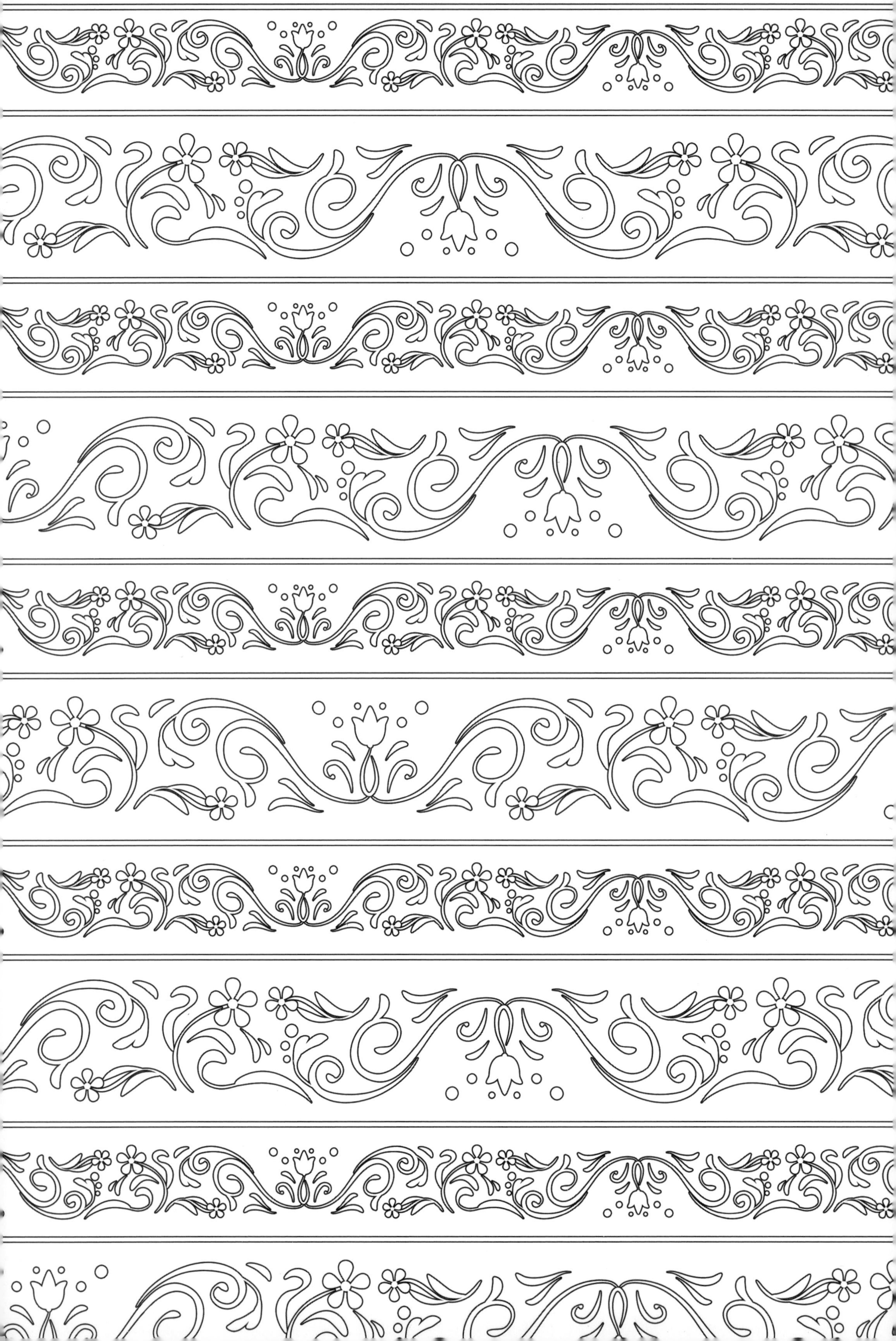

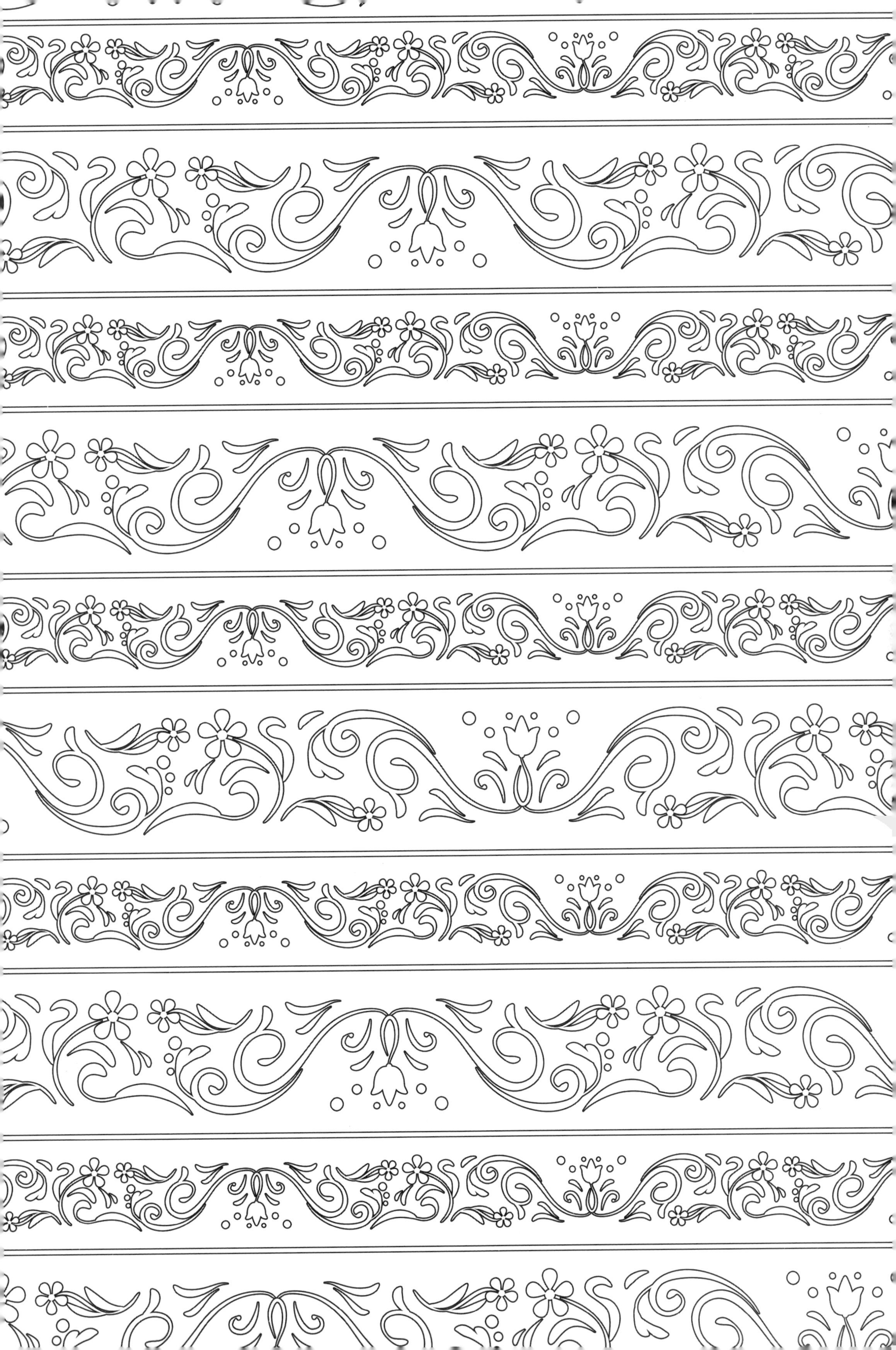

An act of true love will thaw a frozen heart

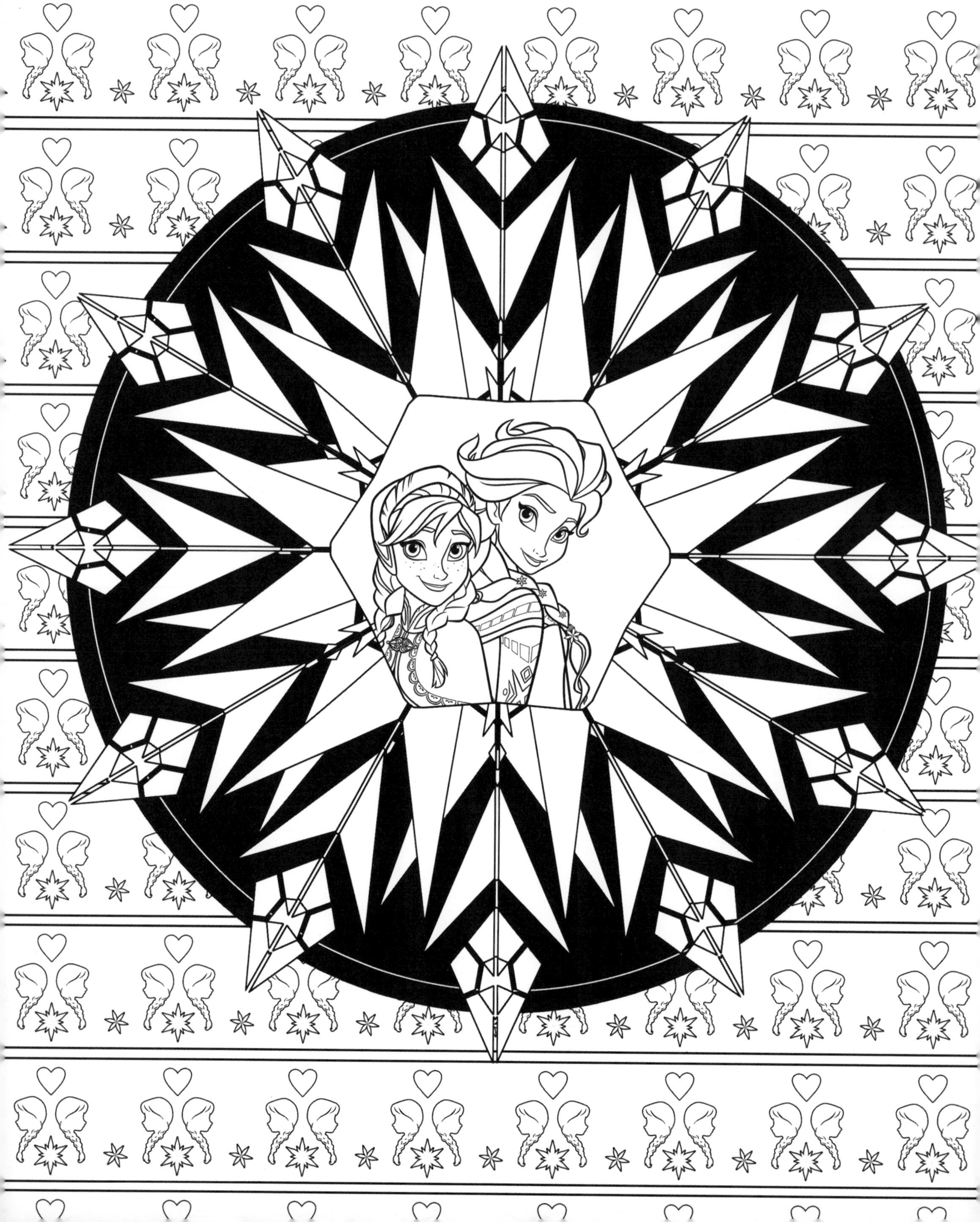

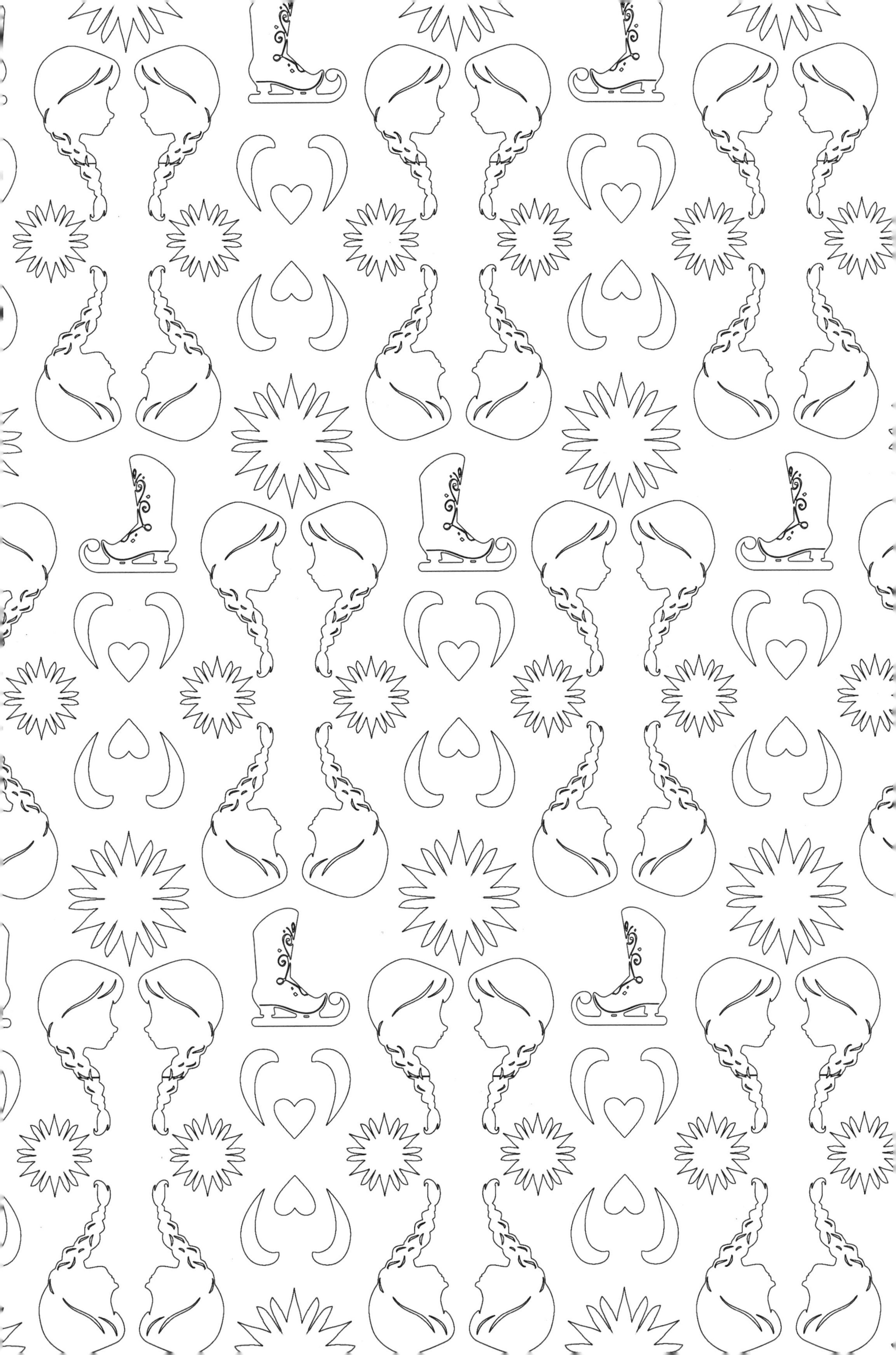